Sun, Sea and Sangria

VICTORIA COOKE

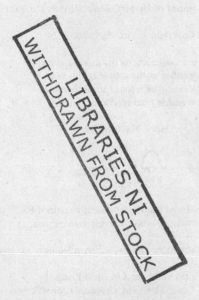

ONE PLACE. MANY STORIES

HQ
An imprint of HarperCollins*Publishers* Ltd
1 London Bridge Street
London SE1 9GF

First published by HQ 2020

This edition published in Great Britain by
HQ, an imprint of HarperCollins*Publishers* Ltd 2020

ISBN: 9780008376215

MIX
Paper from
responsible sources
FSC C007454

This book is produced from independently certified FSC™ paper
to ensure responsible forest management.

For more information visit: www.harpercollins.co.uk/green

Printed and bound in Great Britain by
CPI Group (UK) Ltd, Croydon CR0 4YY

For Dave and Adam, who each inspired this book in their own special way.

Andrea's Sunny Sangria Recipe

One bottle of your favourite Rioja
(I like to have an extra one so I can have a glass whilst
chopping fruit)
An orange
A lemon
An apple
A few strawberries
2–3 tablespoons of sugar
A dash of banana liqueur or brandy/rum/gin or whatever you
have left over from Christmas
(choose one of these – not all)
A cup of orange juice
Ginger ale, soda water or lemonade to taste
A few frozen raspberries

1. Chop the fruit and squeeze a little of the juice from the lemon
   and orange pieces into the pitcher then toss the rest of the
   fruit in.
2. Add the sugar and pour in the full bottle of wine.

3. Add the dash of dusty-shelf booze and chill until you're ready to serve.
4. Before serving, add ginger ale, orange juice, frozen berries and ice, then give it a stir.

Chapter 1

'Where the hell is the dry oil spray?' My chest is tightening. 'We're on in ten and Sammy needs to be glistening like an Adonis and smelling of coconut in five.'

'I've got some olive oil from the restaurant,' Ant pipes up. 'That's what I've used.'

'Yes, well you look like a deep-fried sausage and don't smell much better. Grab a towel and rub it off. It's the twenty-first century, for goodness' sake, and nobody here is auditioning for *The Full Monty*.'

'Yes, Kat,' a few voices mumble. I don't have the time to think about who they belong to, but I do spot one or two other super-greasy torsos.

'Seven minutes to go. Come on!' I'm rummaging through my bag, throwing things left and right in a fit of panic. 'Here.' I produce an old bottle of Skin So Soft from Avon, which I've been using as a mozzie repellent since my mum gave me a bottle in 1997.

'I want you all shimmering seductively and smelling nose-twitchingly floral in three minutes tops.' I toss the spray to my lead dancer, Marcus. 'Go!'

Through the fog and nose-tingling scent of dry oil mist, I check myself in the mirror. My stage make-up looks like Mary

Berry has daubed it on with a silicone spatula, but this glam look is for my bold stage persona. It helps me get into the character of a strong, confident woman who knows what she wants. It should look natural under the lights. Anyway, it's the guys who need to look good out there, not me.

'Okay, huddle up.' The guys gather dutifully around me. 'Right, remember that Sammy has pulled his shoulder, so when you all go into the backflips segment, he will be stage left, grinding. Don't wait for him. Also, Marcus, that thing you did with the eye contact and the winking last night – the audience loved it. I want to see more. Remember, the crowd loves you. Do your best and let's blow this thing up.'

There are some whoops from the audience as the amplified beats of 50 Cent's 'Candy Shop' start. I'm up. I wiggle my curvy hips as I saunter onto the stage and pump the mic above my head in time to the music. The crowd whoop and cheer and the excitement is tangible. Under the glare of the bright white spotlights, I can barely make out the hundreds of people who've come to see the show, but the energy is electric.

'Ladies … and gentlemen,' because there are always a few blokes in the crowd, 'welcome to the Grand Canarian resort complex where we are going to Blow. Your. Mind! There won't be a fire hose or PVC thong in sight, because tonight we're giving you your dream man. Think gorgeous Adonises who can satisfy your deepest desires. Think dreamboat pick 'n' mix. Ladies and gents, think the Heavenly Hunks …'

As the crowd goes wild, my five men come out dressed in distressed blue jeans and T-shirts that struggle to contain their abs. Marcus and Ant lift me into the air and turn me around as 'I Want It That Way' by the Backstreet Boys kicks in and the boys start to dance. It's the same routine we do every night, but each show feels a little different depending on where we're performing. As the boys move to the front, I slip back into the shadows.

'They always bring the crowds,' a male voice with a thick

Spanish accent says. Gaël, the hotel manager, has appeared in the wings beside me.

I smile. It's taken a while to get to this point. When we first started up here, there was just me, Marcus, Hugo and Pauw trying to get gigs (Pauw's real name is Paul but everyone loves to make fun of the fact that despite living in East London his whole life, he doesn't have a cockney accent – it's incredibly hard to just call him Paul now). Most of the big hotels wanted tribute acts or magicians and we just about scraped by in seedy bars.

Things changed when Gaël booked us a couple of years ago for his huge, fancy hotel, on a whim, after a spate of complaining Brits rightfully whinged about a geriatric gymnast who took five minutes and two helpers to do a cartwheel and called it a show. After that, people couldn't get enough of the Heavenly Hunks. The *Canaries Today* called us 'The Chippendales for the Modern Woman'. We're probably piggy-backing off the success of *Magic Mike* a bit, but I don't think their lawyers are worried.

'My favourite part,' Gaël nudges me. He's a skinny, six-foot, heterosexual guy but even he can't help but glue his eyes to the backflips and breakdancing. Pauw does his run of six consecutive backflips as Ant, who's a trained ballet dancer, leaps across the stage in mid-air splits, his long brown hair billowing behind him. The crowd can't get enough of his porcelain skin.

The music slows down and the intro to Ed Sheeran's 'I'm a Mess' kicks in. Marcus appears in an open dark denim shirt that reveals enough of his smooth, toned chest to drive the audience wild. The shirt is paired with fitted, dark jeans and chunky boots. His short dark hair and light-brown skin look beautiful under the light, and the whole ensemble is one of my finest pieces of work, even if I do say so myself. He sits on the edge of the stage, making eye contact with as many lucky audience members as he can manage, whilst his silky voice gives its pitch-perfect rendition of the song. I still get chills watching him and I've seen this act a billion times.

5

'Even *I* am almost falling in love,' Gaël jokes.

'See, that's the point, Gaël. Women don't want cheesy hosepipe-stroking and pant-dropping to the beat of "Hot Stuff". We don't even want to see any naked bottoms.' Gaël shifts uncomfortably, but I'm proud of the act I've put together so I carry on regardless. 'Women want sexy all-rounders. Men with talent. Half the time, the Heavenlies are fully clothed, yet you can practically hear the ladies' ovaries scream.'

'I admire what you've done. You know, if you ever get fed up of managing the Heavenly Hunks, there would be a job here as my entertainment director. I'm terrible at it.' He laughs.

'Thanks, Gaël, though I can't see that happening any time soon.'

I switch my mic back on and step back into the spotlight. 'I don't know about you but I've come over all hot and bothered,' I say over the screaming cheers. 'We've had a hard day today, haven't we, ladies? I mean, I bet some of you even had to fetch your own cocktails from the pool bar, didn't you? Well, we're going to slow things down and treat as many of you as possible to your own *heavenly* massage whilst our talented Hugo plays the piano, just for you.'

The spotlight switches to Hugo, who starts playing 'All of Me'. As dry ice fills the stage, the rest of the guys filter through the audience giving shoulder rubs to as many audience members as possible. Those not having their shoulders rubbed are fixated on Hugo. His black hair shines under the light and his muscles ripple beneath his tanned skin as he hits the keys, his eyes intent on the sheet music. A ripple of excitement washes over me. We put on a bloody good show even if I do say so myself.

As the song finishes, it's time for our pièce de résistance, and okay, the song is nicked from *Magic Mike* but we did our own choreography and I doubt Mike cares. The beat starts and the guys bound across the stage from behind the curtain as 'Pony' kicks in at the chorus, and the crowd are up, out of their seats, singing and going wild. Under the blue-white spotlight, with the rising dry ice, they look like mythical beings.

***

'That was awesome, guys. The manager is really pleased with us and has booked us in for an extra show next month when we're back from Gran Canaria, as well as the bookings we'd already secured for early next year.' The guys cheer and there's a bit of back-slapping. 'We have the show over in Playa de las Americas tomorrow, which is going to be huge, and there's a British news-paper doing a piece on the resort – they want to include a short review of our show, so I want you all bright-eyed and bushy-tailed for the rehearsal tomorrow. That means one drink tops in the bar tonight then bed, okay?'

I glare pointedly at Ant and Hugo. Ant looks sheepish and Hugo looks downright confused. He speaks English fairly well, but he doesn't always catch what I'm saying if I go off on a rant and sometimes I wonder if it's 'selective' understanding. I'm hoping a stern glance in his direction is enough to stop him going home with an audience member or two, tonight at least.

'Love you, Kat.' Pauw leans in for a hug.

'You too. Make sure you get yourself to the doctor's tomorrow and have that mole on your back checked,' I say, unhappy with the raised appearance it's taken on recently. He gives me a salute and blows me a kiss. I shake my head as he walks away.

'Marcus, you left your driver's licence in the dressing area,' I sigh, holding it out to him between my fingers.

'What would I do without you, Kat?'

'I honestly have no idea,' I say drily as he wanders off.

Hugo gives me a sheepish look and waves goodbye as the rest of the guys give me hugs and disperse. When I'm alone, I take a deep breath, gather my things and walk out through the hotel's reception on a high.

Chapter 2

As I walk out into the crisp silence of the early hours, my skin bristles. I feel on edge. A man is loitering across the street. He has a messy bun and a giant camouflage-print Puffa jacket on. Granted, it can get chilly here at night in September but it's hardly the Arctic Circle. My body is tense with apprehension; each nerve ending senses danger. He's watching me whilst sipping something from a bottle. I tuck my bag under my arm and walk briskly past. It isn't until I'm much closer that I realise he's sipping some kind of smoothie drink. I relax a little, as though it's a given that muggers don't really worry about their vitamin intake or care much for liquefied kale. It's silly how our perception of people works sometimes, but right now it's making me feel safe.

Something grabs my shoulder, and my heart catapults out of my chest. I spin, fists clenched, ready to pound seven bells out of Smoothie Man or whoever it is.

When my eyes focus on the person in front of me, I get quite the surprise.

It isn't the camouflaged man-bun-man I was expecting. It's a dark-haired man I don't recognise. Something about his soft-brown eyes, fixed with concern on my clenched fists, stifles my alarm.

8

'Sorry, I'm so sorry.' He holds his hands in the air. 'Just realised how bad it was to touch your shoulder. I didn't want to just shout a random "excuse me" down the street at half twelve.'

'But grabbing a lady on a dark, lonely street at half twelve is okay?'

'Like I said, I'm sorry. I didn't think it through, I just really wanted to talk to you and you left the hotel before I got a chance. Can we start again?' He grins a wide smile and two small dimples form either side. He may have terrible etiquette but he *is* handsome. That thought is quickly overshadowed. What could he possibly want to talk to me about at this hour? I'd send him away but I'm too intrigued.

'What is it?'

'I saw your show tonight and thought it was great ...' He runs a hand through his hair, messing up the longer-on-top side-parting thing that seems trendy these days. 'Anyway, I think I have what it takes and I wondered if you might have an opening for another dancer? I've just moved out here and I'm looking for work. I think it would suit me.'

I get a pang in my stomach. He certainly looks the part despite perhaps seeming a little older than the others, but that's not a problem. The age range of our audience is eighteen to anything goes. I just can't take someone on at the moment. 'Look ...' I look pointedly at him, hoping he'll furnish me with a name.

'Jay,' he says, taking the cue.

'Jay. It's not that I'm trying to brush you off. You certainly *look* the part and if you can dance I'd definitely audition you if I had space ... The thing is, our profit margins are small and I'd not budgeted for taking on another dancer this year. I'm sorry.'

'No, I'm sorry. I shouldn't have hijacked your evening. It was just an idea. I've just got out here and I'm looking for work. It looked like fun, that's all.' He drops his head and turns to leave.

I feel really bad, not that he's my responsibility or anything but when I first arrived out here, desperate, I was given a chance

9

and it indirectly kick-started the Hunks. Perhaps I'm just shattered after back-to-back gigs but I want to throw him a lifeline. I'm sure we probably *could* afford another body on stage and it will give us an excuse to update our posters and fliers.

'I'll tell you what, why don't you come along to a short audition tomorrow and I can keep you in mind.'

The dimples reappear. 'Yes, great. Tell me when and where you want me.'

I shiver. Must be the arctic conditions. I rummage in my bag and pull out a tatty old business card for the bar we rehearse in. 'We practise at three so come at two. Prepare a routine to "Pony" and we'll take it from there.'

'Okay, I'll be there …' he gestures to me with an open hand.

'Kat,' I say and take his hand in mine sealing the arrangement with a firm shake.

'Nice to meet you, Kat.'

Chapter 3

We rehearse in a dance bar about a ten-minute walk away. The owner, Andrea, is a Spanish woman in her mid-forties who lets us use it for free. I suspect it's for the view, but I like to think it's because she's my friend. I like Andrea a lot; she takes no nonsense from anyone.

When I get to Andrea's bar my insides are twisted in all kinds of knots. In the heat of the moment when I'd invited that guy in for an audition, I wasn't thinking. If he turns up and does a routine and he's really bad, I'll feel terrible for giving him false hope.

A cheerful hello breaks through my anxious thoughts.

'Jay, you made it,' I say, forcing a smile. He's wearing jeans and a plain white tee and there's a khaki bag slung over his shoulder. He's got a certain Channing Tatum look going on – I can definitely picture those promo posters.

He shuffles awkwardly and points to the small dance floor area. 'Should I just get straight to it?'

'Yes please, then we'll chat after. I have the music set up ready to go when you're ready.'

He's nervous, I can tell. I don't think he's done this before and I have butterflies on his behalf. Plenty of blokes think they can dance and look sexy simultaneously but it's not as easy as it looks.

Oh God, I've been here before with blokes who think they can but really can't. As the music starts, I'm braced for something terrible.

He walks forwards bending his knees to the beat with each stride, tugging down on the hem of his T-shirt as he does. It's not dancing but he's got presence.

Then, he tears the T-shirt down the front exposing his smooth, tanned chest then throws the tattered tee to the ground. I almost gasp. I don't know why; I watch the guys do this every night. I suppose I just wasn't expecting it. Then he jumps down into a one-armed push up and turns it into a humping action, then he leaps in the air and does a backflip – all in time to the music. It definitely grabs my attention and I thought I was immune to all things hot-guy.

When he finishes, he picks up the tattered remains of his T-shirt and dabs the sheen from his forehead and neck before looking at me sheepishly.

'That's pretty much it,' he says.

'Have you danced like this before?' I ask.

He shakes his head. 'No, I did gymnastics as a kid and a bit of street dancing when I was a teenager but mostly, I just watched a load of YouTube videos this morning.'

I smile at his honesty. 'Well, you pulled it off. You did well.'

He breathes a sigh of relief and his body visibly relaxes. 'So, did I make the all-famous Heavenly Hunks?'

I ponder this. A few minutes ago I was certain he wasn't right for us, but now I'm on the verge of sacking the guys and having him as a solo act. I have to be sure that it's my brain and not my very distracted eyes that wants this guy. I've calculated the costs – we *can* afford him and it will give us a new edge. His brow is furrowed; I'm torturing him here. 'How about a month's trial to see how you get on?'

He smiles and I notice a clean, straight set of teeth and those dimples again. 'Sounds good.'

'Great, I'll go over all the details with you, contracts and whatnot, and then you might as well stay on and rehearse. We'll introduce you into the show tonight if you're up for it?'

The rest of the Hunks start to pile in and Andrea breezes over in a multi-coloured, floor-length kaftan and hugs me. Her musky perfume envelops me as her long, wavy blonde hair tickles my face. 'Kat, my dear, it's so good to see you.'

'You too, Andri.'

I turn to Jay. 'If you want to stay for the rehearsal, we can try and squeeze you into a small part of the show in Playa de las Americas tonight if you like?'

'I'd love to.' He's visibility excited.

'Grab a drink and you can meet the guys,' I say, and he walks over to a table where Andrea has placed some iced water.

'So, a private show hey?' she says, giving me a wink. 'Does he do them for all the girls?'

'It was an audition,' I say drily. 'I'm thinking about expanding the group and making the Heavenly Hunks even bigger and better than we already are.'

'Well the more hot guys you want to bring into my bar, the better.' She flashes me a grin. 'I *actually* thought he might have been your date.'

'What, in the middle of the afternoon to a bar that isn't open yet? Give me some credit. Besides, you know I don't date.'

She shrugs. 'I thought perhaps you'd changed your mind – that's all.'

I roll my eyes. 'No, I haven't.'

'Noted. I'll feel less guilty about ogling the new guy then.' She grins.

'You're still married,' I remind her, laughing.

'And I've done nothing wrong.' With that, she disappears.

'Okay,' I shout to the Hunks who are in the process of welcoming Jay. 'Let's get this show on the road.'

Chapter 4

On stage, each dancer is honed to perfection, but something about Jay catches my eye. Obviously, he had the full-body appraisal in his audition earlier, but to my shame, I'd taken little notice of his face other than a fleeting acknowledgement of his celebrity doppelgänger. His flawless tanned skin looks like caramel under the light and his jaw is chiselled to perfection. Even from a distance, you can see a depth in his eyes. As he dances, I'm drawn to him. I can't tear my eyes away no matter how hard I try. There's a tattoo, a quote of some sort, on his inner bicep that wraps itself around and emphasises his muscles. I wish I could read it.

He's a bit older than the rest; maybe that is what's making me feel so captivated. There's a maturity in him that I don't see in the others – like each fine line on his face tells a story of something deeper. It makes me feel weird. I don't look at the dancers this way; it's wrong. In the end, I convince myself that I'm watching in a professional capacity – I have to see how the new guy gets on and get a feel for the audience perception; nothing more.

The cameraman I've hired to get some new promotional shots of the Hunks stays behind to give me a flavour of what he's captured. He's taken reportage-style shots so they're not posed. Instead, he's captured the Hunks doing what they do best – showcasing their talents on stage whilst looking good. Ignoring the hideous photos of me (think shiny face and hair plastered to my head), I think we've got some great material. I'm excited about making the Hunks an even bigger name in the Canaries.

**

'Jay!' I exhale, loudly. 'For fuck's sake stop sneaking up on me in the early hours.' After Jay's first show, we'd gone for a drink not far from where we live to celebrate but now I'm ready for home.

'Sorry, Kat, I didn't mean to scare you. I found these in the dressing room and thought they might be important.'

I glance at the clear squidgy things in his hands and almost drop dead with embarrassment.

'Thanks,' I say, as heat floods my cheeks.

'What even are they?'

I swallow hard and croak, 'Chicken fillets.'

His brow furrows with confusion. Seriously, what person has never seen these before and why are my cheeks hot? The guys all know I wear these on stage.

'You put them in your bra and they give you a bit of extra va-va-voom. It's part of my stage persona.'

'Ahh.' He glances away and I think the awkwardness is over.

'But why?'

Okay, the awkwardness is *not* over.

'Just to give me a bit of shape while I'm on stage.' I can't believe I'm explaining gel breast enhancers to one of my employees whom I barely know. I look at the sky, wishing a giant meteorite would hurtle down from space and land on me.

'Ahh.' He nods. 'Well, you don't need them. You have a great figure.'

Seriously, a meteorite, please!

I swallow hard and it takes me a second or two to compose myself. In future, I'm booking a taxi to take me home after a show to avoid any more run-ins like this.

'At least one of you is heading home,' I say changing the subject. 'Where are the others?'

'Hugo left with a couple of older women, and Pauw went home with his partner, Phil. Ant was with Sammy drinking cocktails in the bar with an attractive brunette, and I haven't seen Marcus since the hotel foyer.'

I roll my eyes. 'Typical. So how come you're heading home? It sounds like the night is just getting started for the others.'

'I'm just obeying orders,' he says, fluttering his eyelids in an attempt to look virtuous.

'We've another gig tomorrow but I said you could go for *one* drink.'

'I know. I just need my beauty sleep.'

'Is that so?' I give him a sideways look. This is the first glimpse I've had of his sense of humour and for some reason, it surprises me. What else do I need to know other than how his muscles make his T-shirt strain and how his intense brown eyes can cause a lower-abdominal stir in the back of a crowded auditorium?

'Do you always go home alone?' he asks.

'That's a bit personal.'

He laughs softly. 'I don't mean like *that*. I *meant* … don't you mind wandering the streets by yourself at this hour?'

'I'm used to it.'

'I get it. It's the twenty-first century, you're a modern, independent woman who doesn't need a chaperone—' I cut him off with a warning glance and he holds his hands up in surrender. 'All I'm saying is *I* might appreciate someone walking *me* home at night. That guy with the smoothie the other day was pretty dodgy-looking.'

Nice backtracking.

'If you're feeling vulnerable, I'd be happy to walk you home.'

16

I humour him even though he'll be out until all hours having fun with the rest of them in no time at all, once he realises his soon to be acquired 'minor celebrity status'.

'You did well tonight,' I say. He did too. I must admit I was on tenterhooks putting him up there after only one rehearsal. He only danced to one track – right at the end – but I was nervous as heck as he went on stage. I needn't have worried: the crowd seemed to love him.

'Thanks, Kat. When I saw all those screaming women, I was terrified going out there.'

'Those YouTube videos have really paid off,' I tease.

We walk in silence for a little while, and I ease into the feeling of having company on a walk I'm so used to doing alone. My ears still have a soft ringing in them from the loud music of the show, so it feels good to let them recover.

'So, Kat, how come you're not out hitting the bars and chatting up the fellas?' Jay asks unexpectedly. Initially, I bristle, then relax. Somehow, his northern accent – he's from Manchester, I think – makes him sound friendly and cheeky rather than too direct. Besides, he doesn't know me. He doesn't know this is a topic that's not up for discussion.

'I'm here to focus on the business. There isn't time for much else, and I have my work cut out playing mum to the guys. Do you know I had to show some of them how to use a laundrette?'

Jay shakes his head and laughs softly.

'I can't really be doing with another man in my life,' I say honestly.

'Fair enough,' he says.

'So what brings you to Tenerife anyway? The world-class entertainment?' I ask, glad to get the focus off me.

'Nah, I'm just here for the career prospects.'

I look at him with a raised eyebrow.

'To be honest, I'm here for a quiet life. I didn't have all that much to stay in the UK for, and I love the sunshine, the dancing

17

and the buzz of being on stage. During the day, I'm happy just reading by the pool. Boring really, aren't I?' He laughs.

I smile. 'Only as boring as me.'

We arrive at the budget apartment complex that we use as our base here in Tenerife.

'Right, see you tomorrow for the Los Christianos gig,' I say.

'Night, Kat.'

When I get inside, I slump on the bed and soak up the thick silence. My stomach churns with unease. I haven't thought about *him* in a very long time and I don't know if I want to pace around the room or crawl under the covers and hide. After all these years, how can he still have this effect on me?

***

The warmth of love is consuming. My muscles absorb it. It courses through my veins, soaks into my bones and fills up any hollow cavities it can find. It's all-encompassing as I lie here with Iain beside me. I'm safe. There's nowhere else I'd rather be. Even though he can be a bit possessive and sometimes I sense a hidden darkness in him, a mood that he doesn't share, I know it's his insecurity. He worries he'll lose me, that's all, and that's normal, isn't it? It just means he loves me and that's a wonderful feeling.

I understand his fear. I spent so much time feeling like I wasn't good enough for him that I know what he's going through. This is love and our love is so strong that the fear of losing one another is too. I almost hyperventilate when I think about losing Iain, so I know exactly how he feels. Once we're married and he knows I'm his forever, he'll calm down.

***

I sit bolt upright. Sweat is trickling down my head. I check the time and it's just after four. I get up and flick on the air-con

18

before getting back into bed. After all these years, Iain is still in my head and I'm annoyed with myself. My marriage ended over eight years ago. Since then I've picked myself up, moved away, built a business and I don't rely on anyone. I like being in charge of the Hunks. It gives me the confidence to be able to be around hot men without feeling inferior – if anything, mothering them makes me feel stronger. I've come such a long way since Iain and thinking about him makes my scalp prickle. He doesn't deserve a place in my memories.

When I push aside thoughts of Iain, I find myself thinking back to the conversation I had with Jay. It felt weird to be asked about dating twice in one day. It's been just me for so long and everyone who knows me understands that. I get that Jay is new and I shouldn't read anything into it, but I can't help but wonder if he thinks I'm broken. It's not like I've actively avoided men, not in recent years anyway; I've just been happy in my own company and haven't really looked. Nor have I been found.

Eventually, after much tossing and turning, I manage to drift off.

Chapter 5

After the show in Los Christianos, we head to an Indian restaurant for some much-needed post-show sustenance. When the food arrives and we're happily tucking in, Jay taps his glass to get everybody's attention. It seems a bit formal and I notice Ant and Marcus raise their eyebrows in surprise. It's a far cry from the shouting over one another that we've become accustomed to.

'I just wanted to say how grateful I am to you all for welcoming me into the Hunks and making me feel so comfortable, especially you, Kat.' There are murmurs of 'no worries' and 'great to have you on board' from full mouths all around the table.

Jay sips his beer. 'I'm curious, how did you all come to be in the Heavenly Hunks? I saw you guys at the hotel the other night and pretty much chased Kat down the street, but what are your stories?'

'When I first landed in Tenerife, I met Kat in Andrea's bar – where we do our rehearsals – when I'd gone in looking for work,' Paul says. 'Phil and I moved here because we fancied a new life in the sun, and I thought that with my acrobatics skills I'd get a job performing. Andrea told me, rather bluntly, that she already had a DJ and crappy entertainment wasn't her thing. She didn't even watch me perform.' Everyone snickers. 'Kat was working in the bar there and overheard. She looked me over and said she had an idea. Hugo used to be a stripper and Andrea had let him perform a few times – Kat thought the three of us could put together an exotic dance act that was part brawn, part talent. She said something like "think the Chippendales meets Diversity with a dash of Bruno Mars". We did small gigs for a while and built up a bit of a following. Then Marcus joined us and we started to really get the crowds going.'

'I was at an utter loss,' Marcus says. 'Split up from my girlfriend and came over on a lads' holiday. I was such a miserable twat and when it came to going home, I just couldn't bear it. I was working as a joiner for a big housing company and I was sick of the sight of cheap skirting boards. I'd made up my mind to stay, but I had no idea how I'd afford it. Anyway, I was sat in a bar and these two losers,' he winks at Paul, 'appeared on stage with Kat. After the show, I tried to chat her up. When she looked me over, I thought *eyup*, I'm getting somewhere here. Little did I know she was sizing me up for a part in the Hunks.' He laughs.

'I didn't even know you could breakdance then, either,' I say, laughing along.

'To be fair, I didn't even know I could still do it.' He turns to Jay. 'Throwback from my early teens.'

'What about you, Ant? How did you come to be in the Hunks?' Jay asks.

'My mum and I moved over here when I was ten. She met a bloke and moved back to England a few years ago, but I was an established Hunk by then. I wasn't giving that up,' he winks. 'Anyway, I was working in a bar and saw a poster – Kat was advertising for an exotic dancer. But my dance expertise was a little unconventional – ballet.' He coughs over the word to hide it.

'A bloody good one too, and you shouldn't be embarrassed! Ballet is an art form,' I interrupt. 'Sorry, you were saying …'

'You know what the boys are like!' He laughs. 'Anyway, I auditioned and Kat figured out a way to make me use my talents and look sexy. The sexy part was pretty easy though.'

'Nob,' Marcus says, and the others laugh.

'Sammy, how about you?' Jay asks.

'Nobody wants to hear my story.' Sam makes an over-the-top cutthroat gesture with his hand.

'Oh come on, I want to hear it more now,' Jay says.

'I'd been out with the lads, in Playa de las Americas on the bevvies, and we went into this club and these guys came on the stage. Anyway, when "Pony" came on, I jumped on stage and started grinding. A couple of the blokes who worked in the bar came and tried to drag me off stage but I backflipped out of the way. The crowd loved it and thought it was part of the act – women even wanted selfies with me afterwards – so Kat asked me to stay. To be honest, I didn't have much to go back to in England. I was still living with my folks and I didn't have a job so I thought I'd do a gap year. That was three years ago.' He grins.

I smile at the memory. At the time, I was sure I'd made a mistake taking on Sammy. I thought he'd fly back home the minute he felt a little homesick or something didn't quite go his way and I'd have to rejig all the choreography again. He'd surprised me.

After our food, we head to a bar on the strip for a drink with the guys, but slowly they've all dispersed. Marcus is slow-dancing with a blonde, Pauw has gone home with Phil and I have no idea where the others have got to. There's an older guy at the other end of the bar who keeps staring at me and I'm starting to feel quite uncomfortable. His back is stooped as he clutches his small glass of dark brown liquid. This is my cue to leave. I throw back the last of my beer and make my way to the exit.

As I step into the inky-black quiet, I feel a spindly hand on my shoulder.

'Where are you going?' It's the man from inside the bar.

'Home.' I peel his hand away, but he steps forward so his warm, pungent breath fills my airspace.

'Don't I get an invite?' he slurs.

'I don't think so,' I say, trying to move past him.

'How about a dance before you go?' He presses himself against me.

'Excuse me.' I try to sidestep him but he mirrors my movement.

'You haven't even let Billy show you a good time yet.' He licks his cracked, dry lips.

'I don't know who Billy is, but I don't need him to have a good time, thank you.' Something inside is screaming at me to stay calm and not anger this man.

He steps forward again, pinning me to the wall, pressing himself into my pubic bone. 'Oh, I think you do.'

I glance at the bar. People are inside, dancing, lost in their own fun. Nobody gives us a second glance. My chest tightens.

'Get away from me!' My voice comes out with a small tremble, and he laughs. That enrages me, so I shove him back as hard as I can and slam my knee into his crotch. He doubles over in pain. I contemplate going back inside to tell the others what happened, but I know they'll make a huge scene. In the split second it takes to contemplate my choices, Billy is upright again. He grabs my arm.

'You bitch!' he spits, and for a second I don't know what he's going to do. I'm frozen.

'Get your hand off her.' A firm, male voice sounds from behind us. Billy looks up and his eyes widen. Immediately, he releases me.

'If I see you treat a woman this way again, you'll be sorry.' The voice is a low growl and Billy scurries off. I turn, surprised to see Jay, all six feet, two inches of solid muscle. No wonder Billy backed off so easily.

'Thank you. Not just for chasing him off, but for not causing a scene,' I say. The last thing I want is for the Heavenly Hunks to make the front page of the *Canaries Today* for being involved in a mass brawl and that would have happened if any of the other Hunks had come over.

The corner of Jay's mouth curves into a grin. 'You seemed to have it under control.'

'It's not my first encounter with a drunken idiot.'

'I'm sure dealing with drunken idiots is a regular occurrence being the manager of Marcus.'

I smile. He's not far wrong. 'Have you settled into the apartment all right?' Jay is now bunking in with Marcus.

'Yes, Marcus is a messy sod but he makes a great coffee in the morning.'

I agree on both counts.

'Are you heading home?' He tilts his head to the side.

'Ahh, I forgot you needed someone to escort you,' I tease. 'But yes, I'm going for a taxi if you want to share?'

We set off to the taxi rank and chat about how well the show went and how great the Hunks have been at showing Jay the ropes. When we arrive at the apartment complex, Jay holds out his hand to help me out of the taxi. His sleeve rides up revealing the script tattoo on his arm.

'What does it say?' I ask, pointing to it. I've been dying to read it.

'Oh, that. Nothing really. It's just something from my past.'

I squint, trying to read the cursive font, but he moves his arm down by his side, covering it. I'm all the more intrigued now but it's obvious he doesn't want to talk about it anymore so I don't press him.

We reach the staircase that leads up to my apartment. 'Thanks again for dealing with Billy in such a civilised way and not just punching his lights out like the others would.'

Jay frowns.

'Billy was the idiot in the bar.'

'Ahh. Not a problem. I'm just glad you're okay.' Jay's eyes linger on mine for a moment and I feel some sort of connection. It makes me feel uneasy so I try to ignore it. My phone pings, letting me know an email has come in, so I open it for a distraction. It works.

'That's weird,' I say under my breath.

'What is?' Jay asks. I'd not realised he was still standing there.

'Oh, it's a cancellation for the Hunks.' I try to make it sound less dramatic than it is. The hotel that's cancelled has been booking us for years. Only last week the manager was talking about slotting in some more gigs soon. It makes no sense.

'I'm sure there's a good reason,' Jay says optimistically.

'Yeah, he just says that holiday bookings are down on last year and he can't afford to staff the large auditorium through the winter season. It will be fine,' I add, not wanting to worry him in his first few days of employment. He nods in agreement and not wanting to get caught in his headlamp eyes again, I turn to leave.

'Goodnight, Jay,' I say, before heading up to my apartment.

***

Despite having such a terrible night's sleep last night and being absolutely shattered, I still find myself tossing and turning, replaying the incident with Billy in my head.

To take my mind off things, I pick my phone up and start scrolling through mundane Facebook updates to try and empty my head. There are a few posts that make me sit up straight.

RIP Tommy xxx

Best lad. You'll be missed, brother xxx

Too young Tommy xxx

Tommy? Tom Mitchell? I rub my eyes and read the statuses again, then I click on the tagged name 'Tommy'. Sure enough, it's Tom Mitchell's profile. He was in my year at secondary school. He was a bit of an idiot back then: the kind of kid who'd spread embarrassing rumours or call you a name just to get a laugh. He had everyone calling me 'the minger' for about six months but I wouldn't wish *death* on him. He can only have been thirty-seven or thirty-eight. God. I sit back against the cheap imitation pine headboard and keep scrolling. There are hundreds of comments along the same lines. People are shocked, sad and so on. His last status was only a few days ago – he'd booked a holiday to Majorca with his wife and son.

'Jesus,' I say aloud.

I click on the local newspaper feed and look for any articles covering what happened. I know I shouldn't – it's morbid and none of my business whatsoever – but he was my age. I feel almost duty-bound to find out what's out there killing people off so young. We've not hit heart-attack territory yet, and if his death was so sudden, I'm guessing it wasn't a long-term illness.

Bingo.

Father of one, killed in collision at accident black spot
Local campaigners say it was only a matter of time before a fatal accident occurred on this popular A-road and expressed anger that local councillors ignored their campaign for traffic-calming measures last year.

'Oh God.'

His profile picture is of him, his wife and his little boy, who looks about four. Poor thing, it's going to be so hard for him to understand. Before I realise what I'm doing, I'm scrolling through Tom Mitchell's photo albums. Going off his pictures, he had so much to live for. There are pictures of stag dos, nights out with huge groups of friends, him at several weddings, him sky diving,

26

him and his wife at a quaint little Cotswolds' spa. In the most normal and slightly enviable of ways, this guy really *lived*. It's the life I thought I'd have with Iain. Sharing a life of minibreaks and experiences, perhaps even a few kids running around.

I put my phone down on the duvet. Tom looked to have had this wonderful life that's now been torn apart. It's heart-wrenching. I know I haven't seen him in years and he was never really a friend at school but through the pictures, you can tell he had a lot to lose and his family will forever have a hole ripped out of it where he should be. To distract myself, I get up for a glass of water before sitting back down on the bed. Selfishly, I start to think of my own life. If I died right this minute, what would I have to show for it? To the outside world, I suppose the pictures of the dancers and me might look as though I'm living my best life but, really, I'm like their adoptive mother and those pictures generally mark some occasion, like Jay joining the troupe or Marcus's birthday. My entire time here has been mostly work and very little play and if you look between the work pictures on any of my social media accounts, there are just stray cats and sunsets. Should I be thinking about doing something more? Having a focus that stretches beyond work?

I stare at the ceiling for a little while more but I'm wide awake now and can't lie here any longer. Tommy's death and the whole 'questioning my own life choices' thing is hardly the equivalent of swigging half a bottle of Nytol. After slipping on some shorts and a hoodie, I slip outside and walk down the steps to the small, glowing turquoise pool at the heart of the complex. I sit back on a plastic lounger, the cold of it beneath my still bed-warm skin makes my bones ache but the contrast to my warm, cosy bed is welcome. The air is cool with a hint of moisture in it, and goose bumps pop up on my legs but still, I refuse to go back inside. Instead, I welcome the lack of comfort as a distraction and relish the feeling of my head finally clearing with each deep breath I take. The water-churning sound of the pool filter is strangely therapeutic and as I close my eyes, my head clears and I start to nod off.

'I know Europeans like to get up early to reserve sun loungers, but I think you're playing it a bit too safe.'

I dart upright, eyes wide open.

'Jay?' My mouth is thick and dry with doziness and the syllable is a mouthful.

'What are you doing out here?' He sits down on the lounger next to mine and hands me his bottle of water, which I take gratefully. After a long sip, I rub dried drool off the corner of my mouth. Sexy!

'I couldn't sleep so came out for some air, which must have worked wonders.' I laugh softly, handing him back the water.

'Me neither. I head outside a lot during the night,' he says. The droop of his shoulders and the way his eyes drift to the ground make me think there's more to it than just a rough night's sleep.

'Is there something you want to talk about?' I ask. If anything is bothering any of my boys, I want to know about it so I can help.

He shakes his head. 'No, I'm fine. Just a bit of an insomniac. I'm really happy I came out here – to Tenerife, I mean – though I'm also happy I came out here tonight too.'

The bit he adds to the end jars me. What does he mean he's happy he came out here tonight? Politeness. It has to be.

'Good, but if anything does ever bother you, promise that you'll talk to me,' I say, ignoring what he said about being glad to be out here.

'Will do. How about you? You're out here in the middle of the night. What's on your mind?'

I'm about to brush it off as he did, but when I glance at him, the moonlight catches his face and he's looking at me with the burning intent of someone who actually wants to listen. It's a strange feeling to trust someone who you hardly know, but it's been a while since I opened up to anyone, so I try it for size.

I draw a deep breath. 'Do you ever wonder if you're truly satisfied with your life?'

He regards me for a moment, perhaps checking that I'm asking a serious question, and then lies back on his lounger and rolls onto his side to face me.

'Of course. It's one of the reasons I'm out here – the pursuit of happiness.'

'But do you think it will make you happy? Like, if you died tomorrow, would you close your eyes and float into the blackness feeling like you'd done enough with your life?'

'Blackness? Why isn't there a light?' He looks alarmed.

'Okay,' I say. 'Light, if that makes you feel better.'

'It does.' He smiles. 'Er, I don't know. I don't really have any ambition career-wise. I just take each day as it comes. Obviously, I won't be a Heavenly Hunk when I'm a wizened old geezer, but I'd be game for the Aged Adonises if the opportunity arises.'

I laugh softly. 'The Aged Adonises; I like it. What about putting down roots, like a house and family and all that normal stuff?'

He shakes his head. 'I think I'm going to like being on the road. The Canaries has year-round sun and I'm a simple guy so that will do me. Just because it's normal for other people to settle down and have a family, doesn't mean it has to be for us. We define our own normal in the confines of what makes us happy. How long have you been out here, Kat?'

It takes me a minute to run the calculation. 'Eight years.'

'And you've been happy all that time?'

I nod.

'So why change it?'

I sigh. 'I wouldn't even have questioned my life this morning, but a bloke from my year at school died suddenly yesterday. I read about it on Facebook – I guess that's why I can't sleep.'

'God, I'm sorry, Kat.'

'No, it's fine. I mean, it's sad and everything but he wasn't a close friend. He was more of a bully back in school if I'm honest.

Anyway, he had all the *normal* boxes ticked – married with a child, and did all these exciting, memorable things – and not only will he be missed by tonnes of people, he also died knowing he *lived*.'

'You mean hanging out with hot male strippers every day isn't living?'

'Touché. I suppose to my Facebook friends back in England I'm living the life of Riley – whoever Riley is or was. But, seriously, I'm not really moving forward, if that makes any sense?'

'What do you mean?' Jay avoids bringing up marriage again, and I appreciate the sentiment but the prompt for more depth makes my skin prickle with unease.

'Sorry, I shouldn't be burdening you with all this "woe is me" stuff. I'm your boss and this is hardly a great introduction into the Hunks.'

'I'm happy to listen. Try me.' He's lying casually on his side, head propped up on his arm, eyes on mine. I feel hypnotised, compelled into talking about things I normally lock away. It's so confusing – it's not even like he's pushing me to talk, it's just something about his energy. All I know is, I need to put a stop to this; it's unprofessional.

'No, it's fine. I think I just need a good night's sleep,' I say.

Jay's face falls. I've offended him but better this than getting too close. I say a quick goodnight and head to my apartment.

Chapter 6

The following evening, we're doing a small show in a local bar. It's an un-ticketed event but the owner pays us a bit of cash and the social media coverage is usually worth it. My only problem this evening is that the place is so cramped that the front row only need to bow their heads slightly to manage a salty lick of Marcus's abdomen and I have a strict 'no touching' policy. There's no dressing room, so we get ready in the toilets, which means I can go in the ladies and be by myself a while. As I'm walking in, the bar manager calls me over.

'Sergio, is everything all right?' I ask.

He furrows his brow as though whatever he's about to say pains him greatly. 'Kat, you know we love having the Hunks here? The problem is, our footfall is dropping. I had to send all my bar staff out on the streets to drag people in tonight with the promise of a free shot and the situation is getting worse. I can't guarantee we can afford to host the Hunks for the next few months.'

When I look back at the audience, I notice the chairs have been purposely shoved forward to make the room look busier and a bar man is wandering around handing out red coloured shots. I manage to nod an acknowledgement but a heavy weight drops in my stomach. This is the second cancellation this week.

'Oh, okay. I'm sorry to hear things are quiet but I understand. Let's hope things improve soon.'

He puts a hand on my shoulder, 'I'm sorry Kat. As soon as things pick up, we'll get you booked back in.'

'Of course, thanks for letting me know, Sergio.'

When I get into the toilets, I slump against the wall and check the booking calendar. We still have plenty of gigs; we should be okay.

After the show, the guys go off to have some drinks but I spot Jay approaching me as I go to leave.

'Not going out for a drink?' I ask.

'Nah, I'm shattered. I told you anyway, I'm too old for all of that.'

I smile. 'Well that makes two of us. Come on then, I'll chaperone you home.'

He grins sheepishly, picking up on my reference. 'So, are you feeling any better about life?' he asks as we set off.

'Yes,' I say, hoping we can draw a line under it, although part of me is intrigued by Jay. He's the same sort of age as me and he's just come over here. What's he running from? Divorce?

'Good, as long as you're happy, don't worry about fitting into a box.'

The truth is, all day I've been thinking about my life. In a few years, I'll be forty and if I do want to settle down with a house and kids and stuff, time won't necessarily be on my side. I have to be sure the decision I made eight years ago is still right for me.

'I don't know how to be sure,' I say. 'You're in a similar position – does it not worry you to think this could be it?'

He clenches his jaw. 'I made my peace with being alone a long time ago.'

He picks up pace and I find myself almost running to keep up.

'Are you okay?' I ask, taken aback by his sudden clamming up.

'I'm fine. I'm not the one questioning life – I'm happy to talk through your problems but please don't try and put them onto me and make out we're in a similar position. With all due respect, we're not and I'm fine.'

'I … You're right. I'm sorry,' I stammer and I hate myself for it.

'No …' his tone is softer now, '… I'm sorry for sounding grumpy. I think moving so far south has given me a bad *latitude*.'

I cast him a sideways glance and see he's smirking. I shake my head.

'That was terrible,' I say, laughing softly and we fall into an amicable silence. He's every right to keep his personal life private but I can't help being drawn to his story, even though it's obvious he doesn't want to share it. When we reach the square outside our apartment block I sit on the wall of the fountain and to my surprise, he sits down next to me.

'It's normal you know.'

'What is?'

'Thinking about having a family and stuff. I'm the one who is probably a bit *different*.'

'No, each to their own,' I say. 'I have been married before.'

'Oh.' He doesn't pry but I find myself wanting to give a little more.

'It didn't work out and I've become a much stronger person on my own. I'm independent both financially and emotionally and I don't want to jeopardise that. That's why I'm scared to venture back into the world of dating.'

He doesn't reply; instead, he nods.

'It sounds silly out loud but I have my reasons.'

'You could always try it – one date wouldn't mean settling down,' he says. I know he's right but it scares me so much.

'It's just all that stuff with Tommy dying that's made me feel like this. I was fine before that. I guess it's just shaken me up.'

'Try it. Plenty of people use Tinder these days for casual dating. It doesn't have to mean anything.'

'I guess not,' I say without conviction. 'I just don't think that sort of stuff is for me.'

Jay furrows his brow, seemingly unconvinced. 'How long have you been single?'

I don't need to run a mental calculation for that. 'Almost nine years.'

Jay whistles through his teeth. 'Have you honestly not been on a date in all that time?'

I shake my head. 'I've not felt the need to. I've always had the Heavenly Hunks to keep me busy.'

'That's fine if you're happy. Forgive me for saying, but you can't have been short of offers.'

Heat creeps up the back of my neck. 'It's just not something I'd considered – I love having my independence and being in charge of my own destiny.'

'Fair enough,' he says and I like that he respects my choice. 'I meant what I said last night. I don't mind listening if you want to talk about it?'

I look him in the eyes to anchor myself to the spot. The conversation is awkward enough that I want to bolt, but maybe talking will be good. I haven't sat down and talked about this with anyone before and I did feel a little bit better after chatting to Jay last night. I sit on the wall of the pretty fountain outside the hotel, allowing the gurgling patter of the water to momentarily fill the silence. Jay follows.

'I just don't know if I'm treading water and going through the same motions without really evaluating if being alone is still what I want, or what I *might* want in the future. I just worry that maybe one day I'll wake up older, regretting not doing more of the "normal" stuff.'

'So, I get it if you're happy being single, but you're obviously not as convinced as you thought you were. Why not go on a date and see how things pan out? If you don't feel comfortable or whatever, no harm done.'

I scrub the soles of my shoes on the crunchy gravel. It makes a satisfying noise. 'I didn't really have many friends at school.'

I pause, waiting for him to say something, but he doesn't and I realise I'm relieved to be able to carry on.

'I wasn't pretty or cool, and most of the kids found it hilarious to call me names. It never really went much beyond that but still … Anyway, by the time I started uni, I'd discovered make-up, highlights, *hair straighteners* and the joys of buying my own clothes rather than the ones my mum picked up in the C&A sale. I started to get … offers.' I repeat Jay's word but almost choke on the awkwardness of it. I glance at Jay who is, to his credit, wearing his best poker face.

'I met Iain.'

'Your husband?'

I nod. 'He was good-looking, a bit of a Jack-the-lad with plenty of charm, but a good laugh. Everyone knew him, and if there was a big night out or a party, the first thing people wanted to know was: would Iain be there? Then at a party one night, he asked me if I fancied going outside so we could chat properly – "21 Seconds" or something was probably rattling out of some tinny portable CD player – and I jumped at the chance. I couldn't believe he'd noticed me.'

'It sounds like you didn't give yourself enough credit,' Jay says.

'Well, I was a young woman, swept up in the affections of one of the hottest guys on campus. We dated on and off. He'd always dump me and then turn up in the middle of the night, crying because he'd made a mistake. After uni, we ended up together properly. He was a bit jealous and possessive then, but at the time I was flattered. I thought it just meant he really cared.' I wriggle uncomfortably – the discomfort has less to do with the stone fountain wall threatening to bestow haemorrhoids upon me, and more to do with the words falling out of my mouth.

'I made a mistake. I love you, Kat.' Part of me is annoyed for opening the door but the other half of me is so glad to see him.

35

When he dumped me, it was like a bear had clawed a hole in my chest. I couldn't breathe. Now that he's here with tear-stained cheeks and big puppy eyes, telling me he's sorry, I know I'll forgive him.

'Please listen to me, Kat! You know you won't find anyone better. Most guys like skinny girls with blonde hair. I'm different, Kat, I love you for who you are.' He takes my hands and pulls me closer. 'Not everyone can see past looks and really see the good in someone.'

I swallow hard. He's right. When I go out, I see those skinny girls he's talking about and when I look in the mirror, I see exactly what he means.

'Kat, forgive me. I love you.' He presses his wet, salty lips to mine and I find myself responding. We can put all of this behind us now. It's our new chapter.

I shake the memory away.

'He proposed. I was thrilled and we got married. Long story short, I didn't do the dating thing, ever, so you can see how looking to start now is a little bit scary for me.'

The corner of Jay's mouth twists. 'I can, but you can't let that hold you back forever. Not when you have doubts about whether you've chosen the right path.'

'No. In fact, I'm going to look at my options,' I say decisively.

'So, you're going to try a date?'

Saying it like that makes me freeze. I'm about to protest, but I pause. What do I have to lose? A few hours of my life?

'Yes,' I say, taking out my phone. 'I'm going to try one of those dating app things.'

I can't believe how easy it is. Download the app, sign in with Facebook and *voila*, in no time at all I'm flicking through pictures of guys like they're in an Argos catalogue.

'You don't mess about.' Jay laughs as I'm swiping left through several pictures.

I shrug, then pause with my finger hovering over a photograph of a guy who looks all right.

'Who is it?' Jay asks, leaning over.

'A guy who works in a bar near here.'

'Sounds like he has all the right credentials,' Jay teases.

'I'm going to do it. I'm swiping right,' I say.

'Good for you,' Jay says. 'Listen, I'll leave you to it.'

'Night, Jay … and thanks for listening.'

'No problem. Night, Kat.'

When Jay leaves, my phone pings. 'Oh my God,' I mutter. He's got in touch already. He's called Mike, he's thirty-nine and he's asking if I want to go out tomorrow.

'Mike,' I say aloud, allowing my lips chance to get used to the word. Then I type:

Okay, when and where?

The reply is instant.

Lunch, tomorrow at the La Grande Grill in the Tropicana Resort Hotel.

I nod. Lunch seems quite informal. I can cope with that.

Okay, let's do it.

Dating aside, it was nice talking to Jay. He's a good listener but doesn't take life too seriously. I hope our friendship continues to grow.

***

The next day I am much less calm.

The yellow sundress I've always felt half-decent in looks sackish and seems to wash me out. The red one that I thought would bring out the blue in my eyes is too tight, and the beige one makes me look naked from afar, and not in a hot Instagram way but more of an erotic potato sort of way. This leaves the corn-flower-blue skater-style dress. The lines are quite flattering but it *is* a little shorter than I'm comfortable with. I check my watch. I need to leave in ten minutes; I just need to pick something. It's either the yellow or the blue. I change back into the yellow. No, it adds ten pounds and only a belt could save it. I slip back into the blue. No way. It sends the wrong message. I now have five minutes left so throw the yellow one back on and scramble for a belt. It will have to do.

I spot my chicken fillets on the side and shove them in my bra for some added oomph. The fabric of the dress pulls much tighter than my stage dress does and when I glance in the mirror, I have a certain Dolly Parton vibe. I'm not sure I like it. From nowhere, Jay's words hit me: 'You don't need them. You have a great figure.' Perhaps I'm sending out the wrong message here. This Mike guy has to meet the real me, not the 'on-stage' me. I pull them out and smooth the dress back down. It's only a first date, after all.

I'm quite close to the hotel entrance when I realise I'm running. I slow down and adjust my dress, which has ruched up and gathered above my belt. When I tug it back down, I realise I was probably flashing my knickers to innocent bystanders at some point, and I'm glad to be of an age where only a full-bottom brief will do. I smooth down my hair and enter through the revolving door. It's a nice hotel, the kind that smells of something fresh and Jo Malone-y when you walk in, and it has an amazing calmative effect on me.

I ask the concierge where the Grill is and, following his instructions, make my way down some steps and outside onto a terracotta-tiled terrace. The pool is bustling in the heat of the day and the sunlight charges each ripple of water with a bright, sparkling burst. It's the kind of place Iain would have brought us to in our early days, just so he could take a load of pictures and show them off to all his faux-friends on his MySpace account, or whatever it was back then.

The restaurant is starting to fill up, and a few people mill around the entrance waiting to be seated. My stomach twists. I'd felt okay-ish up until this point, but now the group ahead have gone in and it's my turn, I'm terrified. I could turn to go, but that would be cruel, leaving someone sitting there alone like a lemon. I couldn't do that to a person, and besides that, my stomach thinks my throat's been cut. I can talk to another human over lunch.

'Madam, do you have a reservation?' the waiter asks.

'I, er, yes. I'm meeting someone. Mike?'

The waiter flips the booking sheet over, dramatically scanning as though he doesn't quite believe that: a) I have a booking or b) I have a date.

His eyebrows lift with relief. 'This way, madam.'

I follow him apprehensively, purposely leaving a gap between us. I want to see Mike before he sees me. I'm not sure why – perhaps if I'm not overly enamoured, I'll have time to arrange my face into something that less resembles disappointment.

'Damn,' I mutter under my breath. All I can see is his short, well-groomed blond hair – his back is to me. There's nothing wrong with his back, but now I've lost my advantage. If I'm disappointed it will show on my face and there's nothing I can do about it. I have that well-known affliction, resting bitch-face. If I'm not forcing a smile, I look miserable, even when I'm not miserable, and any thought that presents itself in my head etches into my expression. Realising I'm starting to panic, I take a breath and move around to face him.

'Hi.' I hold out my hand formally. 'I'm Kat. You must be Mike.'

When I see his face, I'm taken aback. He's not bad. His bright blue eyes twinkle affably under the soft lighting of the restaurant, and his teeth are white against his suntanned skin. A wave of relief rinses through me.

He's chewing on some bread and wipes his mouth on his napkin before standing up to hug me.

'That's me. Nice to meet you, Kat,' he says, pulling away. I detect a soft Welsh accent.

We take our seats and he pours two glasses of white wine from a carafe in the centre of the table.

'So, what is it you do? Sorry, it's a cliché to ask but it was the first thing that popped into my head.'

I smile. 'That's okay. I manage a dance act – the Heavenly Hunks – you've probably seen our posters dotted about if you work in a bar.'

'Oh yeah, the sexy dance group?' His tone is layered with titillation.

I feel my cheeks flush, which irks me because I'm not at all embarrassed about my work; in fact, I'm proud of it. I'm just not comfortable with the lewd way in which Mike said it.

'They're an all-male exotic dance troupe,' I correct him.

He raises his eyebrows in a way that suggests he doesn't see the difference. I glug my wine and pretend not to notice.

'And you're a barman?'

'That I am. Been here for the best part of six years now.'

I nod along and sip my wine, hoping that in the few seconds it takes to swallow it I'll come up with something riveting to say.

'Will you stay here much longer?' That wasn't riveting at all.

'Probably. We'll have to see how it goes.' He takes a drink, and I swear I see him wink at me but convince myself I'm mistaken, for the sake of the afternoon and the fact I'm starving and we've not even ordered yet.

'The seafood platter looks good,' I say, as one of the waitresses carries one by.

A waiter approaches us to take our order and Mike jumps in first. 'We'd love the seafood sharing platter please.' He looks at me for confirmation and I nod, not quite sure if it was sweet that he ordered on my behalf or a little bit controlling.

As we wait for our food, the small talk dries up, and in turn, so does our carafe. We order another, and half of that has gone by the time the platter arrives.

When I look at the prawns, I realise I'm a little woozy. This is not good; I need to keep my composure. I look at Mike, happily holding a prawn by its tail whilst chewing the body. I force my eyes into focus. He is good-looking but there is something off about him and the vibe is all wrong. Perhaps I'm too used to being on my own and I'm being too picky. I can't expect to meet the perfect guy on my first date. I decide to ignore the twinge of disappointment and give him a chance. Besides that, we're not kids anymore, so perhaps that spark just doesn't happen for older people. Perhaps a nice meal and a bit of benign conversation are all I have to hope for.

'You're really beautiful,' he says, all of a sudden.

The back of my neck tingles and I smooth down the hair that covers it.

'Thanks. You ... er, you are quite blessed in the looks department yourself.'

Quite blessed? I'm going to need the rest of the carafe if I'm going to feel less cringe-tastic about saying that!

I steer the conversation to our favourite 'day off' activities on the island and how often we visit the UK and such, and before I know it, the platter is finished.

I did it. I went on a date, and aside from a few initial bumps at the beginning, it was actually okay. I allow myself to feel a little smug.

'So,' Mike pipes up, 'you must be quite a saucy little thing putting together your whole exotic stripper shebang thingy?' He winks. I'm certain this time.

I gawk. There's no other word for it. Just as it was all going so well.

'Excuse me?'

'Well, come on. I won't judge, but you've got to admit you must be a little bit naughty?' He skims his tongue across his lips.

A thousand ants crawl across my skin. I almost don't really blame him. I blame Hugh bloody Hefner and his reputation – he's tarred us all. Like you can't work with attractive, semi-clad people and not have them all in your bed.

I've gone off Mike. A lot.

'Mike, thank you for a ... mostly pleasant afternoon. Here's my half of the bill, but I must be going now.' I toss forty-five euros down on the table, which I reckon is about right, including a tip.

His practically salivating jaw slackens. As if he really did think I was going to start telling him how saucy I am. Midday dirty talk over some discarded prawn tails and clamshells with a guy I've only just met? No thanks.

'Sorry, did I misread the signs? I thought we were having a good time getting to know one another.'

No apology then?

'I just don't see a second date on the cards for us.'

'What about finishing *this* date properly?'

I have no idea what he means by *properly* – okay, I do but I'm blanking it out. 'I've got a long day of doing all the accounts tomorrow; I have to keep a clear head. Sorry.' I bite my tongue before I can automatically say 'Maybe another time'.

Before he has time to speak, I say, 'Bye,' and leave, making a conscious effort not to run.

Chapter 7

The next morning, as I open my curtains, I see Jay sunbathing by the pool. I lather on some sunscreen and throw on a bikini with a kaftan over the top and march down as meaningfully as my Havaianas will allow.

'I need a word,' I say, kicking the leg of Jay's sun lounger to rouse him.

He groans. 'Kat? Everything okay?'

'Not really. That guy, Mike, was a real creep.'

He sits up, concerned. 'Mike? The guy you went on a date with?'

I nod.

'What did he do?' Jay sits up straighter.

'He implied that I must be kinky because of my work, and believe me, If I had a quid for every time someone made an insinuation like that, well, I wouldn't be rich but I would be able to buy a signature cocktail from the fancy bar down on the waterfront.'

Jay rubs his chin, trying hard to conceal a smirk. 'Ahh. Okay, so he was a creep. Plenty more fish in the sea. Anyway, why are you narked with me?'

I sigh. 'Sorry. I guess you were the one who made me feel like it was a good idea.'

'Because *you* were curious.'

'I'm sorry. I'm just so annoyed that I gave in to this whim when I'm okay being single.'

'You're not going to meet your soulmate after one date, Kat.'

'I know. Maybe my expectations were too high,' I say, slumping on the lounger next to him.

'No, he sounds like a nob. Sorry it didn't work out,' he says, patting my shoulder.

'It's fine. I guess my only real experience of dating comes from Hollywood movies and not the real world. I'm clearly not the greatest with men.'

'I know the guys here really respect you.' He pauses for a second. 'Has nothing really ever happened with you and one of them?'

'God, no!' The thought horrifies me. 'I'd never mix business with romance. I may need to fire one of you one day.' I give him a mischievous wink.

'Bloody hell, should I be worried?' he says playfully.

I shrug. 'Maybe.'

'In that case, I better get myself off to rehearsals.' He stands up and walks to the edge of the pool before diving in.

Funny place to rehearse.

He comes up for air and reads my expression. 'What? I haven't got time to shower.'

As I shake my head, he swims over to the edge and heaves himself out. Water droplets sparkle on his taut, bronzed skin as he rubs his dark hair with his towel. Even though I see his naked torso almost every night, this feels strangely intimate so I look away. As I do, I see Pauw approaching, looking fresh in a white Ralph Lauren Polo shirt tucked into navy chino shorts.

'Morning, lovely.' He kisses me on the cheek. 'And hello, sailor,' he says, giving Jay the once-over.

Jay cocks his head to the side and pouts seductively.

'Oh come on, you're not my type. You don't cut your hair nearly often enough and quite frankly, you're a bit of a diva.'

Jay raises his eyebrows with bemusement but doesn't reply.

'Have you been to the doctor's yet?' I ask Pauw as Jay lies back on his lounger.

'Yes, yes. He's going to remove it and send it off for analysis as a precaution. He thinks it's probably healthy and I'll get a scar—'

'But if it *is* anything sinister, you'll have done the right thing.'

'Very true. So …' Pauw clasps his hands together. 'Where are the rest of our troupe? I didn't see them at the gym today.'

'Coming down any moment now if they know what's good for them.'

Right on cue, Marcus and Sammy emerge followed by Ant and Hugo. All four of them look like they hardly slept.

'Time to shine. I want you to give it one hundred per cent today, boys. It's our last show on the island tonight, so we'd better make it a good one.' I clap three times to emphasise just how wide awake I want them to be.

Marcus rubs his hair. 'Kat, love, can I grab a strong coffee first?'

I check my watch animatedly. 'Yes, if you can rewind time, get up fifteen minutes earlier and make yourself one. If you can't do that, then no. Sorry, it's rehearsal time.'

Marcus pulls a face but doesn't argue. No doubt consciously saving himself the 'this is why we're the best in the business' speech I bandy around when I'm stamping my authority.

When we get to Andrea's, she's behind the bar putting the float in the till.

'Hi, Andri.' I throw my bag down on a barstool.

'Are we having a drink?'

'Just coffee please, Andrea. I have to keep a clear head. Can you do me a favour and brew some for the guys too? I think they're going to need a kick up the backside today.'

She ogles each of them. 'Their backsides look too good to kick!' With that, she winks and walks off. I set up the music and drag a few tables away from the edge of the dance floor to create a bit more space.

'Have you seen this?' Andrea appears beside me and hands me a leaflet.

I glance at it. 'The Canary Islands Entertainment Act of the Year,' I say, reading the bold lettering aloud.

Andrea nods, a huge grin spreading across her face. 'I think you and the guys are in with a real shot of winning. Look at the prize.' She turns the flyer over.

I squint at the smaller lettering, then my eyes goggle. 'Ten grand and a chance to perform in Las Vegas!'

That would be a nice little lump sum for each of us and a great gig. Not to mention the publicity that could help generate some much-needed bookings. I haven't told the guys business is getting quiet yet, but I'm starting to worry. Aside from the cancellations, we don't seem to be generating many new bookings.

'Yes, the prize money is raised by all the tourist businesses across the islands – the hotels, bars – even I've donated and the gig in Las Vegas has been put up by some hotshot from the entertainment world. We get some free publicity from a local TV station and the *Canaries Today*, plus a UK tour operator will tailor a package holiday around your show. I'm thinking hen do packages to see the Heavenly Hunks would be a sure-fire winner.'

'What do we have to do?'

'There is an audition in a couple of weeks over in Maspalomas, Gran Canaria. From there, you have to get through a couple of rounds, and there's a final here in Tenerife, which local people are invited to watch.'

She goes back to the bar for the coffees and I read the leaflet once more. This is a huge chance to really put the Heavenly Hunks on the map. I'll see what the guys think later.

'So, what's new?' She lays out the cups and makes a broad gesture to the guys to show the drinks are for them before pulling out a chair and sitting next to me.

'Oh, not much.' It sounds so dull, so I add, 'I did go on a date last night.'

46

'Kat! On a date! Oh my goodness. With whom?'

I fill her in on the Mike situation.

She shudders. 'Eurgh. Why do men think that's how we work?'

'Because, that's how *they* work. You know, Andri, I'm not even sure dating is for me after all. It was a bit of a whim really. I've been single so long and happy the whole time too. I've got all the freedom I want to form my own opinions, make my own choices, go wherever I want …'

Andrea puts her hand on mine. 'You know, Kat, if you find the *right* man, none of that should have to change.'

I ponder that thought. It's a nice idea, and perhaps there are characters on TV who live their free independent lives with their modern-world partners, but it's not reality. Not in my experience.

'So, anyway. Why the change of heart? Why start now?'

I draw a breath. 'An old school acquaintance of mine died suddenly a few days ago. It got me thinking about my life, and I guess I feel like I'm just treading water a little. I'm getting older, that's for sure. Look.' I prod at my emerging crow's feet for emphasis. 'But I've not got much to show for my life. I guess I thought I might like to do the whole settling-down thing, maybe have kids even. It sounds stupid when I say it all out loud.'

'It's not stupid, Kat. There's no harm in trying. Just because the Mike guy was a douchebag, doesn't mean your next date will be.' I shake my head at her phrasing. Andrea's perfect English comes partly from the fact that she watches a *lot* of American films and TV.

'I know that. I just don't know if I want to dedicate any more of my time to weeding out the Mikes.'

'I have a guy who is perfect.'

Another blind date? Do I really want another night of prawns and perverts? Okay, that was harsh; the prawns were great.

I'll humour her. 'Perfect how, exactly? Is he made out of chocolate and huge packets of cheese and onion crisps?'

She casts me a sideways glance. 'You and your cheese and

47

onion crisps. He's a local businessman. Never married but he's had a series of serious relationships. He's good-looking, *wealthy* and kind.'

Whilst wealth is obviously an important factor in keeping Andrea in her diamante-encrusted kaftans – which have unfathomable price tags – it isn't to me. I earn what I need and I certainly don't want anybody else's money.

'He's kind, you say?'

'The kindest. He rescued his dog from a shelter and donates lots of money to charity.'

Hmm, I'm not sure that's the comprehensive, all-encompassing definition of kindness, but there doesn't seem anything inherently wrong with him thus far.

'Will he even want to go on a date with me?' Andrea can sometimes get ahead of herself and I want to be sure this isn't her own romanticising.

'He will love you, Kat. I've set him up on dates before. He'll thank me, I promise.'

I frown, not at all convinced. 'Okay, something casual like sundown drinks or lunch. We're going on tour tomorrow so it will have to be when I'm back.' She's tapping furiously on her phone and I don't know if she's even listening. Her phone makes a *zoop* (for want of better onomatopoeia) sound as a text message sends, and then she looks up and nods.

'Okay.'

The guys take a coffee break. They're already sweaty.

'Might not need the coconut oil tonight, lads,' Jay says, catching my eye.

'Pongy blokes don't get rebooked,' I say, pointedly.

'I'm winding you up!'

I flick a towel at him but miss. 'I'll get you next time. Now drink up, quick loo break and back to it. I want to wrap up in the next hour so you can all go and get some beauty sleep this afternoon.'

The next hour passes well. The guys are on form and I make a few minor tweaks to the choreography to make things look a little smoother in light of the smaller stage we're on tonight. When they're finished, I gather them around.

'What do you think about this?' I hold out the competition leaflet Andrea gave me and wait a few moments whilst they all scan over it.

'I say go for it. It's over a grand apiece and a trip to Vegas. It looks like it could mean some great publicity for doing what we do anyway. I'm up for it,' Marcus says.

'I'm in,' Jay adds.

Sammy and Ant agree too. I look at Pauw, anticipating another yes.

'I'm not sure,' he says.

'Why ever not?'

His shoulders sag. 'I have a bit of a phobia of competitions.'

'You? But you love being on stage.'

'I love being on stage, but it's different being up on stage and pitted against other acts.'

'I hadn't thought about it like that.' I look at the other guys. 'Listen, you guys go and get some rest; I'm going to have a chat with Paul.' I pronounce his name properly to be more sensitive.

'We'll be doing the competition together, and I really think we could win,' I say when the others have gone.

Paul sits down on a chair next to me. 'I just get super-nervous, Kat. I think if I force myself up there, I'll screw it up for you all.'

'Don't be daft. We're a team and you're an amazing performer. Can't you just tell yourself it's a show, not a competition?'

'What if I fall flat on my face?'

'You're a trained acrobat and an experienced dancer – if you fell flat on your face it would be incredibly graceful and look like part of the act anyway. Look, it's never happened before, so why would it happen in a competition?'

He shrugs. 'I sound ridiculous, don't I?'

'A little bit,' I say, adding a warm smile.

'I entered a school talent comp when I was in year nine.'

'Brave,' I add, thinking back to my own teenage school years.

'I was doing so well in front of my mirror each night. I sounded good. I was doing Craig David's "Fill Me In" and I had a little dance routine and everything.' He clasps his hands together.

'And what happened?' I ask softly.

'I got up on stage and saw all those people. It was the whole school, teachers *and* parents. I was terrified. Anyway, when the music started, I counted the beats in. My heart was racing and I could hear that too. My hands started to tremble and I took deep breaths but it all got worse. Somehow, I managed to get the first line out on time but it was high-pitched and out of tune. I remember thinking it wasn't even my voice that I could hear. It was awful but I carried on because that's what you do. I thought if I pulled it all together and people heard what I'd heard in my bedroom when I practised they'd forget about my ropey start, but it just got worse. For some reason, I couldn't get into the right key and I kept getting brain-block with the lyrics. In the end, the sight of people laughing was too much. I ran off stage in floods of tears. For weeks after that kids stopped me in the corridors to either impersonate my awful singing or say things like "Bet you wish you'd got someone to *fill in* for you".'

I put my hand on his knee. 'But that was when you were a kid. The pressures are different when you're that age. You're a confident man now.' It seems a bit hypocritical of me to offer this advice when I've let my own high-school woes dictate part of my life before now, but I don't go into that.

'I know. I guess that fear is just embedded.'

'We will get through this together as a team. We'll be there by your side.'

'I know you will. Thanks, Kat. You know the worst thing about it all?'

'Things got worse?' I say with soft humour.

'The winner was one of the popular football kids who rapped "Slim Shady" – he had no musical talent whatsoever. He knew the words though.'

'He had confidence,' I say. 'Confidence gets you further than any talent or skill. You've had a good eighteen years of being on stage in some form. You already have the confidence you lacked as a kid.'

He smiles. 'Thanks, Kat. I just panicked. I'm going to do this. For you, and the boys.'

'Good!' I say, patting his back. 'Now go and get some rest.'

'I will. Do me a favour though – don't tell the guys, will you? Pauw is bad enough – I don't think I'll cope with them calling me Craig David for the rest of eternity.'

I laugh softly. 'My lips are sealed.'

He hugs me and leaves. Whilst I'm gathering my things Andrea comes over, grinning like the Cheshire cat.

'What's that look for?' I ask.

'Well, I've just spoken to Alonso, and he's free *today*!'

'I can't do anything today. I'm working later and I've a tonne of stuff to sort out.'

'Your show starts at ten p.m. and you already look fabulous. He's going to be at the Hawaiian Beach Bar in half an hour for sundown drinks as requested.'

'Half an hour?'

Andrea rummages in her glossy tote bag and pulls out various beautifying items. 'Here, live spontaneously!'

With that, she walks off. I study the things she dumped on the table. A brush, some bits of make-up (not all fathomable), perfume, antiperspirant and chewing gum. If I didn't know Andrea was happily married, I'd say spontaneous dates were *her* thing.

***

The mirror reflects a person I don't recognise. Sparkling eyes, glossy hair and a healthy glow. The woman is smiling, full of confidence with just a hint of familiarity – a flashback to more carefree times perhaps? I've put in a huge amount of effort for tonight. I've been to the MAC counter and had my make-up done and even had a blow-dry in a Saks salon. The floaty dress I borrowed from a friend, and the gold strappy sandals were a charity shop steal. It's not often I feel this confident; most of the time I'm back to being the invisible frumpy kid nobody likes.

I hear the front door open and I jump to my feet, smoothing down the wrinkles in my dress and grabbing the cake with '3 Years' written on it in pink icing. Okay, the cake is cheesy, but Iain isn't big on anniversary gifts so I went for a small gesture that would at least taste good. He works so hard that I want to make tonight special for him. I've booked a table at the curry house in town that he loves and filled the fridge with his favourite beers and snacks.

I wander downstairs hardly able to contain my grin. Iain is already slumped into the squishy sofa cushions, so I creep up behind him and hold the cake out.

'Surprise!' I bend down to kiss the side of his face. 'Happy anniversary.'

I walk around the sofa to face him. His expression is more irked than surprised.

'It's three years today.' My voice falters at his expression. He's almost sneering.

'Is it? Is that why you've done that to yourself?' He flicks his hand in my direction.

'I, er …' My insides squirm.

'God, you look like a dog's dinner.' He laughs at his own joke and slugs one of the beers I'd got him.

'It's just a look I was experimenting with. I didn't do it, it was just one of those free make-up counter things.'

'Well, I'd be flabbergasted if you'd paid to look like that. Where's that dress from?'

'Oh, a girl at work said she thought it would suit me so gave it to me to try on.' My cheeks burn as I try to play down my efforts.

'Looks like you've spent the day working with the blind.' He chuckles, and for some reason, I do too.

'I booked the Bay of Bengal for seven if you fancy it?'

'A dinner date with Coco the Clown? An offer I can't refuse,' he says drily, popping the lid off another beer. I notice a half-eaten box of chocolates on the side and can't help but feel a little miffed, which I shouldn't really because he wasn't to know I'd planned anything special. That's the risk of a surprise though, isn't it?

I force a smile. 'I was going to have a wash and get changed. You were just home a little earlier than expected.'

'Don't get changed, love. You know I love you anyway, and at least I don't have to worry about other blokes giving you the eye at the pub later.' He winks.

I scurry upstairs as tears prick my eyes. My phone is on the bed, flashing with a text message. It's from Ellie at work.

You looked stunning today, babe. I bet Iain thought all his Christmases had come at once when he saw you. Have a great night xxx

Hot tears escape. As I feel them taking the oily make-up down my face with them, I hit delete.

***

I head into the ladies and get to work. I don't bother with much of the make-up, and quite frankly the 72-hour eyebrow liquid terrifies me. I mean, what if I painted them on wonky? Would I have to stay like that for 72 hours? I'm sure the whole eyebrow trend was manufactured by the make-up industry as a way to sell more products. In the Nineties, we all plucked our eyebrows to a pencil-thin line; then, once we'd all bought tweezers, sales must have dropped, so they had to invent eyebrow liquid to sell to us instead. It makes sense if you think about it. Anyway, I'm not falling into that trap. I've got enough body parts to worry about without adding eyebrows to the list.

I pop a chewing gum into my mouth and gather up Andrea's mini-makeover salon.

'How do I look?' I say, plonking the cosmetics on the bar. She's restocking the fridge but stands up to get a good look.

'How you doin'?' She winks.

'Ahh, so you're binge-watching *Friends* again.'

She giggles. 'Yes, could it *be* any funnier?'

I give her a weary look.

'Okay, sorry. You look stunning. Now get yourself down to the bar!'

Chapter 8

I can't believe I'm on my second date in as many days. My mother
would say there's a name for people like me, but I don't care –
I'm here and I'm doing this. Andrea said to look out for a tall,
well-built man in a dark navy suit. The bar is quiet given that
it's only four o'clock in the afternoon so I spot him straight away.

'Hi,' I say. 'I'm Kat.' Andrea was right; he *is* incredibly handsome. His hair is probably chin-length but is neatly slicked back
with product.

'Kat! Nice to meet you.' He jumps up and swiftly moves around
to pull out my chair.

Heat flushes my cheeks. 'Thank you.'

'You're looking radiant.'

'Thank you,' I repeat, as the back of my neck tingles again.
Weird. I don't think I'll ever be one of those women who can
take a compliment gracefully.

We mull over the drinks menu in silence, and when the waiter
approaches us, Alonso speaks to him in Spanish.

'Is there anything you'd like, or shall I order you a surprise
cocktail?' he asks. He does seem polite and at least gives me a
choice, which is good. Fingers crossed no laden remarks about
my work will ensue.

A surprise cocktail? I'm intrigued. Is he a strawberry daiquiri or a Moscow Mule kind of guy?

'Surprise me,' I say, and why not? It seems to be the theme of the day.

'So, tell me about yourself. How long have you been here? Where are you from in England?' His English is very smooth, beautifully laced with his Spanish accent.

He leans forward and rests his arms on the table, so I settle into my seat.

'I'm from Yorkshire originally. I got married but that didn't work out, and I came over here about eight years ago to make a fresh start. I presume Andrea already told you what I do for a living?'

'She did.' His face doesn't slacken into some creepy leer like Mike's did, which is a start. 'I think it's great what you do. I've heard all about the Heavenly Hunks and think it's fantastic what you've achieved.'

My chest puffs a little and I look him in the eyes. 'Thank you, that means a lot. I've worked hard and the guys are just fantastic. I really enjoy it.'

The waiter brings our cocktails over and places them down on little white serviettes. He puts some peanuts in the centre of the table and walks off.

'You know what they say about bar nuts?' I pull a face.

He frowns. 'No, what do they say?'

'That they're bacteria-ridden because of all the unwashed hands that have been in them. Although, I think I might have learnt that fact from a movie at some point.' Ben Stiller springs to mind.

'These here are fresh, I can guarantee it.'

'How can you be so sure?'

'This is my bar,' he says casually, before grabbing a handful of peanuts. 'We put out brand-new nuts with each order.'

'Ahh, okay. So these are safe?' I grab a handful of my own. 'I was just about to ask what you did. Andrea said you were in business.'

'Yes, the bar business. I have a chain of cocktail bars throughout the Canary Islands, so I travel around a lot and work long, unsociable hours. I suppose that's why I'm still single.' He forces a laugh, and I find myself warming to him.

'That makes sense,' I say. I suppose it would be easy to write a guy like Alonso off as being a bit of a player. I imagine if I ever did settle down, the hours I work could be an issue too. It's not something I've worried about before.

I take a sip of my cocktail. 'Mm, this is good. What is it?'

'It's one I picked up when I travelled to Ibiza. It's Aperol, soda, cava, mint and orange. An Aperol twist on the mojito. I call it the Aperol Zest.'

We chat over the drinks and Alonso orders us another round. Before I know it, it's seven o'clock.

'Goodness, I didn't realise the time. I'm going to have to go and get ready for the show tonight.'

'Of course. I'm heading over to one of my other premises too; I have a new manager to meet with, but I've enjoyed meeting you. I'd like to do this again if you would?'

I get a flutter of excitement. Mike was attractive until he opened his mouth but Alonso is next-level handsome. It's hard to believe someone like him is even asking someone like me. I'd half expected him to end the date with a polite 'I'll see you around'.

'I'd love to.'

We swap numbers, and when I stand up, I feel a little woozy. I'll have to have a strong coffee when I get back to the apartment.

Alonso escorts me outside and stops by a very low, very expensive-looking red sports car. I don't know or care much about cars but even I know that it's fancy.

'I'll see you soon.' He leans over and kisses my cheek before opening the door.

'Bye,' I say. He starts the engine and there's a thunderous roar. 'Bloody hell,' I mutter under my breath as he drives off.

On my way home, I catch up on all my messages. Ant can't find his white T-shirt, Andrea is desperate to know how the drinks went, and then there are a few emails.

Dear Kat,

I say this with a heavy heart, but we're going to have to cancel the next block of shows booked across our chain. Our bookings have really taken a hit this year and I can't guarantee we'll sell enough show tickets to break even. I'm sorry. I hope things turn around for us all soon.

Best wishes,

Marco

General Manager

Sunseeker Resort and Leisure group

My heart thumps in my chest. 'What the ...?' I whisper.

The Sunseeker chain is four hotels. Each one had booked four shows over the winter season. That's sixteen shows wiped off our calendar before Christmas, coupled with the two other cancellations I've already had. Even with the ten per cent cancellation fee imposed, I can't afford to keep me and the guys in accommodation if I don't think of something to fix this mess.

Chapter 9

'Okay, everyone. I have something to tell you.' We're waiting for a minibus to pick us up and take us to the ferry port. My stomach is knotted, but the words are out there now, no turning back. I've got to be up-front and honest about the gigs that have been cancelled.

'Actually, so have I,' Pauw interrupts. I wasn't expecting that. It's taken me all morning to work up to telling them about the cancellations and now Paul has taken the wind out of my sails.

'After you,' I say. I'm not procrastinating in the slightest. Honest.

'I just wanted to say to everyone that I'm sorry I was so down about the competition yesterday. If you guys want to do it, I'm in.'

There are a few cheers from the others, and Ant slaps him on the back.

'You never know, if we get some good publicity we might get on *This Morning* with Holly and Scofe,' Marcus says.

'That's it – you dream big,' Jay teases. As he laughs, his eyes catch mine and linger for a second.

'Anyway, what did you want to say, Kat?' Sammy asks. I can't go and spoil this high everyone is on now. Maybe I'll give it a day or two, and broach it then.

'Taxi,' Hugo says as the minibus pulls up by the entrance to the apartment building.

'Okay, Gran Canaria, here we come!' Marcus shouts, and with that, the moment is well and truly gone.

Once we're on board the ferry, everyone scatters about. Food is sourced, beer is sipped and headphones are plugged in. I take a seat by the window and check my phone. There's a text message from Alonso, which surprises me in a good way.

Hi Kat, just wanted to wish you a safe journey to Gran Canaria. It would be great to catch up soon. Alonso xx

I double-check – yes, two kisses. There's a little fluttery feeling in my chest.

Before I tap out a reply, I check around me. I'd like to keep this private for now.

Thanks – it's supposed to be calm seas ahead! I'd love to catch up. We're in Gran Canaria for 2 weeks, then we fly to Lanzarote for a week but we'll sort something out xx

With a fizz of excitement, I press send before I regret the kisses.

'Hey, Kat, I got you a beer.' Marcus slumps in the seat beside me.

'Cheers, my dear.' I smile. Marcus is mixed race with shaved black hair and the most intense green-brown eyes you've ever seen. In fact, you shouldn't ever see them – you should never look directly at them because if you do, you're in trouble. The kind of trouble that requires peeing on a stick and a serious chat with your parents. The age gap between him and me, however, is great enough that I'm immune to this allure.

'You've been in love, haven't you, Kat?'

This is a surprising question coming from him.

'Yes.' I draw out the word. I suppose I was at the time.

'I think *I'm* in love.' He throws his head back against the headrest.

'What? With who?' I can't hide my surprise. This is Marcus the man-slut we're talking about.

'Don't judge me, but it was a girl I met after a show a few nights ago.'

I roll my eyes. 'A one-night stand?'

He gives me *a look*.

'Well, come on,' I say with a sigh.

Marcus proceeds to tell me at great length about the girl in question.

'We chatted for hours and then we went up to her room and—'

I hold up my hand. 'Don't need to know that bit, Marc.'

The corner of his mouth lifts. 'Anyway, *we talked*, all night. The other thing did happen, but it wouldn't have mattered if it didn't. Now I can't stop thinking about her. She's in my dreams and everything but she's going home to England soon.'

'Do you know what I think?'

'Am I going to like it?'

'I don't care.' I cast him a sideways glance and he grins. He likes it when I'm direct. They all do and although it makes me feel really old, I am almost a mother figure to some of them. 'You're not in love. You're infatuated because you actually connected with someone using more than your penis.'

He opens his mouth to protest and I hold up my index finger. I'm not done. 'If you spent more time trying to connect with women on a verbal level, you would see that and you'd get far more from it than a few minutes of fun.'

'Minutes!' He feigns outrage.

'Just stop sleeping around. If you're feeling lonely and want to be with someone, go on some dates and don't go further than a goodnight kiss for the first few … at least!'

'What if you're wrong and this girl is the one.'

'*This girl* is going back to another country soon. I think the fact you feel like this about her shows you're ready for something more. I know it's easy to have a one-night stand out here. The rules don't feel the same as they do back home and let's face it, you're not short of offers, but it's meaningless. What about the poor girls too? They might sleep with you but many of them probably expect a call back or a date afterwards or something.'

He shrugs. 'It's just mutual fun. It's all consensual, Kat.'

'I know, and God help you if it wasn't. You'd be praying to be locked up if I got hold of you before the police! I just mean, if a girl watches your show and you have a drink with her after, and one thing leads to another, she might feel you value her more than you do.'

'I always just assumed they wanted the same as me.'

'Some might, but not everyone. If you have to do it, at least tell them first that you won't call them again – let them decide if a one-night stand is what they're looking for too.'

'I suppose what you're saying makes sense. But what if this girl is the one?'

'Did you get her number?'

'Yes, I always do.'

I roll my eyes. 'And then never call anyway? Well, give it a few days and if you're still thinking about her, call. If not, delete the number.'

'I suppose I could do. She'll be back home by then though.'

'Feelings are feelings. There are plenty of ways to stay in touch and have a long-distance thing.'

'I don't know how you do it.'

'What?' I say.

'Manage to change my whole opinion about something in just a few minutes.'

I wink at him. 'Older and wiser.'

'Thanks, Kat. I think it's time you got yourself a good seeing to as well.' He grins.

'Oi! That's enough of that.' I tap him playfully on the back of his head. 'Now bugger off and give me some peace.'

He laughs and jumps up. 'See you in a bit.'

When he's gone, I close my eyes and it isn't long before I drift off.

***

'You're home late,' I say as Iain walks in. It's half seven and I know for a fact his office is always locked up by six.

'It's not that late. Just got a bit of extra work done, called for petrol and that kind of thing.'

I shrug. There's no point pressing him and turning the conversation into a row.

'Did you take the glass to the bottle bank?' I ask instead.

He creases his brow and reels in a way that suggests I'm nuts. 'You were supposed to be doing that.'

Wait, what? We had a conversation about it last night and I specifically told him I couldn't because I was doing a sponsored cycle to work. He said he'd do it. I can't tell if he's genuinely forgotten the conversation or if he's trying to defend not doing the job.

'Kat,' he says softly as he sits on the sofa beside me, 'I'm getting worried about your memory.'

He can't be serious. 'What?'

'I think you're under a lot of stress at work and it's taking its toll. I know you're working hard to try and prove yourself but ...'

'What?'

'It's hard for me to say this to you and I'm only saying it because I love you.' His tone is calm, almost soothing. 'I think you're finding it so hard because you're just not good enough. Like if I tried to swim the channel – I could put my all into it but I still wouldn't make it.'

'But—'

'Shh, it's okay. I'm here for you and I'll keep us afloat financially.' He pulls me into a hug. When I try again to remember the conversation about bottles, it's foggy. Maybe I did say I'd take them after I got home from work. Did I make the whole conversation up in my head? What if Iain is right – what if I'm losing my mind?

**

I jolt forwards. The ferry's horn is blasting as we approach the dramatic cliff-lined coast of Port Morgan, and people are already gathering their things. Ant and Pauw stand nearby laughing. My stomach knots. I still need to tell them all about the cancelled gigs, and soon.

We dump our bags in the large apartment I've rented. It's a three-bed and the living room sofa converts into a double. It's a bit of a squeeze for us all but I wanted to keep costs down. Nobody questions it.

The hotel we're performing at tonight has let us use their entertainment lounge to rehearse in, so after unpacking, we head over.

'If we're going to enter this competition, we need to give it our all in rehearsals,' I say when we get there. 'I want to see sharp, seamless transitions, crisp moves and accurate timings. Remember the beats and if you get a mental block – backflip, or grind if you're Sammy and can't. Any questions?'

When nobody replies, I go into my introduction and we run through the show from the top.

'Kat.' Ant's voice is low when he comes over to me during a comfort break.

'What's up?' I ask.

He looks around to make sure nobody else is listening. 'It's a bit embarrassing really, but I was just wondering if there's any chance of a pay rise, for me and the boys I mean. We've been talking and we know you pay us all fairly and everything, but if we could maybe charge more for tickets or if there's anything in the pot or whatever ...'

I feel to the heat of blood rushing to my face.

'It's just that a few of us would like to think about next steps, getting on the property ladder and what have you. We can't stay at the apartment complex forever – it's been fun and everything but I sort of feel like I want to have my own space – furniture and stuff.'

My chest clenches. It hadn't even occurred to me that the guys might want to put some roots down, which is quite blinkered now I think about it, since that's exactly what I've recently decided I want to do. The timing is bloody awful though.

'Guys, listen.' I pause until they're all looking my way. 'There's something I have to tell you all, and it's not good news.'

I pull up a seat, and there's a series of loud clangs and scrapes as the others do the same. When we're sitting in a rough circle, I take a deep breath. 'There are some problems with tourism. Brexit, the local economy here and whatnot have caused some uncertainty, and after the collapse of BeachLuxe Holidays a couple of weeks ago, fewer Brits are travelling abroad. The hotels are getting nervous and the Sunseeker Leisure chain have cancelled all our shows. I expect a few more may follow suit. Things might get tight for a while.'

I look around the group, making eye contact with each of them in turn. Ant's face is twisted with either sadness or anger, Pauw looks sulky, Marcus is staring at his shoes, Hugo looks confused and Sammy expels a puff of air, causing his lips to blow a frustrated raspberry. Jay is looking directly at me with the most hopeful expression of the lot.

'Kat, don't worry. We're all fit and healthy – we can get day jobs if we need to, can't we, lads?' He looks around the circle, trying to rally support. The others nod along, some more enthusiastically than others.

'Yes, yes we can,' I say, trying to sound positive. 'There's also the competition, and even if we don't win, it will give us more exposure and maybe score us some gigs at new venues. We're going to be fine.'

'You've never let us down before, Kat. I trust you,' Marcus says.

'Thanks, Marc – we'll be okay, I'm sure. I just wanted to keep you all up to date. Let's go and get some rest, and put on a kick-ass show tonight!'

They amble out, all slumped shoulders and shuffled steps. I

know it's come as a shock to them after everything has been going so well, but we'll get through it.

'Kat?' I turn around to see Jay pulling on a fresh T-shirt. It glides over his defined torso like silk.

'Everything all right?' I ask.

'Yeah, I just wanted to check on you – that didn't look like an easy thing to have to say. Fancy a walk?'

I check my watch. An hour wouldn't hurt. 'Okay then. Where to?'

'Beach?'

We step outside into the bright sunlight. After being in the windowless cabaret lounge, it almost burns my retinas. One of these days I will remember my sunglasses. We walk through the pool area in silence past sunbathers and their cocktails, the children in the little pool with their buckets, and the waiters buzzing around collecting discarded glasses. Living here, I don't often feel the need for a holiday like this, but right now, the idea of being as carefree as these people is appealing. We cut through a gate to the private beach and sit on a lounger. The tide is coming in and waves crash against the sand. It's one of my favourite sounds.

'I feel that we've not had much chance to catch up recently and wanted to make sure everything is okay with you. You're always looking after everyone else and nobody ever really looks out for you.' Warmth courses through me.

'I'm the Heavenly Hunks' manager. It's part of the job description, I guess,' I say light-heartedly, though it's one of the most thoughtful things anyone has ever said to me. I'm starting to cherish this new friendship with Jay. It's a comfort I never knew I needed.

'Don't worry about the cancellations. I meant it about day jobs. We all love working in the Canaries and we'll do what it takes to make it work.' He smiles reassuringly.

'I can't help but pin my hopes on this competition. If we win, at least you lot will have a bit of cash to tide you over.'

'*We* will.'

'Sorry?'

'Well, *you* have things to pay for too. If you're planning to split the money, it should be split seven ways.'

'I don't want any of the money. I've let you all down.' I glance down at my balled-up hands.

'Don't be daft. It's not your fault tourism is struggling. Unless you're secretly that corrupt CEO guy from BeachLuxe Holidays and have been siphoning cash for the past seven years, that is? In which case, you definitely look better without the beard.'

I chuckle. 'Hmm, don't get me started.'

I pick at a pimple on my arm and watch a seagull swoop down over the water. 'The seagulls in England are lazy now – you don't really see them hunting, do you?'

'I can't say I've paid all that much attention. Though we don't get many in Manchester.'

'They're not bothered about catching fish anymore. They swoop in and nick poor unsuspecting folks' chips and ice creams instead.'

'Kat.'

'What?'

'Don't worry about the money and the shows.'

'I'm not worried – I just want to make sure you're all okay. That *we're* okay.' I add the last part to spare another lecture about looking after myself.

'Good. Then we'd better get rehearsing for this competition!' With that, he stands up. 'Are you coming?'

I lift my head and smile at him. 'No, I'm going to sit here for a while.'

He nods and gives a wave before he leaves, and I sit, pondering for a moment. I've always felt a sense of responsibility to the guys that extends way beyond the expectations of a boss. I've got ten years of life experience on some of them. Even the older ones don't really seem any further evolved if I think about it, but Jay is different. He treats me like a human being and not someone there to make sure his laundrette bag is collected or chuck him a few aspirins after a heavy night. He takes an interest in me and I'm not used to that. When we're together, I feel like I could stay talking to him forever. I find myself wanting to spend more and more time in his company.

Chapter 10

Just before our first Gran Canaria show kicks off, I gather the guys around to let them know I've officially entered the Heavenly Hunks into the competition.

'The first auditions are in Maspalomas the day after we were due to leave, so I've changed our ferry and accommodation bookings so we can stay for it. We have to condense our show into fifteen minutes so I want you all thinking about what we should include – the parts that really get the crowd going. I have some ideas but I want this to be a team effort. Now get out there and show 'em what you're made of!'

I've taken on board Jay's comments, about looking out for myself too, and I think we should all take ownership for the competition – that way if we win, we all win; if we don't then we'll have all given it our best together. I've also been thinking about how a fifteen-minute segment will work. It should be easy to condense if we have some overlap. Marcus singing whilst Hugo plays piano and then maybe some grand jetés from Ant and so on. The set starts to build in my head and I know we can make it work.

After my intro, I watch the set and scrutinise the audience, looking for the bits that get them excited versus the parts that have them checking their phones or heading to the bar – thankfully there isn't much of that, but it happens from time to time. Whilst there are always whoops when the shiny torsos come out, it's the more talent-driven aspects that have the crowd's bits a-fluttering, and the eye contact is a winner – I can practically see their hearts race as each one of them gets to feel like the only woman in the room for a second or two.

My phone vibrates and I sneak a peek in my pocket. It's a message from Alonso.

I'm going to be in Gran Canaria at the end of the week (work trip). Would you like to meet for a drink? I'll be over for a few days xx

My throat tightens. He never mentioned a work trip when he texted last. Surely he knew then? Do work trips to coincidental places tend to pop up out of the blue?

***

'You nearly ready or what?' Ellie shouts through the cubicle door.

'I'm trying to have a wee, but I can't do it if you're at the door listening.'

'Stage fright? Don't worry, it's a thing. Anyway, hurry up! It's five p.m. and it's Friday!' The excitement coming from her is infectious.

'I know, I'm coming.' I haven't been out for drinks after work for a long time. Everyone else seems to do it every week, including Iain, but I always seem to have things to do. I flush the chain and open the door.

'Finally!' Ellie groans. 'Here, try this lippy.'

I smear on the dark pink stain and pout in the mirror. It seems weird getting ready to go out in the loos at work. It sort of reminds me of my uni days.

Ellie turns me to face her. 'Love it!'

My chest fizzes with excitement at my new friendship. I finally feel like I'm putting down some roots in this town.

'Okay, let's go.'

We walk into reception giggling because Ellie wobbled over on her ridiculous heels and a figure in front of the revolving doorway stops me dead in my tracks.

'Iain?' My stomach clenches. Is everything okay? Is my mum okay? In the split second it takes for him to answer, all sorts of scenarios play out in my head.

'Hi.' He smiles sheepishly and I take a breath. Obviously, nothing terrible has happened. 'I thought we'd said we'd meet for dinner tonight?'

'Iain, I told you I was going out for drinks tonight,' I say softly before glancing at Ellie who's doing a good job of inspecting the fire safety poster on the wall.

'I think I'd remember,' he says, cocking his head to the side. 'We had a whole conversation about eating at that new Italian place. Look, if you don't want to go, it's fine, I've got a shitload of work to do.'

I remember the conversation. He'd told me a new place had opened and we said we'd go but not tonight. There's no way I'd have agreed to tonight because this night out has been on the calendar for weeks.

'Iain—'

'Forget it.' He throws his arms in the air. 'Have fun on your night out.'

'Iain, please. It's a misunderstanding, that's all. We can go another time.'

'Yeah. Anyway, these are for you.' He hands me a bunch of white lilies. My favourites.

'Hang on,' I say, before turning to Ellie.

'Ellie, you don't mind if I give tonight a miss, do you?'

She looks at me for a minute like she's trying to determine if I'm being serious. When I don't flinch, she replies wearily, 'You go. There are plenty of other people going out tonight.'

'Thanks, Ellie, I'll be out next time, I promise.'

She rolls her eyes and heads for the door.

Chapter 11

I haven't replied to Alonso. I want to speak to Andrea first. The sludgy feeling of unease I have about him coming over here probably stems from the fact I don't like surprises. I hate them and the thought of someone springing themselves on me makes me wary. I won't get rid of the niggling seed of doubt until I know this is a normal trip for him, that he isn't just making excuses to see me.

The phone rings three times before she picks up.

'Andrea, hi,' I say as soon as she answers.

'Kat? Is everything okay?' I hear a puff as she takes a drag of her cigarette.

'Yes, fine. No.'

'Oh?'

'It's Alonso. He's coming to Gran Canaria.'

'That's great – the two of you should hook up,' she says with indifference.

'Why is he coming?'

'Work, I guess. He has two bars over there, so he goes all the time.'

That's the answer I wanted to hear. 'So, this last-minute trip is normal for him?'

'Of course. Staffing problems, training, premises review, marketing and that sort of thing. He has to go to his other bars at the drop of a hat sometimes. He has to be visible to his staff or they'll take advantage – I'm always here, aren't I?'

'I suppose so. It just seemed like too much of a coincidence. I wasn't sure if he booked the trip especially to see me, and it felt a little too much too soon, that's all.'

'I think things like that only happen in the movies.'

'You're right. I'm an idiot. Don't tell him I had this mini-egotistical-meltdown, will you? I'm mortified enough that you had to listen to it.'

'I get it. Dating is new to you.'

'Kind of.' Andrea doesn't know the whole story and it will stay that way. One of the reasons I instantly clicked with her is that she never asked me why I got divorced – when I told her I'd left my husband, she gave me a knowing nod and poured me a glass of sangria. From that moment on, I knew I could start afresh without judgement.

'Relax. Have a drink with him and see how you feel. Take it at your own pace. Listen, I have to go – one of my waitresses has just dropped a tray of tea lights, not lit, thankfully. Speak soon. Mwah.' The line goes dead.

'You missed the after-show huddle.' I turn around and see Paul emerging from the hotel entrance.

I wave my phone at him. 'Had a call.'

'I've had ten missed calls off Phil. Probably can't find the corkscrew or something.'

I raise my eyebrows in mock-seriousness. 'Better call him back ASAP then. He'll be tearing his hair out.'

He laughs. 'What hair?'

'Good point.'

'Jay did the after-show talk-down. He was terrible. I think your job is safe.' He winks and puts his phone to his ear.

As Paul wanders off chatting to Phil, I tap out a reply to Alonso.

73

Sounds good. When you arrive, let me know what free time you have available and we'll work something out. X

I have to put myself out there. I stuff my phone in my pocket as the guys start to filter out.

'Great show tonight, team,' I say as they approach me. 'I have some good ideas for the auditions but I want to hear whatever thoughts you have too.'

'I'm happy with your judgement, Kat. You get to see the show from our point of view and the audience's. You know what works,' Ant says.

'Totally your call, Kat. You see more of the show than we do – just tell us when we look good.' Jay winks. Heat floods my cheeks. He carries on talking about some of the bits he thought worked well when he saw us in Tenerife. When Jay looks me in the eye, I realise I'd stopped listening. He could have introduced unicycling were-rabbits and I wouldn't have the foggiest. I give my head a subtle shake.

'Don't you think?' he says.

'Er …' I'm pretty sure I know him well enough to be confident he didn't introduce a unicycling were-rabbit, and the first half of it all was exactly what I'd envisaged. I can only say yes or no (or admit I wasn't listening). 'Yes, great!' I say.

'Perfect. Anyone else got any ideas?' Jay looks around the group, obviously picking up on the fact I'd lost concentration a little. There are headshakes and a few mumbles of 'Sounds good to me', then they say their goodbyes and disperse. Jay stays behind.

'I hope I didn't sound like I was taking over just then. I got a bit carried away.'

'No, I may have been inclined to put Deep Heat in your coconut oil if I thought you were.' I hand him my notebook with all my ideas jotted down.

'Well, there you go, you'd already thought of everything,' he says, scanning the pages. 'Are you walking back?'

'What?' I glance at him. 'No after-show drinks or allowing yourself to be chatted up by the fans?'

He furrows his brow. 'I told you, I'm not like that.'

I give him a suspicious look but don't question it any further. It's none of my business really, is it? We set off towards the apartment.

'Just because I'm a stripper, doesn't mean I want to take a different woman home each night,' he says, clearly catching my look.

'You're an exotic dancer,' I correct him and he laughs.

'My updated CV says *semi-clothed professional titillator*, actually.'

'Oh dear God, triple Z-lister fame has gone to your head already,' I tease and he laughs.

There's definitely more to Jay than just a hot body and awesome dance moves. The simple fact he manages himself for a start and doesn't rely on me to cluck over him, but also, he doesn't take himself too seriously and I really don't think he has a clue how good-looking he is. I'm so used to looking after the dancers, and used to them letting me, that Jay stands out. He doesn't seem to need me to look out for him and there's something quite nice about that. He's an equal.

'Yeah, maybe a little. Anyway, I love being a Hunk; I shouldn't need a CV.'

'Until you're past it,' I tease.

'Hey, I'll be *exotic dancing* right up until the point in time I need a hip replacement and after that … Naked waltzing is a thing, isn't it?'

'I think it's frowned upon in these parts.'

'Damn.'

We chat for so long, neither of us realise that we've passed the turning for our apartment complex. When we realise we giggle and turn around, blaming each other for the distraction.

'How did the date go?' Jay's question takes me by surprise.

'With Alonso?'

He nods. 'Andrea mentioned it after you'd gone – I'd gone back to pick up my hoodie a few hours after rehearsals.'

'It went well, a lot better than the last one that's for sure. He's a nice guy and didn't put any pressure on me for anything more than drinks, which I appreciated.'

Jay shoots me a raised-eyebrow look. I find myself wanting to carry on so stop walking before we reach the apartment. Jay stops too.

'As I said back in Tenerife, I haven't ever dated and I don't really know what I'm doing. Since that date with Mike, I read a load of horror stories about Tinder dates that had gone wrong. It seems people expect far more from a first date nowadays, which goes some way to explaining Mike and his behaviour. Dating still terrifies me.'

Jay reaches out and places a comforting hand on my shoulder. 'Hey, you just do whatever you're comfortable with. This Alfonso guy sounds like he's been decent, so what have you got to worry about?'

I don't correct Jay when he gets Alonso's name wrong because what he said was so right.

'He does seem like a decent guy. I just don't know what he thinks of me. Maybe he finds me boring because all I did was chat about normal stuff like work, and drink cocktails. There was no ...' God, it's embarrassing to even use the word, '... romance as such.'

Jay shrugs. 'What's wrong with getting to know someone first? You've been married but you've also been single for a long time. I think you're qualified to make decisions that suit you.'

The word *married* sends a chill down my spine.

'Married,' I echo. 'I'm not sure what I had counted as a marriage.'

'Oh?' he says but doesn't push me any further. I'm grateful for that but I find myself wanting to say more regardless.

I sit down on a bench at the side of the pavement and draw a breath as Jay sits beside me.

'My husband wasn't what a husband should be.'

'He didn't … hurt you, did he?' The muscles in Jay's jaw twitch beneath his skin.

I shake my head. 'No, nothing like that. Sorry, I shouldn't have said anything. It wasn't a good marriage but it was a long time ago and I'm completely over it.'

'Sorry if this is overstepping the mark here, but if it's put you off ever being with someone else, are you over it?' Jay says softly.

'Yes.' The answer comes out like a sharp bitc. Instantly, I feel terrible.

'Sorry. It's none of my business.'

'No, I'm sorry, it's just … Let's drop it, okay?'

'Agreed.'

Chapter 12

'Sweetheart. I'm worried about you.' Iain wraps his arms around my waist as I'm washing the last few dishes from dinner.

'Oh?' I ask, confused.

'It's all the time you're spending with that Ellie girl from work.'

'Why?' I turn to face him. 'Since moving so far away from my mum and dad I've felt pretty lonely. You're usually at work anyway so it's not as though having a few cups of coffee over lunch is impacting on us in any way.'

He places his arms around my neck and kisses my cheek. 'No, of course not. God, I'm so happy you're finally making friends. You've seemed really down since we moved here and I want you to meet new people.'

'What's the problem with Ellie then?' I ask, bewildered.

He presses the knuckle of his index finger to his lips as he ponders how to spit out whatever it is that's bothering him. 'Okay, I'm just going to come out and say it.'

I wish he would.

'I think she's using you.'

'That's absurd. Why ever would you think that?' I say with a nervous laugh.

'I realise how it sounds, but you're so good at what you do, you have a business degree and you're intelligent. She's an office girl trying to claw her way up the ladder.'

'But we hardly talk about work,' I protest in disbelief.

'So she never asks about your projects?'

'Well, sometimes—'

'Or picks your brain about work stuff?'

'Now and again.' I fold my arms. 'But—'

'And you're telling me she has no ambition whatsoever?'

'I'm not saying she has none ...'

'Kat.' He takes my hands in his. 'You are good at what you do, but you're too trusting. Too quick to see the good in people, and I'm just looking out for you. All I'm saying is, I've been in business a long time and I know how it works. I don't think you should trust Ellie.'

He walks off, leaving me to think about Ellie. She's so sweet that I can't imagine she's trying to steal my job, but she does ask for work advice every now and then, and I know she'd like to earn more money. It's such a crazy idea, but Iain has been so successful in his accountancy firm and probably does see this kind of thing happen. I'm lucky to have someone like him watching out for me.

I think back to the last time I saw her. We'd met for lunch and she'd gone on and on about being skint and maybe needing to look for another job. Then she was doing all that extra work for my line manager as unpaid overtime. Could she be using me? I suppose it's possible ...

***

The following morning I have a text from Alonso with some options for times we could meet for a drink. I check my diary and confirm that Sunday would suit me best. I feel funny about seeing him again and it takes me a moment to realise that the light feeling in my chest isn't the onset of a heart attack, it's excitement. Jay was right; if I am truly over my marriage, I wouldn't have a problem going on a date. I'm a much stronger person now, but that's because I'm in control of every aspect of my life and my guard is up, surely?

I go for a walk around Maspalomas, browsing the shops and wandering the promenade. I spend the whole day alone, doing exactly what I want to do, and then I sit on the beach before taking a dip in the rather chilly Atlantic. As I wrap my towel around me, it occurs to me that controlling *everything* doesn't necessarily mean I'm *in* control. I do something completely out of character and unexpected. I call Jay.

'Kat?' he answers, evidently just as surprised as I am.

'If I try to control every aspect of my life, I'm not actually in control, am I?'

'Sorry, you've lost me.' He sounds groggy from an afternoon nap, not uncommon after a late-night show, and now I feel guilty for waking him.

'I mean, I'm completely in control of everything I do. I'm a well-oiled machine with a predictable routine that's worked for me for years.'

'Yes ...'

'But now, I'm wondering if maybe it's not working for me but I can't let go. I think I want to and therefore I'm in complete conflict with myself, so I'm not in control am I?'

'Has Alfonso asked you out again?'

It takes me a moment to realise that Jay is now more up to speed with the conversation than I am.

'Yes.'

'Then *go*. You can still be in control – kiss him if you want to, don't if you don't. Just take it one thing at a time and remember that it's your choice every step of the way.'

I nod, which is for my own benefit since Jay can't see me. He's right; dating isn't one big entity to say yes or no to. I can pick and choose the components along the way and I can call it all off at any time.

'You must think I'm an idiot,' I say eventually.

'I think you're great,' he says with a sincerity that makes my skin tingle.

I don't quite know how to respond to that so I change the subject. 'How come you're single?'

'You know that thing we do where we don't discuss our pasts …' he says before pausing. 'I'll see you later, Kat.'

Chapter 13

My stomach is filled with tap-dancing ants. I'm meeting Alonso in his bar on the Maspalomas promenade and I'm more nervous about this second meeting than I was about the first. There's more pressure on a second date, isn't there? The first date, you don't really know one another; if it's a blind date you might not have even seen a picture of the person you're meeting, so if you're not keen on the other person, you can quite plausibly go your separate ways, no harm done. A second date is different. You think the other person has potential; you think there could be a spark and you want to find out a bit more. If you ditch someone after a second date, it's because you've dug a little deeper, gotten to know them better and decided you don't like what you've discovered. What if Alonso doesn't like what's beneath my next layer? Once again, I got changed three times before I left the apartment.

When I go down the terracotta steps to the exit, I spot Sammy and Jay doing push-ups by the pool. There's some kind of male-ego competition going on as Ant and Marcus are cheering them on. A few onlookers have gathered too and the business part of me wishes I had a sandwich board or something with the Heavenly Hunks splashed all over it. I head over to say hello. As I get down, Marcus comes over. He's all slumped shoulders and broody-looking.

'What's up?' I ask.

'That girl brushed me off,' he says staring at his feet.

'Oh, Marc, it wasn't meant to be. You'll find someone else. Just take on board what I said and it will happen.'

He nods as the rest of the guys burst into a cheer. Sammy gets to his feet as Jay collapses.

'Told you I'd win, old man,' Sammy teases before looking me over.

'You're not wearing that, are you?' he says, in an unsuccessful attempt to be hilarious. My chest tightens and I'm about to retort when Jay stands up. I feel his eyes on me as he takes in all the effort I've made.

'You look stunning, Kat.'

The back of my neck tingles. 'Thanks.'

I'm vaguely aware that some of the others murmur in agreement as Jay drops his eyes to the ground. I suddenly feel weird and self-conscious but I've no idea why – the guys pay me compliments all the time.

'Hot date, is it?' Sammy asks.

'Yes, I'm going to see Alonso.'

'Is he the bar guy?' Jay asks.

'Yes.'

'So it's *second-date* serious then?' he says lightly, but he doesn't smile as I'd expect.

I shrug. 'If you can class a second date as serious. It's still early days yet but he seems like a nice guy and I like spending time with him.'

I turn to leave but he calls me back.

'Yes?'

'Sunglasses. You always forget them and you're squinting again.'

I get a sense of warmth at the small, thoughtful gesture. 'Thanks, Jay.'

***

I pause outside the bar and push my sunglasses up on my head. My stomach twists. Perhaps this completely wild idea to date was just a bad one from the off.

'Kat!' Alonso walks out past the two large white plant pots that mark the entrance to the outdoor seating area of the bar. A mini palm tree sprouts out of each one. The look of him catches me off guard. He's wearing blue jeans and a white shirt unbuttoned enough to reveal a thin sprinkling of dark hair on his olive-skinned chest. His black hair is soft and falls in floppy waves over his ears.

As I say hello he gives me a polite hug and kisses both cheeks. 'I've reserved a table at the front.'

He leads the way to a corner with white sofas and a white table that offers far-reaching views across the ocean. A waiter comes over immediately to take our drinks orders and we both order an Aperol Zest.

'It's great to see you again, Kat.' Alonso sits back on the sofa and rests his ankle on his opposite knee. He's relaxed, which I take as a good sign. I'm not sure why I notice he's not wearing socks, but I do.

'It's good to see you too,' I say as the waiter places our drinks down with some peanuts.

'I take it these are safe to eat?' I joke, putting a handful in my mouth.

We spend the next hour or so chatting about work. It's pleasant. He's a good man, hardworking, attractive and seemingly has all his ducks in a row, and for some bizarre reason, he wants to spend his free time with me. There are no alarm bells ringing and I don't feel the need to use my Get Out of Jail Free card at any point; in fact, I'm really enjoying his company. The date is like easing myself into a hot bath, uncomfortable at first but then pleasant and enjoyable. I'm not losing control.

Chapter 14

We take our seats in the conference centre of the Maspalomas Grand, which, for tonight, is doubling up as the competition auditorium. The front quarter of the large room is full of entrants. Given the generous prize, I shouldn't really be surprised by that, but I am. Now my stomach is knotted with nerves. There are all kinds of acts: going by the costumes, it looks like we'll be up against everything from go-go dancers and aerial acrobats to ventriloquists and country singers.

'I don't know how they'll even pick a winner,' Ant says, nodding towards the judges. There are three of them, two men and a woman. All of whom are apparently really high up in leisure and tourism. The brunette woman works directly with the Spanish secretary of state for tourism, one of the men is the director of a local hotel chain, and the other man is from the tourist board.

'I mean, how can they decide between an awesome dancer and a fantastic singer?' he continues. 'They don't compare.'

'I don't know, but we're here now and all we can do is our best. We'll see what happens.' As I finish speaking, the music dies down and the woman appears on stage.

Under the spotlight, she shimmers with effortless grace. Her brown shoulder-length hair is perfectly coiffured and her beige shift dress doesn't have so much as a crease. She speaks first in Spanish and I glance down the row to Hugo, Pauw and Marcus, who are the only three besides me who seem to understand any of what she says. I've been nagging the others to learn some Spanish for ages.

'Good evening, ladies and gentlemen.' She switches to English with ease and Sammy, Ant and Jay each sit up straighter now they're able to understand. 'Welcome to our first Canarian talent competition, where we aim to bring you the best our resorts have to offer. Each act has fifteen minutes to wow us. As judges, we will be looking at the whole package: how well the performance is executed, how entertaining the act is, how original it is, and how the audience responds. We will select ten acts today to go through into the quarter-final, six acts will compete in the semi-final, and three acts will be chosen to compete in the grand final. Only one act can be the overall winner and our American judge, Brad, will go through the details of the Las Vegas trip with the winning act. Without further ado, I'd like to welcome our compère, Antonio Velez.'

There's a round of applause as she glides off stage and a charcoal-haired, tuxedoed man appears. He talks a little in Spanish before switching to English. 'Ladies and gentlemen, please welcome act number one, Magica.'

The lights go dark as music starts to blast. It's 'Bat out of Hell'.

'My heart is racing,' Ant says. Mine is too, but I'm nervous on the first act's behalf. The atmosphere is so thick with tension it's palpable.

The lights turn red as a man jumps on stage, swirling his red and black cloak behind him as he does. He throws his giant top hat into the air and catches it, before pausing to look at the audience. It's an indication to clap. Nobody claps.

'Jeez, tough crowd,' Ant whispers.

'To be fair, he hasn't really done anything yet,' I say, although I agree with Ant. Usually, a crowd will applaud the initial opening of an act to welcome them on stage. The fact they didn't is a worryingly bad sign, though I don't want Ant to fret about that.

Magica places the hat on the floor and dances like a bat around it, twirling his cape tails. I'm five rows back and even I catch a glimpse of him easing something into the hat as he attempts to use his dancing cloak to conceal the action. He stands up tall and the music stops. A brilliant-white light illuminates just him and the hat on the floor. He closes his eyes and lifts his head up. His face glows white and his mullet-style hair shines a soft silver. All of a sudden, he casts his wand through the air and firecrackers spit and bang onto the stage floor.

'That was different,' I whisper to Ant.

'I was throwing firecrackers in maths class fifteen years ago,' he replies, clearly unimpressed.

The man bends down and looks in the hat. He stands up and scratches his head.

'Oh God, he's going to do that "pretend the magic didn't work" crap that they do at kids' parties, isn't he?'

I don't answer Ant's question for fear I'll have to say yes.

There's an almighty scream from the front row.

'Hey, this looks like it's about to get quite good,' I say, glad he isn't sticking to the old-fashioned formula. An audience plant makes things interesting, especially when they feign terror.

I wriggle forward in my seat, anticipating the next part of the act, then the whole room lights up. It's not fancy stage lighting though; it's fluorescent lighting. The bright kind that sears your eyeballs when you've been sitting in the dark for any length of time. The kind they put on in a nightclub at the end of the night when they want you to leave.

'What the …?'

The magician scurries off stage and picks something up from underneath a chair that's suspiciously close to the origin of the scream.

'Is that …?' Ant whispers in disbelief.

'An iguana? Yes,' I reply as the magician clutches the wriggling reptile close to his chest.

'If that was supposed to be pulled out of the hat, I think we're better than him.'

A minor kerfuffle follows and the elegant tourism lady stands up to announce a five-minute break.

'I'm going to the loo now. There's no way I'm missing out on the next act,' Ant says.

After he's gone, I see someone take his seat from the corner of my eye.

'We'll find it hard to top a lizard on the loose, although Marcus often tells women he's got a snake in his trousers.'

I splutter, turning my head to see Jay wearing a bemused expression.

'He'd better not,' I say.

Jay shrugs. 'What do you think so far?' he asks.

'I think we've got a bloody good chance, but it's early days yet.'

'Would you jump in my grave as quick?' As Ant returns, the lady judge takes the stage and announces the next act. Jay grins and Ant squeezes past to reach Jay's empty seat further down the aisle as Spandau Ballet's 'Gold' starts to play.

'Why is all the music from my childhood?' Jay whispers. I snort out a shock of laughter because I'd just been thinking the same thing with the added thought that it's all music from before the rest of the guys were born. To be honest, 'Bat out of Hell' was probably before my time but I know it well.

It's an act of imagination and intrigue, apparently. Whatever that means; so far it's two crumbly old blokes and a woman who wouldn't look out of place in a care home.

'This should be interesting,' Jay whispers. In time to the music, bang on the chorus, they all dramatically drop their red satin cloaks to reveal red-and-gold Lycra. Lots of Lycra.

'Those guys up there are revealing more package than I ever

have, and I'm a stripper,' Jay says. I cast him a sideways glance. 'Sorry, *exotic dancer*.'

He does have a point, though. The short, chunkier man with a dark wavy ponytail has a modest bundle, but with the taller man, it's hard to know where to divert one's eyes. When he stands on his tiptoes to balance on the handle of a sword, I honestly don't know how he keeps his legs together.

'I think we should offer him a job with the Hunks,' I whisper to Jay, who looks significantly alarmed.

The start of the Eurythmics' 'Sweet Dreams' refocuses my attention on the stage. The petite golden-haired lady in a red-and-gold leotard brings out a clear Perspex box and places it on a table at the centre of the stage. She dances around it, flailing her arms about in a dramatic and controlled manner. It's not until she shoves her foot inside that I realise what she's about to do.

'No …' I draw out the word with disbelief. The box can't be much more than a foot and a half high and a similar depth. The woman must be knocking on seventy.

My eyes are glued to the stage. I can practically chew the atmosphere it's so thick with tension. Her arm's in now and she's jimmying her shoulder in too. I have to admit it's a little bit gross to watch but somehow so compelling that I can't look away. She pulls in her other leg. There's a lot of yanking and easing and there's nothing remotely graceful about it, but she's determined to get in that box and I think she'll do it too.

'Jeez,' Jay whispers and I glance down our row. Everyone is transfixed. When I look back at the stage, the woman is wedged inside the box. Papery skin squishes up against the clear sides, and if that wasn't enough, she sticks her arm out and swings the door shut.

'I feel a little bit sick,' I whisper. My torso feels like it's been through a mangle.

The audience applaud her and there are a few whoops from people near the back – obvious friends of the entertainers.

The next few acts are really quite good. So good in fact, I start to worry. A sparrow-like opera singer with a hurricane-force voice, and a flame-throwing acrobat who definitely wouldn't pass a UK fire-safety inspection. When the music turns more dramatic, I start to get butterflies. I know what's coming. A large flaming hula-hoop is suspended mid-air. The acrobat eyes it with intent, rubbing his palms together. As the intensity of the beat increases, he throws himself into a series of flips, before hurtling through the ring of fire and landing with more grace than I could manage if I wasn't on fire and really tried.

'God, he's really good,' I whisper, feeling a little queasy. I'm not sure how well we can compete if the rest of the acts are as good as the last two. It suddenly dawns on me that we might not get through to the next round of auditions and if we don't, I honestly don't know what we'll do – I think somewhere in my subconscious, I believed we had a real chance of winning the money and the trip and it would solve our short-term problems. Looking down the row, I see that everyone is watching the show. It's difficult to read their expressions. Are they worried too? We're on soon and I don't want nerves to ruin it for us.

'I'm going to the loo,' I whisper to Jay.

When I get inside the bathroom, I stare in the mirror. My stage make-up looks fluorescent under the harsh lighting and the foundation has started to gather in my emerging lines. To top it off, my face is so shiny it looks like I've spent the last forty minutes doing Bikram yoga – which I've only heard of because I spent a zillion pounds on an imported copy of *Heat* magazine a few years ago when all the celebrities were doing it. I blend the make-up in a little with my finger and blot the shine with a square of loo roll. I look a bit better but I don't feel any more confident. With a deep breath, I head back out just as we're called up.

My stomach feels like I've swallowed a brick whole. I've pinned my hopes on winning this stupid competition when what I should have been doing was working harder at securing some gigs by contacting new venues and increasing our social media presence. I look at the guys bouncing around excitedly. I've let them down.

The compère takes to the stage. He has the charisma of a turnip and I can't help but wonder if he's just here because he owed someone a favour.

'Please welcome the Heavenly Hunks.' He sounds like he's auctioning off defective coffins.

There's a polite round of applause as our music kicks in. It's not quite the same without all the big speakers as I can't feel the bass pumping through my body, and it's a bit stark without all the fancy stage lighting, but I have to get out there and pull this off. I lift my chin up high and strut out.

Somehow, we manage to pull off a good, albeit compact version of our show and when we sit back down, I get the usual little after-show buzz that I've come to relish.

***

'We made it to the quarter-finals!' Ant bounces excitedly as we leave the hotel. I'm still in shock that we made it. The acts seemed to get better and better. There was an impressive magician and a violinist who smashed it. It was touch and go for us and I can't say with confidence that we'll make it through the next round.

'We'd better get practising,' Sammy says.

As they talk about improvements they could make to their performance, I drift off into my own head, trying to formulate a plan to secure more bookings.

'You don't think we can do it, do you?' Jay's voice jolts me from my thoughts. I glance around, relieved to see everyone else is out of earshot or not listening.

'What makes you say that?' I ask, putting a hand on my hip.

'You're chewing your bottom lip and don't seem at all excited about the fact we got through the first stage of the competition.

The other acts were better than you anticipated and now you're worried we won't make the next round.' He looks smug.

'What? You got all that from a bit of lip chewing?'

He cocks his head to the side and the moonlight catches the side of his face, which sports a mock-serious expression.

'Fine!' I sigh. 'I'm worried. A little bit. The gigs are drying up, Jay, and I thought this stupid competition could create a bit of buzz around us again. And then there's the cash ...'

Jay places his hands on my shoulders, forcing me to face him. 'Stop worrying about us. I've told you, we all just want to work in the sun. We love the Heavenlies but we're all more than capable of working two jobs. *You're* the only person *you* should be worrying about.'

I fall into his kind, chestnut eyes. They're deep and calming and somehow I'm able to absorb what he's saying. I take a deep breath and nod. I've come this far and I'll be damned if I let everything crumble around me now. We can make it work together. We're a team.

'Thank you, Jay.' We look at one another for a moment. In his white vest, with the post-show sheen on his body, Jay looks every bit the movie action hero who has just averted some huge crisis. Which I suppose in some small way, he has. I realise his hands are still on my shoulders and once I notice, I can't think of anything else but the weight of them. I want to wriggle free, but – at the same time, the warmth of them feels nice.

'Kat.' I spin round to see a smartly dressed, handsome man running up behind us. Jay's hands fall to his sides.

'Alonso? I thought you'd gone back to Tenerife.'

'I did, but I wanted to come and support you tonight. I got here late but I managed to watch you perform. Congratulations on getting through to the quarter-finals. I thought you were great – a very professional act.'

Jay shifts his weight from one foot to the other.

'Sorry, Jay, this is Alonso, an, er—'

'Her date,' Alonso says sheepishly.

'We've been on a few dates,' I clarify, although Jay knows this. 'Alonso, this is Jay, one of my dancers and, er, friend.' It shouldn't feel awkward but it does. I cast Jay a sideways glance and feel relieved when he holds out a hand for Alonso.

'Good show,' Alonso says, giving it a firm shake.

There's an awkward moment of silence. What on earth am I supposed to do now? Alonso is smiling. I think he's waiting for Jay to leave but Jay is smiling too; I think he wants to carry on our conversation. I can't tell either of them to go, and my entire vocabulary has fallen out of my head.

'Kat.' Alonso touches my elbow gently. 'Would you like to join me for a drink?'

I can't think of a reason to say no, so I nod. 'Is that okay, Jay? We can catch up tomorrow.'

'Sure.' He glances at Alonso and then down at his feet. 'I'll get going then.'

Without warning, Jay leans in and kisses me on the cheek. Heat surges through me and my chest tenses. He's never done that before. Was it for Alonso's benefit?

'Night, Kat,' he says casually, before walking off.

'Shall we go back inside to the bar?' Alonso says when Jay starts to jog towards the other dancers.

'Er, yes.' I'm hardly concentrating. Without realising, I raise my hand to my cheek. I can still feel Jay's lips there.

When we reach the bar we take a seat. Alonso ordered drinks as we walked in and I can't say I paid much attention. Why did Jay kiss me? It must have been a territorial thing, a warning perhaps. A 'don't mess with a Heavenly Hunk' kind of thing. I can see that being his style.

The waiter puts an ice bucket on a stand next to the table. He shows a squat, podgy bottle to Alonso who nods seriously. Two champagne flutes appear and I'm vaguely aware that a cork pops.

My hand becomes warm, and I notice Alonso has covered it

with his. Our table is tiny and we're a bit squished together. 'Kat, I just wanted to say well done and congratulations for doing so well tonight. I was really impressed with the act.'

A guitar string twangs in my stomach. I haven't paid any attention to Alonso since he arrived and I should have done. It was wrong of me; he's been kind and generous, plus he's come all this way to support me.

'Oh, Alonso, thank you. You didn't have to buy champagne though. It's only the first round of auditions.'

He bats away my words with his hand. 'Nonsense. The competition is tough. I was genuinely impressed. If we had the space in any of our bars, I'd hire you in an instant.'

Sensing an opportunity, I try my luck. 'Actually, bookings have become a little hard to secure. The large hotels we usually perform at are opting for smaller, cheaper acts. They don't want to book big ticketed events like ours because they're worried about the uptake. I need a few new venues – we'll travel anywhere in the Canaries if you know anyone who could help.'

'Leave it with me. I have a few contacts.'

That's all it takes to make me feel more at ease. I take a sip of my champagne and, as the fuzzy alcohol feeling floods my veins, I relax into the conversation and realise I'm enjoying myself.

'Wow, you're quite amazing,' I say when Alonso finishes telling me the story of how he set up his first bar at twenty.

'You are too, Kat. You started a successful business in a new country. That's a big deal.' I watch his full lips move as he speaks and get a sudden urge to kiss him. Without another thought, I do it. I plant my lips on his. He responds and I soon remember the familiar rhythm. It's been a while but I suppose it's a bit like riding a bike. I'm concentrating so much on what I'm doing that I can't say I'm enjoying it. It's reminiscent of being in the laundrette watching the drum of the machine churn my whites, and I'm worried about the possibility of bad breath and trying not to clang my teeth against his. He pulls away and burrows his face into my hair. I wasn't expecting the ground to move or anything, but I did expect to feel something the first time I kissed someone other than Iain. Perhaps I'm just nervous. It's understandable.

'I wasn't expecting that.' A huge grin appears on his face and his cheeks have a pink flush. It puts me at ease and makes me remember why I kissed him in the first place. I find myself wanting to try it again. Maybe it will be better the second time.

'I have a room here, and you're welcome to stay over if you wish.'

I don't know if it's the alcohol but things twinge and tumble beneath my bellybutton. I want to say yes but I should say no. It's too soon to be staying over and if I couldn't get into the spirit of a first kiss, I doubt I'll manage to pull off a *first anything else*.

I look him in the eye and whisper, 'Okay.'

We don't finish our champagne. Instead, Alonso picks up the ice bucket and flutes in one hand, and takes my hand with his other, gently leading me towards the lift. He presses the button for the top floor, and when the door closes, he moves closer to me and kisses me softly on the lips. With the buzz of champagne in my system, I tug his crisp shirt, pulling his firm body towards me, before the doors ping open.

'We're here,' he whispers, pulling me to an oak door.

'Wow!' I say, taking in the lavish suite drenched in elegant fabrics and soft furnishings. 'I wasn't expecting a palace.'

'It's my favourite suite here. I always request this room. Come and see outside.' He beckons me over to the French doors that lead out onto a large balcony. The moonlight bounces off the inky black Atlantic, and the sonorous sound of waves crashing against the shore heightens the buzz of the champagne. There's something exhilarating about the power of the ocean. I feel alive and ready for anything.

'Alonso, it's beautiful here.'

'Sit, make yourself at home,' he says, gesturing to a heavily cushioned, rather expensive-looking rattan chair set. I sit down as he puts his phone and room key on the table and recharges the champagne flutes.

'You look cold. I'll get you a blanket.'

The sound of cupboard doors opening and closing as Alonso hunts for a blanket makes me smile. I take a sip of champagne and rub my arms to warm them up.

When Alonso returns and takes the seat next to me, he puts his hand on my knee. A familiar and dark discomfort comes back and my skin crawls beneath his touch. His hand is too far up my thigh and it takes everything I have not to hit it away.

'Alonso …' I start, but before I say any more, he lifts his hand off my knee and holds it up.

'Kat, we can take it slowly if that's what you want.'

I breathe a sigh of relief. I think that's what I needed to hear. I need to let go of my relationship anxieties. I like Alonso and he's done nothing to make me think he's anything other than a decent bloke.

'Yes, I think *slowly* sounds good.'

Chapter 15

'So, tell me, what happened in Gran Canaria?' Andrea lounges in her plastic patio chair. The sheer colourful fabric of her kaftan cascades over the acrylic frame, making it look less like an IKEA bargain and more like something from an *Ideal Home* shoot.

'The shows went well; we got through the first round of the competition, which I didn't expect, so I'm over the moon, but some of the acts were amazing so we'll have to pull our socks up.'

She rolls her eyes. 'I'm talking about Alonso. He was there?'

'Yes, he was there.'

'And? Goodness, Kat, you're hard work today.' She lowers her brow accusingly.

'Okay, we met up, we drank champagne …'

'But?'

'But, it's early days. I don't want to take anything for granted just yet. We've agreed to take things slowly.'

'Have you kissed him?'

I pause. This is starting to feel a little like a high-school conversation I was never a part of, but for the sake of not being called hard work again today, I reply, 'Yes.'

'And he's not a good kisser?'

I catch myself grinning. I'm quite enjoying this. 'The first time was a little awkward, but the second time, when we'd gone back to his room, was better. The next morning was pretty good too,' I tease her with the information I know she's dying for.

She gasps so loudly a few people in the beach bar turn to assess the commotion. One man looks like he's poised to leap up and perform the Heimlich manoeuvre.

'Shhh,' I say, glaring. 'We didn't do *that*. We'd had a few drinks, we kissed and he invited me back to his room. We sat and had a drink on the balcony and just talked. All night, in fact – we watched the sunrise and it was so beautiful.'

'Hollywood will be clamouring for the rights to that love story; *Fifty Shades of Magnolia*, I can see it now.' She rolls her eyes. 'So, I guess there will be more dates?'

'Maybe. I hope so. I'm new to all this and now I've been reading up on modern dating and the rules all seem different than they used to. All this swiping left and right and hooking up for the night – I don't know what he wants and, quite frankly, I'm too old to be playing silly beggars.'

She frowns as she often does when I use idioms. 'I think you need to give him a chance. Damn, I think you actually need to give yourself a chance. You've been single a *long* time so *take* your time. Alonso isn't going anywhere – he was born and raised in Tenerife.'

I suppose she's right. Besides that, it's been almost two weeks since I stayed over in his hotel, as we went straight to Lanzarote after that. Since landing back in Tenerife I've been building our online presence, mercilessly uploading teaser trailers to Instagram and YouTube, doing IGTV videos and Facebook stories and trying to make various tweets go viral. Unfortunately, my tweets seem to be about as contagious as a broken arm. All that considered, I haven't given much thought to Alonso. We've sent texts back and forth but it's no wonder there's not much romance blossoming between us. Now I've thought about the night we spent on his balcony, I have a strong urge to see him again. I pull out my phone.

'You know what? I'm going to arrange another date.'

'Good for you!' she says.

Chapter 16

As I leave the apartment complex, I pause to fasten the clasp on my handbag. When I look up, I jump.

'Jay?'

'I know I haven't shaved but I'm not that terrifying, am I?'

'Sorry, I was in a world of my own. What are you up to?'

'I've just finished at the gym and was coming to see if you fancy heading down to the beach or something. It seems weird not having a show tonight – the guys have all gone to watch the match but I wasn't in the mood.' He stuffs his hands into his pockets and twists nervously. His hair is wet and he smells of coconut. He looks me over. 'Sorry, are you off out?'

I twist my mouth, feeling guilty about leaving Jay at a loose end, but then scold myself because he isn't my responsibility. 'Yes, I have a date with Alonso.'

'Another one?'

'Yes.'

He glances at his Havaianas then back to me. 'So are you two becoming a thing then?'

I shrug. 'Not really. It's still early days yet, but we seem to be clicking and he seems really nice.'

I turn to walk off but something holds me back. I glance at

my watch. I'm already running ten minutes late but something about Jay's soulful expression gives me a heaviness in my stomach and I think I know what's wrong with him. He's lonely.

'I know it's not what you're here for, but why don't we set you up on a date? You never know …'

He presses his lips into a hard line and folds his arms. 'Kat, just because you've found this new version of you that's experiencing things you'd written off years ago, it doesn't mean I have to.'

'Okay, I'm sorry.' I turn to leave again, feeling scolded, but I get a niggling bubble of anger. *He's* come to *me* for company, and in the past, he's had no qualms asking me personal questions. What exactly is Jay's deal?

'Why are you so set against meeting someone?'

He regards me for a few seconds too long. My nerve endings seem to light up as his eyes travel over my body.

'I'm not who you think I am, Kat.'

Oh? My chest clenches. A million thoughts whirl through my head, ranging from the alarming to the absurd.

'What do you mean?' I almost trip over the words.

He shakes his head. 'It's nothing. You're going to be late for your date.' With that, he shuffles down the steps and heads towards the apartment he shares with Marcus. It's a second before I can shrug off the strange exchange but I can't process it now; I'm late.

As always, Alonso is the perfect gent. He regales me with tales of when he sank his friend's sailing yacht by crashing it into rocks, and his early mistakes as a bar owner. He takes me behind the bar to teach me how to make some of my favourite cocktails, but all the while, I feel guilty because my mind is on Jay. There's something about him – a melancholy – that's got under my skin. I swear if I fell asleep right now I'd dream about him.

'Thank you for a wonderful evening.'

'It's been my pleasure, Kat.' He leans forward and places his lips on mine and I must admit, I find the rhythm naturally. It's starting to feel a lot more normal, like the rusty mechanism has had a good old blast of WD40.

When we pull apart, Alonso takes my hand in his. 'Goodnight, Kat.'

'Goodnight, Alonso. I'm sorry I need to leave early, I just have this awful headache.' I get a pang in my stomach – lying has never sat well with me.

He bats the air. 'Nonsense, you go home and rest. Perhaps we could go to a picnic on the beach next week. I'll check my schedule and let you know some dates.'

I place my hand on his firm upper arm. 'That would be lovely.'

'Before I forget, I think I have a gig lined up. I'll text you the details when I know for sure.'

My chest lifts. 'That's brilliant. Thank you.'

I kiss his cheek and we say goodbye.

By the time I've walked back to the apartment, I've convinced myself that I need to go and see Jay. He's come from nowhere, joining the Hunks and asking me personal questions, wanting to spend time with me, but he won't give anything away about himself. I need to find out why he's not who he says he is, as a friend but more importantly as his employer. Is he trying to tell me that he's a drugs baron or something? A fugitive? A spy sent to check up on me? *Not who you think I am.* What does that even mean? How does he even know what I think of him anyway? Secretive, for one. The lights are off but I bang on the door anyway.

'Jay?' I shout, banging again.

The light goes on next door and a lady swings the door open. She shouts something in a language that sounds Eastern European and I apologise in English.

'Jay?' I shout again, once her door closes.

Finally, his door swings open. 'Kat? What the hell is going on? Is the building on fire?'

'What? No! I've come to talk to you.'

'Couldn't it wait until morning?' He rubs his hands through his hair and I notice that all he's wearing is a pair of black Calvin Kleins. With his arms up high, his muscles ripple beneath the skin of his torso. Something pleasurable flickers beneath my bellybutton, which I force myself to ignore. I'm not here to check out the talent but the sight of him does take the wind out of my sails.

'Sorry, were you asleep?'

'It's midnight and the lights were out. What do you think I was doing?'

Fair point.

'Sorry, I just … I wanted to talk to you about what you said earlier.'

He looks at me for a moment and sighs, before swinging the door open. 'Come in.' He pulls a dressing gown on and heads towards the kitchenette.

The apartment is small like mine but has the stuffy smell you get when you combine testosterone, overcrowding, and one small window. Clothes are strewn everywhere.

'The mess is all Marcus,' he says, reading my expression. 'Fancy a drink?'

I'm about to say yes when I remember I've had a few already. It would be best to keep a clear head. 'Just a glass of water will be fine. Is Marcus in?'

He gives me a look to say 'are you kidding?' and pours me a glass of water from a bottle in the fridge before opening a can of beer for himself.

I move a pile of clothes off the sofa and sit on the end. Jay pulls out a dining chair from the kitchen table and sits facing me. There's a look of resignation on his face. The maternal instinct I have for the boys kicks in. I need to make sure everything is okay, but also, if Jay is struggling with something, I want to be there for him and help. I take a deep breath.

'I'm sorry, Jay, but I have to ask what you meant before when you said I didn't know the real you.'

'Forget it. You know everything you need to know.'

Of course, he has the right to privacy, but if there's something going on, I need to know. Whatever it is can't be any worse than what my racing mind has already come up with. I just need to know that the guys and the show are safe.

He's holding his beer in two hands, staring at the can like it's the first time he's come across San Miguel.

'I'm an ex-con.'

My jaw slackens. I wasn't expecting that. Jay seems so genuine and honest. Once again, my mind whirls with the possible reasons for incarceration. I remember watching a TV show about prison, I can't remember which, and I'm sure it said that it's bad prison etiquette to ask what landed someone inside. I go for a more subtle approach.

'How long were you in prison for?' I do my best to ensure my face isn't displaying the full extent of my shock.

He rolls his lips. 'Four years.'

My poker face is getting a full dress rehearsal. *Four years.* Does that mean he got out in two? Or does it mean he was originally sentenced to eight? I swallow so hard it hurts the front of my throat, which feels very exposed all of a sudden.

He rubs his face with his hands. 'You hate me, don't you?'

It largely depends on what he did really, doesn't it? 'No, of course not. I'm surprised, and a little hurt you didn't tell me before, but I don't hate you.'

He stares back at his can. 'I couldn't. I never tell anyone.'

'Why? Everyone knows people change.' It's possible, isn't it?

'I'm ashamed of myself.'

I feel like the Titanic has hit an iceberg in my ribcage. I want to hug him despite that being the worst reaction possible. I don't even know if he's taken a few bottles of whisky from Tesco to sell in the pub or battered someone to near death. All I know is the Jay I love talking to: the gorgeous, well-toned, dressing-gown-clad man before me. This is a total mind-fuck, if I'm being brutally honest.

All of a sudden, he throws his face in his hands and lets out a low, guttural scream. I jump. 'This is why I moved away from home. This is why I don't have relationships. I disappoint people. I know what I did is in my past, and I'm not that guy anymore, but it's there like an ugly scar on my conscience and I don't want people to see it.'

'Why did you tell me then?' I ask gently.

'I don't know, Kat, I didn't plan to. There's something about you. I feel like I can tell you anything. I *want* to tell you everything.'

My stomach skitters. 'Then try me. Finish your story.'

He eyes me for a moment too long, obviously unsure, but then he begins. 'I was eighteen. My parents were the sort of parents who grafted every hour God sent just to keep the roof over our heads. My dad went to the pub every Friday and my mum played bingo on a Saturday. Sundays we always had a family roast, no matter how hard times were, and my dad always treated Mum like a princess, no matter what.' The muscles in his jaw flex as he concentrates on the beer can. I'm not sure where this is going but I don't want to interrupt.

'I knew things were bad when I caught my mum sobbing in the kitchen on Sunday over a tin of Spam. She and Dad hadn't been going out and they were arguing more than normal but I'd not thought much of it.' He pauses again to swallow. This is much more personal than I thought it would be.

'You don't have to tell me this. I shouldn't have pushed you,' I say softly.

'Things started to get quite bad. My dad was laid off and they had to start selling things. My mum sold a ring that my grandma gave her before she died.' His voice breaks and I have an overwhelming urge to dart across the room and wrap him in my arms.

He stands up, walks around a bit and then sits back down. 'Anyway, long story short, I went out drinking because I couldn't bear to be at home and see my parents depressed all the time. They'd stopped opening the post because the letters were so red. My brother was away in the army so it was just me and I didn't know how to help them. It hurt to see them like that. I hung out with people who were only interested in getting drunk or high. Those people knew other people who were into bigger things. I never took drugs or anything like that, but I knew who these other people were. They were car thieves, burglars and drug dealers. I knew they needed help hiding the money they made and I came up with a bit of a plan that would help us all.

'It was just a stupid suggestion over drinks on a car park one night, but they listened. I suggested a second-hand market stall. You could quite feasibly turn over a decent amount of cash in a short space of time and there was no real need to log stock and sales. Someone could buy a second-hand jacket for a few hundred quid, and it could be logged as a "vintage jacket" sale. It didn't matter if it was nicked or from Primark and had been picked up at the charity shop for two pounds. They asked me to do it and offered to pay me a decent amount of cash. It felt good to be able to help my family out. My mum questioned the money but I told her I'd got a job working late shifts for double time in a warehouse. They were made up, bragging about me, their wonderful son, to anyone who'd listen.'

Jay looks up but he still can't bring his eyes to meet mine. He stares at the wall before going back to his beer can.

The tension inside me melts away. I must admit, despite it being a terrible crime, I'm relieved it's for something non-violent and that his motives came from such a good place.

He sips his drink and draws a breath. 'And then we got caught. One of the car thieves gave everyone up when he was arrested. No doubt hoping for a more lenient sentence. Me being naïve, I thought I'd probably get a fine and a ticking-off. I hadn't harmed anyone directly or stolen anything. But it turned out that the money I'd laundered was quite a lot and my involvement was quite a lot too. There were clear victims of the whole operation, and as a result, the judge gave me the most he could. I was sentenced to four years.'

He throws his head back and drains the last of his beer. It's clear a weight has been lifted.

'My mum and dad were so upset. They're good, working-class people with a lot of pride. I'd hurt and embarrassed them and everyone in the community knew what I'd done. The trial was a lot for them – my mum's face when I caught her eye in court still haunts me to this day.' His voice falters. 'It was too much for my dad. The stress brought on a massive heart attack and he didn't even make it to the hospital.'

His mouth turns downwards and he sobs. 'I killed my dad.'

'Oh, Jay.' I want to offer comfort and say of course he didn't but what do I know. What an awful burden to carry around. He wipes his eyes and continues to stare at the bottle.

'I got out after three years. My mum slammed the door in my face when I went to see her, my brother wouldn't talk to me and neither would anyone from the town we lived in.'

My stomach churns. I'm not sure if it's knowing about what Jay did that makes me feel queasy, or the realisation I didn't really know him at all.

'You made a mistake.'

'Killing your father isn't a *mistake*.'

There is no reply to that. Instead, I let the words hang in the air.

'How long ago did you get out?'

'It was over fifteen years ago now.'

I don't know why but that makes me feel a little better, perhaps because I know the crime he committed is so far back in his past I can be sure he's not that person anymore. 'If you couldn't go home, what have you done for all this time?'

'On the inside, I read most days, and when I wasn't doing that, I was working out – my skill set was limited. When I was released, I took on the kind of jobs where a background check wasn't necessary. Needless to say, I didn't become a banker.'

He smiles and even though he's trying to make light of it all now, his shoulders are hunched and he can barely look me in the eye. I know he's ashamed.

'I was a labourer, a gardener, and did other things like that. I had a few girlfriends in the early days but when I told them I'd been inside that was always it – the nice sort of girls I went for couldn't see past something like that. I didn't want to hide it from anyone but I didn't want to burden someone with something like that either, so I stopped dating. Aside from a couple of drunken one-night stands, I haven't been with anyone since.'

'Oh, Jay,' is all I can manage. It's a lot to process but my instincts are usually right and, money-laundering aside, the last part of his story shows he's got some integrity.

'Is that what your tattoo is all about?' I remember how cagey he was when I asked about it last time.

He nods. 'It's stupid but I wanted something to symbolise moving on. It's a Lyndon B. Johnson quote that really spoke to me at the time. It says: *Yesterday is not ours to recover, but tomorrow is ours to win or lose.*'

Jay turns his arm so I can see the tiny script running down his inner bicep.

'I guess I thought it would give me the strength to overcome everything I screwed up and be a better person moving forwards.'

I sense it didn't, but I like the sentiment. 'I really like the meaning behind it.'

'Well …' He grasps his bicep with his opposite hand, covering the tattoo. 'I'd appreciate it if we kept all this between me and you for now.'

I nod. 'Of course. I appreciate you telling me, and it won't go any further. As far as I'm concerned, it's in the past. You made a mistake, paid the price and you've learnt a lesson. There's no need to tell anyone else, even though I doubt the guys would judge you if you ever did tell them. We've all done things we regret.'

He stands up and takes his beer can to the bin then looks at me, shifting uncomfortably.

'Thanks for not hating me.'

I look at him, so vulnerable, and my insides turn to liquid. Instinctively, I walk over to hug him. His skin is warm and smooth. When I pull away, I look him in his chocolate-opal eyes but he looks away.

'I couldn't ever hate you.' The thought of anyone hating this beautiful man is inconceivable. Every aspect of him is perfect bar one blot on his record. 'You're a good person, Jay. You listen; you care about people. You're there for me.' I step around him, forcing him to look at me. This time he holds my gaze, and before I know it, he leans in and places his lips on mine. They're warm and soft and his kiss is gentle yet firm enough to show he means it. My chest explodes with electricity as my body gives in to him like we're each made of magnetised matter. But, this is wrong on too many levels. So wrong. I pull away.

'Jay,' I whisper, terrified.

His eyes are heavy with sadness and he steps back. 'I ... I'm so sorry. I don't know what came over me.'

I place the palm of my hand on his smooth chest and look up at him. He has about eight inches on me and I feel small, almost childlike. 'I like you, Jay, but this is wrong. I'm your boss and I can't be involved like that with any of my guys – it's not professional. It's not right. Besides that, I'm seeing Alonso and you're my friend.'

He puts his index finger beneath my chin and tilts my head up. His eyes are full of pleading. 'I have feelings for you, Kat. I have for a while now. I feel like we have a real connection.'

The words pierce my gut. 'You can't, Jay.'

'I've tried to ignore it, but seeing you with that guy has …'
He drops his forehead to mine and takes a breath.

'Jay.' I mean it as a warning but it comes out too soft and breathy.

'Do you not feel anything for me?' His voice is almost a whisper. My chest aches and my stomach stirs.

'It doesn't *matter*. I can't allow myself to, Jay. I'm your boss. Can't you just accept I have a professional rule and move on?'

'Please, Kat, can you honestly say you don't feel a spark when we're together?'

He's the picture of beauty. Almost naked in front of me bar his loosely tied dressing gown, his flawless skin, soulful eyes and full mouth. 'Yes.' I almost choke on the word and I can tell he's about as convinced as I am by the answer.

'You look good on stage, you get the crowd going and I'm glad I selected you in the audition, but, no, personally, I'm not attracted to you in that way,' I say with more conviction this time.

'Fine,' he says. His answer is short but thickened with the heaviness of his hard-set jaw. 'Parameters clearly defined.'

'Goodnight, Jay.' I walk to the door, half expecting him to stop me, but he doesn't. It's not until I reach my own apartment that I can relax. Slumping against the wall, I throw my head back.

'Jay, you idiot,' I say aloud.

Why did he have to go and complicate things like that? Of course, I'm attracted to him – who wouldn't be? But he had no right bringing it up and drawing attention to the fact. He knows my rules about not dating the dancers. Screw that, he knows how I felt about dating full stop. I've shared everything with him recently, and he had no right to try to turn our friendship into something more. It feels like a betrayal.

When I'm back in bed, I can't get Jay out of my head no matter what I try. I listen to music but I picture his face. I play stupid games on my phone but then get mad at myself when he creeps back into my mind. In the end, I do the one thing that should help. I text Alonso.

Hi, can't sleep. Just wondered if you were awake? xx

He replies moments later.

Hi Kat, I've been at the bar cashing up after closing. I was about to go home but I can call over and keep you company if you like? Good intentions only ;) xx

I smile. Maybe taking the next step with Alonso is what I need to do. If we don't connect physically, how can I really expect to connect with him on any other level?

I'd love you to. Your intentions don't have to be all that good ;) xx

He responds immediately.

Be there in 15 xx P.S. I got the Heavenly Hunks another gig. A friend of mine has a hotel in Los Christianos and wanted something new. It fits with the dates you wanted to book in Tenerife. I'll give you the details later.

I put the phone on the side and jump out of bed. Even though I haven't slept I still have the stale, cottony taste of morning breath in my mouth from the two minutes I must have dozed for, and I should have a quick shower before he comes, just in case. I should also swap the old T-shirt I've been using as a nightie for some proper PJs. When I've taken care of all that, I go to pour a glass of wine, but, given the time, I'm not sure what that might look like so I settle for a glass of water. When I hear the knock on the door, I realise I haven't thought about Jay once in the last fifteen minutes.

Chapter 17

There's an incessant hammering on my front door. I check the time; it's noon. We're not rehearsing until three so God knows who this is or what they want. The bed next to me is empty and I vaguely recall Alonso waking me up a few hours ago to say goodbye. We'd stayed up talking all night again and kissed a LOT, but he stayed true to his word and didn't push me for anything more and my admittedly skimpy short-pyjamas stayed on until after Alonso left. I was roasting so went back to sleep in my underwear. The frantic knocking comes again and I jump out of bed – it could be an emergency. Wrapping a towel around myself for modesty, I almost trip over my discarded PJs as I dart to the door.

'Jay, what's going on?'

'I would have come earlier but I thought you might need your rest.' His arms are folded across his chest. Is he mad at me for something? I thought we'd dealt with everything last night.

'Why? What's happened?' My voice is thick with sleep.

'I saw him leave.'

It takes me a minute to process what he's talking about.

'Alonso?'

'Who else?' he says drily.

'Have you just turned up to hammer down my door and judge me for spending time with Alonso?'

His shoulders sag. 'No, I'm sorry. I actually came to apologise for last night. I don't know what's gotten into me.'

I tug his T-shirt. 'You'd better come inside.'

When the door is closed he sits down on the chair. I notice him glance at the crumpled nightwear on the floor and I feel a twisty pang of guilt so scoop them up and throw them into my laundry bag.

'I don't know what has gotten into you either,' I say, and regret it instantly. I know exactly what's gotten into him – I made him talk and his emotions got the better of him.

'I don't think Alonso is the right guy for you.'

'Well remember all that talk about me going out there and trying dating out? I am and I'm enjoying myself.'

'Good,' he says without conviction. 'I *want* you to be happy. I just … I hope you didn't do anything you might regret last night because you were angry with me.'

I look at the floor. 'It's none of your business what I did or didn't do last night.'

He stands up and walks over to me. When he's about a foot away, he ducks, moving into my eye line. He doesn't even touch me yet my skin tingles at his proximity and every part of me wants to move closer so our bodies meet.

'I just don't want to see you get hurt.'

'I know what I'm doing.'

Jay steps back and nods. 'Okay, I behaved like an idiot last night but I meant what I said; I have feelings for you, Kat. You're different to anyone I've ever met.'

Irritation flames in my ribcage. 'You know what, Jay? You have no right to tell me that now I'm with someone. I've taken a huge step forward with Alonso, and you're part of the reason I felt brave enough to do that. Now you're here trying to make out it's all a mistake because it doesn't fit your agenda. Your agenda that just popped up at two in the morning by the way.'

He sighs, defeated, and throws himself back down on the chair.

'You're right, I'm sorry, *again*. But for the record, it didn't just pop up at two in the morning. I've been keeping my feelings quiet for a while. I think you're amazing.'

My stomach stirs.

'I love how you came here and built up the Hunks by yourself. I love how you care about people and I love that you grabbed the bull by the horns and downloaded Tinder to try dating after so many years of not wanting to. You're special, Kat.'

Tears feel like tiny needles jabbing my eyes.

'Do you have proper feelings for this Alfonso guy then?'

'Alonso.'

'I don't care.' He shakes his head. 'Do you love him?'

'No.' I don't know why but anger burns inside me. I shouldn't be explaining myself to Jay. I don't know why I am.

'Does he make you happy?' he asks.

'Yes, of course he does.'

'Does he *really* though?' Jay's tone is firm now. 'If he does, I'll leave now and I won't mention it again.'

'Yes!' My voice is loud and surprisingly steady.

'Does he light a fire inside you?'

Fire? 'He's a good guy!' I'm shouting now.

'Does he fill you with excitement, make you feel alive?' Jay's eyes are ablaze. The passion in them makes me falter.

'I don't—'

He stands up again and walks over to me slowly. 'Does every nerve in your body light up when he does this?' Slowly, he leans in and presses his lips against mine. There's plenty of time to stop him but a part of me doesn't want to. Fire fills my lower abdomen, my skin tingles and my blood fizzes through my veins. Every molecule in me reacts to the heat from Jay's body, and the urge to press my body into his is impossible to fight.

I pull away, thumping my fist against Jay's firm chest as I do.

'How dare you?' I yell. 'How fucking dare you? Get out!'

I shove him through the door. He doesn't make it easy but he doesn't resist either. Once he's out, I slam the door shut.

***

'You know what I've said about your friends. You can't let them walk all over you, Katelyn. You know I'm just looking out for you.'

'Iain, can't you just drop it? All I did was lend my friend twenty quid.'

'No!' He slams his hands on the table and I jump. 'I'm sorry, Kat. Don't be frightened.' His voice is softer as he moves towards me. He's close now. His warm breath engulfs my face. It's minty but I detect a hint of coffee and day-old aftershave. He lifts his hand to my face and cups my chin gently, rubbing my cheek with his thumb.

'Don't cry. I didn't mean to shout at you. I just love you so much.' His hand tightens on my face. 'I can't stand to see people treat you like shit. You are everything to me and I just want people to respect you. The story you told me about school, about not fitting in and being teased, it broke my heart. I just want to protect you, my love.'

I think back to that conversation we had when our love was new and we stayed up all night telling each other everything. I remember his red-rimmed eyes after I told him what the other kids used to say to me. The memories didn't hurt me anymore; telling him was part of letting him in and getting to know one another. I didn't think he'd take it quite that badly, but seeing him get so emotional over it was one of the reasons I fell in love with him, because he cares so much about me. My stomach twists. Iain can see things I can't. Perhaps if he'd been at my school looking out for me, life would have been different.

'You're right. I'm going to say no to lending any more money. I'm not a pushover, not anymore.'

He smiles and pulls me in. Pressing himself against me, he kisses me hard and the solidness pushing against my hip tells me that he wants me.

'Let's go to the bedroom,' I say, yanking him towards the stairs.

Chapter 18

'What on earth is the matter with you?' Andrea wraps her arms around my shoulders and squeezes gently.

I wipe my eyes with the back of my hand and sniff. I'm in the corner of her bar and thankfully the place is empty, aside from a few people having lunch on the outside terrace.

'Has Alonso done something wrong?' she asks softly.

She walks over to the bar and I hear her pour some liquid into a glass.

'No, he's been great.'

She presses a small glass into my hand. 'It's tequila. It will take the edge off,' she says, knocking one back herself. 'Sorry, I didn't bother with the salt and lemon.'

'Thanks, Andri.'

'So, are you going to tell me why you look like a panda?'

'It's one of my dancers – Jay?'

She raises her eyebrows. 'Okay, what did he do?'

'He told me he had feelings for me.'

'And that's so bad because ...'

'Because we work together and I'm seeing Alonso and he has no right to push the boundaries like that.'

'Okay, so did you tell him he'd overstepped the mark?'

'He kissed me, Andri!'

She studies my face. 'And you didn't want him to?'

'Of course not. I'm seeing Alonso and I'm his boss!'

She folds her arms. 'So he kissed you without permission?'

I can tell she's angry. 'Yes, but only for a second. He was upset. Don't worry, I gave him what for.'

'That's my girl!'

'So, when he's not behaving like an ass, how do you feel about this Jay guy?'

'We get along really well and of course, he's hot as hell.'

She gives me a knowing smile. It's no secret that Andrea admires the view when we're rehearsing.

'We have become quite close recently but I thought it was as friends. That's what I'm so annoyed about – I really enjoy spending time with him and now he's gone and done this.'

Andrea puts a gentle hand on my knee. 'I get why you're upset and things might be a little awkward for a while but he's the one who caused this. You shouldn't feel bad.' I think about what I've told her so far, and I see her point.

'It's complicated.' I shake my head without the vocabulary to answer. I suppose in some way, I opened the can of worms that is Jay's emotions.

'As far as I can tell, the only reason this would upset you is if you have feelings too.' She shrugs.

My knee-jerk reaction is to protest. But I imagine any of the other guys confessing feelings for me – I'd think it was cute, I'd let them down gently, and we'd forget about it and move on. So why is it so different with Jay? Granted, I do find him attractive … 'But he's an employee,' I blurt.

She shrugs again.

'And I'm seeing Alonso. He stayed over last night.' I clamp my hand over my mouth but it's too late – her eyes pop out on stalks.

'You slept together?'

'No, but we fell asleep cuddling.'

'So now we have Fifty Shades Lighter,' she says drily.

'It was nice.'

'And do you have feelings for Alonso?'

I think back to lying in bed in his arms. He smelt good and did all the right things, but if I'm honest, I didn't get any warm gooey feelings in my chest and I hate myself for it.

'Not yet,' I say sadly. 'But it's still early days isn't it?'

'I would have thought you'd feel something by now.'

'I know,' I say, my spirits dampened. 'I need to give it one last go. Maybe we need to do something different, have some fun. So far all we've done is drink together. Maybe we should do something a little more "out there". We could rent a pedalo or go to the waterpark or something. Alonso is always a perfect gent but I think it's time to scratch his surface and see him with his guard down. I'm going to drag him to the beach for a swim. If we have a laugh together and I don't feel anything after that, I'll know for sure and I'll call things off.' I glance at my watch. 'If I'm not back when the guys arrive can you start them off?'

She shrugs. 'Sure.'

'Thanks, Andri. You're a star.' I kiss her on the cheek.

I walk the short distance to Alonso's bar. With every step, I have the overwhelming urge to turn back. Is a banana boat a stupid idea? It's probably better to make plans first isn't it?

I find myself outside Alonso's bar, frozen. Is it a good idea to go in there and drag him off in the hunt for a deeper connection? The place is open, his staff are in there, and he's probably working really hard. Will he think I'm an idiot? As this moral quandary progresses, I see him step outside to the bar terrace. The image isn't quite right. He's holding hands with someone. She looks young, early twenties perhaps, and she's very pretty, with long dark hair and a white halter dress that sets off her tan. She spins around and cups his face in both her hands before kissing him tenderly. My stomach turns to ice.

I feel like a voyeur, and I try to look away but the shock is too much. I'm not hurt exactly but in many ways I am. I feel ridiculous. I feel like I carried a watermelon. I slump against a post. All this time doing well on my own and I finally let a man in again who proves me right. Men treat women like crap. I almost want to run over there and give the girl a good shake – or at least warn her. The poor thing is looking at him with besotted adoration. When I find myself still staring, I have to physically remove myself so I can't watch. I practically run back to Andrea's bar until I cross the threshold and smash into her.

'Wow, steady,' she says, putting her hands on my arms. 'I guess Alonso didn't fancy renting a pedalo? Was he okay?'

I let out a dry laugh. 'He's fine. Better than ever, you could say.'

'Oh?' She furrows her tidy brow.

'I didn't tell him, because when I got there, he was *with* someone else.'

'What?' Her eyes goggle.

'You said he was a decent guy.'

'He is. I mean, he has short-term flings, but because of the hours he works, I just assumed the women wanted more than he could offer and things fizzled out. I had no idea he would do something like this.'

'I think it's less to do with the hours he works and more to do with the meandering contents of his pants.' There's little point dwelling on it and at least it's over before it really started.

'I'm sorry, Kat,' she says.

'It's not your fault.'

'I feel responsible; you're not okay.'

'I'm fine.' I clap my hands together. 'Right, are my boys here?' I ask, but before she answers, I hear the music start. 'Ahh, I'll see you later.'

She heads to the bar area. As I approach the guys a few of

them wave, nod or smile to acknowledge me. Jay, on the other hand, can't look me in the eye. I try to ignore him and slip into a seat near the stage. As he dances, his eyes are to the back of the room. His jeans are pulled low enough I can see the fine hair beneath his navel and the carved-out structure of his abs. His naked chest glistens slightly under the lighting and I try to focus on his face as his muscles ripple with each movement of the grinding motion he's performing.

I rummage in my handbag just for something else to look at and I notice Alonso has sent a text.

Enjoyed spending time together last night. I'm busy for a few days but will arrange that picnic soon xx

I clench my jaw. I'll bet he's busy! I'm angry but I realise something. I'm not upset. I should feel something more but I don't. I'm embarrassed and annoyed with myself for being proven right about men, but I'm not upset about losing Alonso. One thing that's really grating on me is Jay. He knew I had no connection with Alonso before I'd properly realised myself. I hate that he saw that and I don't know why.

The boys take a break. When they approach the table where the refreshments are, I don't feel like getting involved in the usual banter so I head outside for some air.

'Kat, wait.' Jay jogs to catch me up.

'Not now, Jay,' I say wearily.

'I can see you're upset and you have every right to be. If Alonso makes you happy that's great. I care about you, Kat, and that means wanting you to be happy. I've been a dick.'

I force a smile. 'You have, but I'm not upset with you.'

'What is it then?'

'You were right,' I say.

'Oh, Kat, I'm sorry. I hope you didn't take any of what I said on board. It's too soon for feelings.'

'It's not just that. Alonso is just what I expected.' I shake my head. 'I knew it. I knew I'd be disappointed if I went down this stupid rabbit hole of dating and there he was today, hand-in-hand with someone else.'

'What an idiot. I'm sorry, Kat.'

'It's fine. He's just confirmed what I always knew. I'm happier being the only person I need to count on.'

'What did he have to say for himself?'

'I haven't even confronted him yet. I panicked and dashed back here.' I start to get a bubble of anger. 'But I'm going to!'

'Good on you.' He pauses. 'Can we be friends again?'

I nod. 'Pull anything like that again, with me or anyone else, and you'll be sorry.'

'Noted.'

After rehearsals, everyone disperses and I find myself wandering alone along the grey, sandy beach of Costa Adeje, taking in the salty air. I call Alonso because I don't want to see him and create a scene. He doesn't answer but I get his answerphone. For a second, I deliberate and almost hang up but in the end, I realise I'd rather leave a message and never speak to him again.

'Hi, Alonso, I saw you with the girl in the white dress today. I'm too old to play games and be taken for a ride so I don't want to see you again. If I catch you cheating on the girl in the white dress, I'll make sure she knows exactly what you're doing. Oh, and you can shove your gigs up your—' The beep cuts me off. At least he'll get the gist.

I get my feet wet, and when I find a quiet spot, I sit down and take in the view. With things ending the way they did with Alonso I feel a little bit at a loss. It's not so much that he was seeing someone else. It's why I went there in the first place. Why was I trying to force myself to feel something for him? Was Andrea right? Are my feelings for Jay stronger than I'm letting on? Was I trying to mask them? The best thing I can do is go back to the way I've always lived since being out here. A seagull lands on the sand in front of me. It watches me, probably hoping for some food. I let out a small, humourless laugh. Yesterday I had the undivided attention of a handsome rich man; today I have the undivided attention of a seagull hoping for food scraps and I'm just fine with that.

***

'*I need to get some food in for tomorrow,*' I say as I unload the dishwasher. Iain is grinding coffee beans and I have to shout over the noise.

'What for? Can't we just eat something out of the freezer?' He adds two heaped spoons of coffee to the boiling water he's already poured into the cafetière.

'Leftovers for my mum and dad? We can do a bit better than that, can't we? I was thinking homemade spag bol and some of that nice cheesy garlic bread – the one that looks like a pizza.' I put the plastic items on the drainer; they never dry in the dishwasher.

'Your mum and dad?' Iain pulls his face so far back he gives himself a double chin.

'Er, yes. They're coming to stay, remember?'

'Tomorrow?'

'Yes, we had a conversation about it, didn't we?' Now I think about it, I can't really remember. I remember talking to Mum about it, and I remember that I was going to tell Iain but then he wasn't home and maybe I just rehearsed the conversation in my head. I do that sometimes.

'No, Kat. All I remember is the conversation where we decided we were going to have a quiet month. You know work has been hectic, and sometimes it's nice to just come home and not have to make polite chitchat with anyone.'

He has been working hard recently. 'I'm sorry, I must have got my wires crossed. I'll tell them you're feeling off. They'll understand.'

He puts a spoon down with force and shakes his head. 'We're not the kind of people who lie or let people down, Kat. If you've

123

invited them then you've invited them. They'll have to come now.'

He pours himself a coffee and walks out with a huff.

I feel terrible.

***

A sense of loneliness prompts me to do something I don't often do. I call my parents. Our fractured relationship never really had the chance to recover after Iain convinced me to push them away, and then I came out here. We email a lot and speak every now and then.

I listen to my mum, taking comfort in the normality of their everyday lives. Dad's been building a bird box in the shed and Mum has been potting seedlings ready for bedding plant season. They say they're planning on coming over, which is a surprise. The last time they came was about four years ago and they hated the airport experience so much that they haven't been since. I never get long enough between gigs to go home anymore and haven't been back for about two years. When I put the phone down, I feel a little better, like it's not just me against the world.

124

Chapter 19

The lights are bright for the final act. All six dancers are on stage for the finale, each tanned and naked from the waist up. Dry ice rises to their knees and the tempo slows. They all start grinding to the beat. It's nothing new; I've seen them work the crowd with the hip thrusts and eye contact a thousand times. It's what pays the bills, but there's something different about Jay tonight. His hips thrust deeper and his eyes linger on those of a chosen few. It's not like him. To the untrained eye, there's nothing unusual about the performance, but I can tell something is off. Jay has intent in his deep brown eyes.

Tonight's show went down a storm. It's at a venue in Playa de las Americas that attracts a lot of hen parties, and there's always a good atmosphere. We put on a show here roughly every six weeks and it's always a sell-out. We have a night off tomorrow so I give the guys the go-ahead to go out and have fun. I need some sleep anyway since last night was a write-off, and they do deserve a break.

Jay went with them, and I know it shouldn't, but thinking of him out there gives me a knot in my stomach. There was definitely something that had changed in his performance tonight; he seemed more into it than he's ever been. I know he wasn't intentionally trying to make me jealous as he didn't know I was watching him. Perhaps he's changed his mind about the whole not-dating thing and it was his way of putting himself out there.

As I'm walking back to the apartment, my phone rings.

'Hi, Andri,' I answer casually, but it's not like her to call so late – her bar is normally at peak capacity by now.

'I just wanted to make sure you're okay. I feel so terrible for lining Alonso up.'

'Oh, Andri, honestly, I'm fine. To be truthful, it's what I've come to expect from the male of the species, and until one proves otherwise, I'll continue to do so.'

'They're not all bad, honey.'

'Well, I'm done searching.'

'And how have things gone with this Jay guy? Are you still on good terms?'

I glance around to make sure he's not lurking behind me because, let's face it, he has precedent. 'He's apologised but things haven't been the same.'

'He's probably ashamed of himself.'

'Probably. He'll come round,' I say.

'So, he's still not giving you any twinges down below?'

'Andri!' I gasp.

'Oh, come on,' she says. 'Even Javier gets twinges when he watches them.' Javier is her husband.

'I think he's moved on to brighter things,' I say, hoping to put an end to the conversation.

'Already? Why do you think that?'

'He was … different … tonight at the show, and he went out with the guys afterwards and he never does that.'

'Maybe he just fancied a drink,' she says optimistically.

Or, maybe he's realised that not all women will run a mile if he tells them about his past and he fancied playing the field again.

'Yes, maybe,' I reply without conviction.

126

'You said no, so what's the problem anyway?'

'Shouldn't you be busy working?'

'Kat!' she barks. 'I *am* busy, but not so busy I won't come and shake you.'

'It feels weird, that's all.'

'What does?'

'The thought of Jay going out tonight.' Part of me thinks he's doing it to make a point. The other part of me thinks that he's realised he's ready to start dating again. I don't think for a second he just decided to go out drinking all of a sudden. Whatever the meaning is of his newfound desire for nightlife is, it makes my insides twist.

'He's not doing anything wrong.'

'I know that. I suppose I'm used to him not bothering with women and now he is—'

'You realise that *you* want him.'

I pause then whisper, 'It's against everything I stand for: my professionalism, my integrity, my loyalty to the other guys.'

'The heart wants what the heart wants,' she says, and I know it's from a movie but give her credit because what else would she say in this context?

'So what do I do?'

'Tell him.' I hear her take a drag of a cigarette. She only smokes when she's stressed.

'I know you're frustrated with me but I can't. What would you do if it were you and one of your bar staff?'

She cackles wickedly. 'If he looked like your Hunks? Do you want the PG13 version or the uncut X-rated version?'

'Thank you for your help,' I say, sarcasm oozing from every word.

'I'll see you soon, honey.' She blows a kiss down the phone and hangs up before I get a chance to reply. I laugh and put my phone away. By the time I reach our apartment complex, I feel too wound up to go to bed, so I go and sit by the pool and allow the soothing sound of the filter to relax me. It's a quiet night aside from the chirping of the crickets in the gardens.

I don't know how much time passes, but I hear voices approaching, male and female. There's laughter too. My heart starts racing. If it's Jay, he might think I'm waiting up for him and I'm not, I'm most definitely not. I look left and right but there's nowhere to hide, so I slink as low as possible on my lounger. I recognise Sammy with a stunning brunette on his arm. She's all flowing hair and long gorgeous legs – all the better to walk home on in the morning no doubt. I relax. One down, four to go, providing Pauw hasn't had a row with Phil and decided to stay here and crash on someone's floor again. Then comes Marcus and Ant both unaccompanied by any guests. Maybe Marcus took my advice after all.

That leaves Hugo and Jay, and since they're not that close, I can't imagine they're together. My heart sinks. I should go to bed; being out here isn't doing my blood pressure any good. I stand up and head through the gardens towards my staircase.

'Kat?'

My heart pumps blood around my body so hard it reaches my ears and deafens me. I clench my fists so my fingers don't tremble before I turn around, terrified of who Jay might be with.

'You look like you've seen a ghost,' he says, softly. It takes me a second to register he's alone.

'I … I wasn't expecting you back so soon.' I manage to hold it together long enough to get the sentence out.

'How much do you think I can drink?' The corner of his mouth curves up into a lazy smile that makes my insides feel like mush.

'Some of you were enjoying more than just beer.'

'I told you – I'm not into picking up girls if that's what you're implying.'

I look at him, his face sincere.

'But—'

'Were you worried?' He's still amused and clearly enjoying this.

'On stage tonight you were really going for it and I thought you'd changed your mind and were …'

'You thought I was trying to attract women? God, I should really rehearse in front of a mirror. I just had a lot on my mind that's all.'

I manage a smile. 'I don't know, I wondered if maybe I'd made a mistake.' As soon as the whispered words come out, I regret them. I glance around to see if the ground has an opening big enough to swallow me.

His smile vanishes. 'What do you mean?'

He's making me work for this and I can't say I blame him. 'When I thought you'd gone off doing …' I flap my hand '… the stuff the other guys do, I felt …'

He folds his arms impatiently. He's actually going to make me say the words.

'I suppose … I felt a little bit … put out.'

'Put out?'

His dancing eyes embrace me. 'Yes, like maybe I didn't *want* you to do the stuff the other guys do.'

He glances at his feet and kicks a stone, relieving me of the intensity of his eyes. When he looks back up I feel like a rabbit caught in his headlights.

'I've told you before, I don't want to do the stuff the other guys do,' he says finally. I let out a sigh of relief that he doesn't ask me to explain my answer, but the good feeling is short-lived when I realise what he's saying. This whole ordeal, confessing his feelings and whatnot, has made him realise that he doesn't want a relationship. I'm okay with that.

Am I okay with that?

He steps closer and cups my face in his hands. I burn under his gaze. 'I want *you*.'

As he leans in, I close my eyes. He presses his warm, soft lips to mine and kisses me. It's slow, and for the first time since we started talking I sense his uncertainty, so I grab his T-shirt and pull him in closer so our bodies are pressed together. He responds by kissing me harder, more urgently. His hands move down my spine to the arch in my back, sending tingles through each of my vertebrae.

I don't want to stop, but I become suddenly aware of my surroundings. Any moment now, one of the guys could walk past and I don't want any of them to find out about whatever this is. I pull away.

'We shouldn't do this here,' I say, my voice all breathy. 'Come up to my room.'

'Well,' he kisses me on the lips, 'it's late,' he kisses me again, 'and as much as I want to go up to your room and tear your clothes off, I want to do this properly.'

I don't know if I feel disappointed or relieved, but I can't deny that it makes sense so I nod in agreement.

'How about I take you out on a date?'

My chest leaps. 'I'd love to.'

He takes my hand in his. It's warm and big enough that it engulfs mine. 'Tomorrow is our night off. Fancy doing something then?'

'Yes, perfect.' I flash him a shy smile.

'Shall we say six?'

'Sounds good.' I squeeze his hand. 'But, Jay, can we keep this from the guys for now?'

'We can do, but they really won't care.'

'You haven't been around long enough to know how close we all are. They might think you'll get special favours or something.'

'Well, I hope one day I *do* get special favours.' He grins devilishly and I bat him on the chest with my free hand.

'You know what I mean.'

He exhales loudly. 'Kat, I know you're close, but I've been sharing rooms with these guys. They just want you to be happy. Marcus asked me the other day if you and I had slept together because he could sense some tension between us.'

Guys have that intuition too? 'And how did he seem?'

'Fine! He didn't care. Pauw and Ant wouldn't care, Hugo probably thinks you're with one of us anyway, and Sammy only thinks about sex – he'll wonder why it's taken so long.'

I sigh. He's probably right but it doesn't sit well with me as an employer nor as a woman figuring things out. I don't need an audience. 'Well, can we at least spend some time seeing what this thing between us is before we do tell them?'

'Of course.' He kisses my forehead. 'We should get some sleep. I'll see you tomorrow.'

He bounces down the steps to his apartment, leaving me shivering with the breeze and the remains of his touch.

Chapter 20

The next morning, I'm once again awoken by frantic hammering on the door. I think I need to put some sort of sign up or have the outside of it clad in velvet cushioning or something. When I swing the door open, I'm surprised to see Paul.

'You're out and about early,' I say, before noticing the worry on his face. 'What's wrong?'

'You need to see this, Kat.' He thrusts a newspaper at me. It's English. The *Daily Mirror*. I frown at him and he nods at it, prompting me to look. I unfold it, and to my horror, the front page is almost entirely covered with a photo from our show a few weeks ago. The moment the photographer has captured isn't the best. Marcus is centre stage and has his hand on his crotch, licking his lips. It must have been a split-second combination. The Heavenlies don't really do crotch-grabbing but this looks bad. It looks seedy.

I shake my head. 'It's fine. Must be a slow news week.'

'Have you read the heading?' Paul says, jabbing at the page. My eyes fall on the huge black lettering – like grown-ups need size fifty font! Seriously.

SUN, SEX AND STRIPPERS – *How sex-mad Brits are flocking to book raunchy Spanish getaways*

'Oh, God,' I mutter. 'But for every person who thinks it's an outrage, there will be another rallying their girlfriends for a long weekend away.'

'Read the rest of it,' Paul prompts.

Over a decade after the success of The Full Monty, *British women still can't get enough of male strippers. Women have been flocking in droves to the Canary Islands to see the British strip act, the Heavenly Hunks, for years. Local businessman Julio (not his real name) said that 'sex sells' in the resort of Playa de las Americas. Julio, who runs an erotic bar in the resort, said British men are by far his biggest market, so he's not surprised that British women are also lapping up the lads. We asked local mayor, Santiago Barolo, if he thought these sex businesses were a problem for the area. 'I think so,' he said. 'This is a nice, family place and these acts and bars are giving us a bad reputation. The women at these events become inebriated and cause problems in the local area. The people here want tourists to respect our beautiful towns. A holiday should not be about sex, it should be about experiencing the local culture and seeing the beauty of somewhere new.'*

Local hoteliers who have in the past hosted Heavenly Hunk events are starting to look for more wholesome family entertainment.

A smaller picture is embedded in the text. It's a woman throwing her bra at some male strippers who are most definitely not mine.

'That's quite the attack,' I say swallowing hard.

'I know. It's rotten, isn't it? It doesn't paint us in the right light at all.'

'Don't worry about it, Paul. Today's newspaper is tomorrow's chip wrapper.'

'I know, but bookings have dropped. What if this is the beginning of the end for us?'

I put a reassuring hand on his shoulder. 'It's just a coincidence. The press are just catching up with our success. This is what they do – jump on something that emerges in the public eye and manipulate some salacious story just to sell papers. Tomorrow they'll be slagging off the next big reality TV star.'

'So, you don't think this will turn people off us?'

'Not at all.' I force a smile and roll out another cliché from my 'it will be okay' bank: 'There's no such thing as bad publicity.'

'I'm glad we've got you, Kat.' He smiles reluctantly back. 'You can keep the paper, by the way.'

Throughout the day, the guys come to me in dribs and drabs worried about the article. I try to stay positive, but when Marcus appears with a grave expression, I know that's not going to keep me going for much longer.

'What is it?' I say as he sits on the edge of the pool beside me. The sun is hot and the cool water on my legs is just what I needed.

'Have you been on Twitter?'

'What? No! Why?'

He hands me his smartphone.

#saynotosunandsex is trending.

'This isn't …?'

Marcus nods. 'It's not just about us though, it's about other resorts with exotic dancers and party holidays, stag and hen dos and so on. They're attacking everyone.'

'That's nothing new – the press have been slamming party resorts for years.' I scroll the hashtag, where a barrage of people have shared the article and commented, with the general consensus being that we've turned the whole of the Canary Islands into Costa del Blackpool.

'Oh God, that nasty Barry Peters has jumped on the bandwagon,' I say, scrolling the page. Barry is an opinionated arse who unfortunately has his own TV and radio show.

'Why am I not surprised?' Marcus says. 'Go on, what's he have to say?'

For years men have been lambasted for visiting strip clubs to the point it's become a taboo. Only fair that women are held to the same scrutiny. Why is it okay for women to objectify us men? #equality

'Eugh.' I shudder. That man makes my skin crawl. I've never once considered the show to be more than a bit of fun. I scan the thread.

@RealBarryPeters hear hear!

@RealBarryPeters if they want equality, they can have it! Got to deal with the bad as well as the good.

@RealBarryPeters First decent thing you've ever said!

@RealBarryPeters Difference is, the show is a bit of fun and the blokes have clothes on most of the time.

@RealBarryPeters Well said!

@RealBarryPeters I doubt anyone's ever objectified you, you crusty old git!

'Typical Twitter. It'll blow over soon.' I hand back his phone whilst trying to ignore the gnawing sickness in my stomach. Don't people get it? Female strippers have been degraded in the past, treated poorly and sometimes made to do things they don't want to do. There are many safe places to work as a female stripper now but there's a history. Nobody is treating these men with disrespect.

'Look, #sayyestosunandstrippers is trending too. There are some very sensible points of view.' I show Marcus the phone to make him feel better. I'm hardened to how cruel the press and gossip magazines are, but the younger guys are not used to how nasty people like Barry Peters can be. I need to keep an eye on their wellbeing until it's blown over. Marcus reads a few tweets out.

Grown adults can do what they want in a safe environment.

135

As long as people are happy to do the job and they're treated with respect, who cares?

If you don't like it, don't go! #itssimple

'See, plenty of people who see our point of view too. We can't be in the public eye and not expect a bit of stick now and again.'

'I guess you're right.'

'Look, it's only because we had a bit of publicity a few weeks ago. It will be forgotten about in no time.'

'Hey, Kat.' As Marcus leaves, Jay comes over. 'I heard about the article. How are you doing?'

It's quite nice to be asked how *I* feel about it. Everyone else has approached me either in a blind panic, or seeking reassurance (or both). 'It's fine, some of the guys are panicking as they've not dealt with bad press before.'

'Everyone will be talking about something else tomorrow.'

'Yeah,' I say. 'I know you can handle it, I just feel bad for the other lads. You all put your heart and souls into your performances, and then there's all the gym training and keeping up your fitness levels. It's bloody hard work, and people dismiss the act as some seedy tat.' I realise I'm ranting, but what surprises me more is that Jay is letting me. He glances behind him and when he realises nobody is there, leans in and kisses me on the cheek. The feeling lingers even when he's pulled away.

'It will blow over. Barry bloody Peters will have his nose in some other business by tonight. And if you think our lads will listen to him, you're not giving them enough credit.'

'You're right. I'm protective of you all, that's all.'

'Anyway, I'm off to have a shower. I've got a hot date later.' He winks and walks away.

***

There's a stampede of ants in my stomach. I've made an effort with my make-up, which sits somewhere between full-on stage face and none at all. I bought a new red sundress that fits me properly and doesn't make me look like a sausage. I think I look okay, but I sent a selfie to Andrea, just to make sure, and she said she thought I looked stunning and Andrea doesn't sugar-coat anything. So panicking over how I look is off the list of things to worry over, but there's still so much to think about. Lipstick on my teeth, saying the wrong thing, not having anything to say at all, snort-laughing at his jokes, accidentally breaking wind when I lean over to get the sauce. I need a paper bag.

I sit on the bed and take a deep breath. I'm worrying over nothing.

'This is Jay, my *friend*.' I throw my head into my hands. If this goes wrong, I lose one hell of a dancer, and the one person I've grown incredibly close to.

There's a knock on the door, and an anvil crashes to the pit of my stomach. For a split second, I eye up the bathroom window, wondering if I could a) squeeze through it and b) survive the two-storey drop. The door creaks open slowly. Damn, I didn't lock it. Sammy called in earlier to borrow my sun cream as he and the rest of the guys are heading to the waterpark for the afternoon. Bugger the two-storey drop – what's a broken ankle in the grand scheme of things?

'Kat?' Jay pokes his head around the door. He's covering his eyes with his hand. 'Are you decent?'

I glance at the window once more. 'Yes, come in.'

He steps around the door and my breath is stolen in an instant. I've never really seen him make an effort like this before. He's been for a haircut. It's shorter at the sides but left longer on top and styled with something non-gooey. He's wearing a white shirt with the long sleeves rolled up. The buttons don't gape, but it's obvious they can only just contain his chest. He's left the top two open and the white fabric sets his tan off spec-tacularly. His faded black jeans are tight on his thighs but not too tight in a skinny-jeans sort of way, and he smells delicious – I'm getting hints of bergamot, basil and lime.

I stand up and smooth down my dress.

'You look beautiful, Kat,' he says as his eyes wash over me.

'You've turned out pretty well yourself,' I manage.

'Shall we?' He holds out his elbow for me to take, so I grab my handbag and link my arm through his. He's making this surprisingly easy.

'Where are we going?' I ask as we leave the complex.

'It's a surprise.' He presses a car key and a black convertible Mini by the kerb bleeps. 'Hop in.'

'You've rented a car?'

'I have.'

He spends a few minutes trying to figure out how to make the roof go down and then puts up the windows to offer some protection from the wind before setting off. We head towards Guía de Isora.

'It's been a while since I jumped in a car and headed off down the coast,' I say, remembering a time when our shows were only on at weekends and I was still living off my small divorce settlement.

'Me too. I know you're worried about bookings and the newspaper article and everything, but having the night off once in a while ain't so bad,' he says, driving with one arm draped over the steering wheel. At this precise moment in time I can't disagree.

After about twenty minutes, Jay turns off towards Playa de Abama beach before parking up at the very swanky Ritz Carlton resort hotel. I look at him quizzically.

'I don't think I'm dressed for this,' I say, wondering what he's got planned.

'Oh, we're not going in there. He nods towards the hotel. 'We're going down there.' He gestures down towards the beach.

'Is that not a private beach?' I ask, hoping he realises there's a chance we'll be turfed off.

'It's fine. I know the manager here.'

When we climb out of the car, I work my fingers through the knots in my hair while Jay puts the roof back up. Then he opens the boot and pulls out a picnic basket and cool box. I feel a little flutter of something when I realise how much thought he's put into the date at such short notice.

We make our way through the stunning hotel and down the steep, winding steps towards the private beach. It's fairly quiet now since most of the hotel guests have left to dress for dinner. A few die-hard sunbathers remain, catching the last of the dusky rays, and there's the odd young couple sipping cocktails, but most of the sun loungers have been packed away for the night. We walk across the sand around a walled corner to the left, which is more sheltered from the breeze and the remaining beach-goers.

Jay lays out a thick blanket and starts unpacking plastic plates, glasses and various food items from the basket. The sun is low in the sky now and casts its golden shimmer across the calm water. It's almost too bright to look at. There are rocks in the water that act as breakers, so the water by the shore is calm and inviting. I'd love to be like one of those carefree girls you see in the movies. The kind who'd give in to the lure of the ocean and just run into the water just to feel the freedom of it. I suppose I'm already outside my comfort zone and pushing myself into new things just by being here. Why not tick another box on my bucket list?

'I want to go in,' I say impulsively.

'Really?' Jay looks almost as surprised as I am. 'Before we eat?'

'I don't know. It looks so gorgeous with the sun bouncing off the water like that; it's surreal. I just want to get in.'

'I suppose we can have a paddle.'

'A paddle? You softie. I'm going in!' I slip my dress over my head and stand up in my matching black bra and knickers. Jay looks positively shocked.

'Oh, come on, there's nobody about. Besides, it just looks like a bikini from afar.'

139

He grins, stands up and starts to wriggle out of his jeans. 'Okay, it's not like I'm shy.'

Thankfully, he has boxer shorts on, something the other guys don't tend to wear, as I've discovered an uncomfortable number of times in backstage dressing rooms. He might know the manager here but I think skinny-dipping on his fancy beach could be a bromance-breaker.

I head towards the shore, walking in, to where the water laps the sand. It's not as warm as the golden glow suggested it may be, but I can't back down now, not after I've made Jay strip off. I go in deeper and Jay follows.

'Bloody hell, it's like the North Sea. Are you sure?'

'It'll be fine once we're in.' I laugh, but I want to scream with each step I take as the water rises higher and higher. In the end, I just dive in. It's exhilarating.

'Bugger,' I say, popping up. 'I forgot about my make-up.' But when I turn around, Jay is nowhere to be seen.

All of a sudden, there's a mighty splash next to me as he leaps out of the water.

'You're right, it's lovely.'

I turn onto my back and scull around, enjoying the feeling of weightlessness.

'I needed this,' I say.

'A swim?' Jay asks as he catches me up.

'Spontaneity I mean. There's something so therapeutic about the ocean, isn't there? It washes away your troubles. Temporarily, of course.'

'You know you live a ten-minute walk from a beach, don't you?'

'I know. I guess you take things for granted when they're too readily available.'

'Maybe you could make a pact with yourself to visit the beach at least once a week.'

'Maybe I will.' I dive under and swim out a little bit more. As

Jay stands up next to me, I realise the sun has dipped a little lower and the temperature seems to have dropped a few degrees.

'You look cold,' Jay says, taking in my goose bumps. My teeth start to chatter and my tummy rumbles.

'I think I'm ready for whatever is in your hamper.'

He raises his eyebrows suggestively.

'That was not a euphemism!' I splash him, and he dives at me but misses and plunges underwater. It gives me a few seconds head start as I race out of the water. When I land on the shore, my legs feel like lead weights.

Jay isn't too far behind me and steps out with much more grace, brushing the water off his golden skin and shaking it from his hair. Diet Coke break, anyone?

We sit down on the blanket and Jay unpacks some Manchego cheese, Serrano ham, olives and cold tortilla plus a few mini cartons of nondescript white wine.

'Juice boxes for grown-ups? I like it!' I laugh softly, taking one. 'Oh, it has a straw and everything.'

'I can't believe you haven't seen these before. They sell them everywhere.'

'I haven't looked, to be honest. I'm an in-grab-the-crisps-out kind of shopper,' I say, popping the straw through the foil seal. 'They may be a bit low-brow but they're blooming convenient.'

'You may think they're not classy ...' he wags his finger '... and you'd be right, but I read somewhere that they were invented to get the young people drinking wine, so you could say we're being hip.'

'I'll take that.'

'Besides that, I didn't have time to find plastic wine glasses.'

The sky is blue-black now, and so is the sea. The only reason I can tell them apart is because the moonlight reflects off the water. A slight breeze makes me shiver.

'You're cold. Here.' Jay pulls a blanket out of his hamper and wraps it around my shoulders, moving my sticky sea-salt hair out of the way. Then, he wraps his arm around me and pulls me into the bulk of his body. He smells all salty from our swim earlier and his skin is still cold.

'Jay?'

'Yes?'

'I'd like to do this again.'

'Me too.' He kisses the top of my head.

'But can we keep it quiet still? I'm not ready to tell the others yet.'

'Whatever you want, Kat.'

Chapter 21

'God, I'm nervous.' Sammy is jiggling around like a Nineties raver on acid. We're at the heavily marbled and incense-infused Grand Palace, Lanzarote, for the quarter-final of the Canaries Act of the Year competition. I managed to squeeze us in two small shows that just covered the cost of travelling here, so I have everything crossed that this won't be a wasted trip.

'Is it me, or are all the other acts ten times better this time around?' Pauw asks.

'It's you,' Marcus snipes. I sense he's nervous too, and this is what he does under pressure – he lashes out.

'Are you kidding?' Ant glares at Marcus. 'Old Lycra Bollocks has splashed out on a new kit – we need to be on top form.'

'Lucky for us, we don't need our kit,' Marcus mutters.

'I still think we could have added something else,' Ant says.

'Just shut up and do your stuff,' Marcus says.

'Who are you telling to shut up?' Ant snaps.

Marcus squares his shoulders, taking a step closer to Ant.

'Lads, calm down. It's a bit of Lycra for God's sake. We're all feeling the pressure, but they're the same act. They were good last time and so were we. It's why we were all chosen,' Jay says.

'I get that we're all a little bit on edge but fighting amongst ourselves won't help. We need to act like a team.'

Marcus relaxes his shoulders and Sammy slaps him on the back. I'm glad Jay chipped in because I'm busy chewing my fingernails to the quick and don't think I could have stopped long enough to offer anything helpful. I've run all the account projections for the winter season and they're not looking good. Even with the pie-in-the-sky ten grand from the competition, we'll struggle to make ends meet, and that's if the bookings start to roll back in for the summer. If not, we may well have to don Lycra and squeeze ourselves into Perspex boxes.

The lights dim and we take our seats. Jay allows the others to pass him, shuffling down the row so that he can sit with me. When the compère comes on to introduce the acts I feel Jay's hand cover my own, which is gripping the side of the chair. It tingles beneath the warmth of his touch. I look sideways and raise my eyebrows at him.

'What?' he asks. I glance past him at the five faces that are glued to the stage and realise that not one of them has so much as batted an eyelid in our direction.

'Nothing. It's just new, that's all.' I relax into my seat, allowing myself to enjoy the feeling. It's been a week since our picnic on the beach and I still can't get used to these stolen moments. Jay thinks we should tell the others, and we will, in time.

We sit through the opera singer's performance, and when she reaches her dramatic crescendo, Jay gives my hand a little squeeze. My heart flips.

In the interval, I break away to get some water from the bar and I hear a familiar shriek.

'Kaaaat.'

I turn around, glad to see Andrea's friendly face. 'What are you doing here? Who's looking after the bar?'

'I wanted to come along and support you. My ship can sail itself for a few days.' She pulls me into a hug and kisses both

144

cheeks. 'My husband and I are having a long weekend away now the mad summer rush is over. We both needed the break.'

'I'm glad he's managed to tear you away from the bar!' I say. 'When are you up?'

'There's a dance act on and then us.' I take out a few euros to pay for my water.

'Are you nervous?'

'No.' I shake my head, but Andrea is already one step ahead and has hers cocked to the side. 'Okay, a little,' I admit.

Andrea places her hand on mine, the one clutching the cash, and asks the waiter for two shots of vodka.

'Andrea, I can't down a shot of vodka! I'm working.'

'That's right.' She grins. 'You'll down two.'

When we return to the seats, I make the guys shuffle up to make room for Andrea. A few of them look pleased she's made such an effort to come. I think they welcome the moral support. I, on the other hand, have about seventy millilitres of Dutch courage flowing through my veins and just want to get up on stage. I feel great. As my arm brushes against Jay's, I tuck my hands underneath my legs. The guys wouldn't notice a bit of discreet hand-holding but Andrea certainly would.

The male–female dance act are up next. The woman glides around effortlessly in the man's strong arms, her simple white dress billowing gracefully as they sail across the stage. He lifts her horizontally into the air, and the crowd gasp as he turns her around, her back arched slightly to stay balanced.

'What I wouldn't give for her core strength,' Andrea whispers.

'What would you do with it?' I ask. 'Actually, don't answer that.'

As the dancers come to the end of their sequence, there's a standing ovation. We're up next, and as the buzz of the vodka wears off, that familiar concrete feeling fills my torso. Sammy's eyes are still glued to the stage. He'd better keep it together throughout the performance.

'No pressure then.' Jay whacks Sammy on the back, breaking his trance. Fortunately, he smiles and his shoulders relax.

'We'd better give it our best,' he replies. Phew!

'Wish us luck,' I whisper to Andrea as I squeeze past her.

'You don't need it,' she says, though after the performance we've just seen, I'm not sure about that.

Behind the stage, I fuss over the dancers. Pauw's hair isn't falling right and Ant's skin lacks sheen. 'Where's the dry oil?'

'Here, catch.' Marcus tosses the bottle and it catches the side of my eyebrow.

'Ouch.' The pain sears through me and the stress almost becomes too much as I clutch my face and fight back tears. 'Marcus, you nob!' I yell.

'Come with me.' Jay takes me by the hand and leads me out of the backstage room, into the cool, dark corridor.

'Just breathe,' he says, reaching up and moving my hair out of my face. 'It's probably going to bruise but you'll live, I promise.'

He plants a kiss where the bottle hit and I feel all the built-up tension in my chest melt away. 'I'm sorry, I just …'

'Shhh.' He presses his index finger to my lips. 'We're all feeling it tonight. I don't know what it is – it's not even like it's the final. Anyway, don't apologise to me—'

'I know, I know, I need to say sorry to Marcus.' I never lose my cool like that. Perhaps it's the pressure of keeping me and Jay a secret on top of the money situation that's making me on edge. 'Thanks, Jay.'

'Thought you needed a minute, that's all.' The side of his mouth curves upwards, and my chest fizzes with warmth as I head back inside.

As soon as I lock eyes with Marcus he comes over. 'Kat, I'm so sorry—'

I hold my hand up to stop him. 'I'm the one who should be sorry. It was an accident and I shouldn't have snapped. It did bloody hurt though.'

146

'Sorry, Kat. I know what will cheer you up.' He grins, slowly peeling away the white towel wrapped around his waist without revealing anything. He gyrates and hums the *Full Monty* theme tune as he's doing it.

'I hope you're wearing—'

'Ta-dah.' He drops the towel and I cover my mouth in shock. He's sporting the most outrageous, ruby-red sequinned thong I've ever seen.

'What the hell is that?' I try and fail to keep a straight face.

'I thought we needed a secret weapon.'

'I hate to break it to you, M, but your *weapon* is hardly slipping under the radar in *that*.'

'Listen, it's a cheap shot, but I just wanted to mix it up a little bit. I know we're a much classier act than your run-of-the-mill strippers, but a quick flash of this will just spice it up a bit and be a bit of a nod to our people.'

I frown. *'Our people?'*

'Strippers I mean.'

'You're exotic d—'

'I know. Just let's try it; otherwise, our entire performance will be exactly the same as last time.'

'Okay, if you want the public to see you in that, be my guest.' I walk away, shaking my head. Might as well fit in with the current public perception of our show.

On the sofa, Sammy and Hugo sit ready and waiting. I flick my eyes over them. 'At least you two look good.'

The compère knocks on the door. 'We need to get you on stage right away.'

As the door closes, I take a deep breath. 'Okay, guys, we've got this. Let's do our thing.'

The usual whoops, cheers and backslaps are enough to get my adrenaline pumping, and when the music starts, I storm the stage like I own it.

Chapter 22

Everything went well. Contrary to my belief, the crowd did go wild for Marcus's red thong, and when Andrea stood up to clap at the end, plenty of people followed suit. The judges are just about to announce their choices for the semi-finals. As we wait, I start to feel nauseous.

The glossy, well-heeled female judge takes the stage, her navy court dress setting off the tones of her caramel skin perfectly.

'The acts tonight were another fine display of the range of talent we have to offer here in the Canary Islands. We are lucky to have such a varied selection of entertainment, and we believe it's one of the reasons we are a much favoured holiday destination. Unfortunately, only six acts can go through to the semi-final. Now, without further ado, I shall announce the acts.' She shuffles some A6 postcards in her hands.

'In no particular order, the first act to go through to the next round is … La Leona!'

The crowd erupt. Five people behind me jump up and down, cheering and yelling in Spanish; evidently friends and family. La Leona is the opera singer with bags of talent and lungs the size of giant marrows. It's hardly a shock she's made it through.

'Next is Espectacular.' The dancers – again, no surprises there. For a moment, even I wanted them to win.

'Then we have Flexibility.' That's the acrobatic act with the Perspex-box contortionist who still makes my insides wince when I think about it. To be honest, I didn't expect them to get through, and it leaves just three spots for the semi-final.

'The fourth act to go through is Ted Sheeran.' No prizes for guessing what his act involves. He is actually really good and people of all ages and genders seem to love him. We, on the other hand, have the slight problem of appealing to a female-heavy audience.

'Act number five is Daydreamz'. They're a mixed gender dance act with a lot of talent but if you've watched as much *Britain's Got Talent* as I have, they probably haven't got anything too distinctive about them.

'Shit,' I whisper under my breath. There's one spot left and the magician act isn't through yet. They were good tonight. My heart is crimped in a vice. I daren't look to my right. If the guys see my face, they'll panic. I fix a gracious, happy-for-everyone-else smile on my face and look directly at the judge.

'And last, but certainly not least, the act that got a few of us hot under our collars …'

I squeeze my eyes shut. *Please don't say the fire-eater.*

''The Heavenly Hunks!'

My heart jumps. I jump. Everyone is jumping.

'Yes!' Jay punches the air.

It takes a moment before I realise what's happened. 'Oh my God, we did it!'

Sammy grabs hold of me, lifts me in the air and spins me around. 'You beauty!' he shouts.

'See! Oh ye of little faith,' I tease as he puts my feet back on the ground.

'I just want to at least see the final, Kat. I was stressing. I'm sorry, I was a tit.'

'You certainly were.' I raise an eyebrow.

He laughs, showing his perfect white teeth.

I shake my head and go to congratulate the others. 'Well done, team. Listen, there was a bit of panicking tonight and some tension between a few of you. We don't need that. We're a team – we win together and we lose together. If anyone thinks we can improve our act before the semi-final, let me know. Otherwise, we stick to our winning formula. I don't want to see any beef between you lot again, got it?' I lock eyes with each of them in turn. They all nod and there are a few mutterings of 'Sorry' and 'Got it, Kat.'

'Okay. Good,' I say, jutting out my chin. I'm not used to having to reprimand them, and the next sentence comes out a lot easier. 'Now then, who's getting the drinks in?'

'That will be me.' I turn to see Andrea walking towards us, arms out wide, her floaty green-and-gold sleeves draping off them. 'It's the least I can do to thank you for the pleasure of that performance.'

It occurs to me that Andrea has never actually seen our show properly, with the costumes and the torsos and lighting and everything. She's only ever seen our rehearsals at the bar. We shuffle out of the entertainment lounge to the hotel's terrace bar, but before we get there, Jay takes my hand and pulls me back.

'Are you guys not coming?' Ant asks.

'We'll be there in a sec. I just have some ideas I want to run past Kat,' Jay replies. Ant shrugs and walks off.

'What's up?' I ask once we're alone.

'This.' He pulls me in and plants his full lips on mine. I let myself enjoy the warm feeling for a moment, then I pull away.

'Not here.' I glare at him but he ignores me and takes both of my hands in his, pulling me back in closer to his body and I can't resist.

'Well, I was thinking that since everyone is on such a high … we could tell them we've been spending time together.' He entwines his fingers with mine and gives me a wide-eyed look. I get it; the sneaking around is a pain, and I don't think there will be any major drama, but, until I know where this is going, it seems a bit premature. I'm still getting used to the idea myself and making an announcement seems a bit too formal. I just want to keep things special and uncomplicated for a while.

'I do want to tell them, Jay, I really do, but not until the competition is over. I don't want to rattle anyone or jinx it. When the competition is over, we'll know more about each other and where this is going too.'

He sighs. 'I guess you're right. I just want to be able to do this all the time.' He plants little kisses on my forehead, nose and mouth and I giggle like a schoolgirl.

'That's sort of the point. You doing that all the time isn't going to win us the competition. It's a distraction – for everybody.'

He groans. 'You're right. But you're a distraction for me.' He leans in but I push him back playfully.

'It's two weeks, if we're lucky. If we don't make the final it will be over next week.'

'You better get me a drink to cool down then.' He fans himself and grins as we head to the bar area.

'I'm beginning to think something's going on with you two,' Marcus says as Jay and I sit down. I laugh uncomfortably.

'Cava!' Andrea appears with a bottle of fizz, and I've never been more grateful to see her.

'Fill me up and let's get this celebration started.'

Chapter 23

The sun streams through the window. I'm vaguely aware of hot skin pressing against my back. Rubbing my eyes, I roll over.

'Morning, beautiful.' Jay kisses my forehead tenderly.

I try to remember how he ended up in my bed and I can't. I peek under the covers and gasp. 'I'm in my underwear.'

Jay laughs softly. 'That makes two of us.'

'Did we …'

He shakes his head. 'You wanted to, but I'm a gent and you were hammered.'

'Cava. I remember lots of cava.' My head is pounding.

'And that was just the beginning.'

I sit up and the room starts to spin. Without warning, bile rises, and I dart to the bathroom just in time.

'There were Jägerbombs too,' Jay calls from the bed.

'Shut up!' The thought alone is enough to make me retch – I'm too old for Jägerbombs.

'Sorry, do you want me to hold your hair?' I look up and Jay is leaning casually against the doorframe. Even through my watery eyes, he looks good. All he has on is a pair of black Calvin Klein boxers, the fitted sort that grip his muscular thighs and leave little to the imagination. It's wrong of me to imagine *that* whilst kneeling over the toilet with vomit dribbling down my chin. This is not my finest moment.

'No, just go away and don't look at me.' I shoo him away.

He chuckles and mutters something about a glass of water before disappearing, leaving me to hit rock bottom in peace.

After a shower and a thorough brush of my teeth, I feel almost normal. I leave the bathroom and sit on the bed towel-drying my hair, as Jay is filling two cups with boiling water in the kitchen.

'I made coffee,' he says.

'Please tell me it's made with Alka-Seltzer.'

'No, but I also found some full-fat Coke and there are some out-of-date Alka-Seltzers in your cupboard.'

'You are what women want,' I tease.

'Oh, really?' He climbs on the bed and straddles me then plants little kisses all over my face.

'You didn't bring any of the promised goods. You need to do better than that to defend your title of "what women want"'

'Fine.' He huffs dramatically and goes to the kitchenette to find the tablets and fetch the coffee. I close my eyes and lay my head back. I don't think drinking is for me anymore. The recovery period is too long.

'Here you go, m'lady.' He hands me my coffee on a saucer with two small pills at the side and puts a can of Coke on the bedside table.

As I take my pills, my phone rings. It's a local number. 'Hello?'

'Kat, it's Gaël from the Grand Canarian.'

'Gaël, what can I do for you?' I ask, sitting up straighter.

I hear him pull in a lungful of air. 'There is no easy way to tell you this, Kat. I'm afraid I'm going to have to cancel some of the bookings we'd made for the Heavenly Hunks.'

No. No. No. 'What? Why?'

'Fewer people have booked the events than usual. Tourism, on the whole, has taken a hit. There are less people coming over from the UK this year and British people are our main customers.

I'm sure it will blow over by next year and we can get going again in the spring.'

There's no point in arguing our case. We're not like other acts that hotels just put on free for their guests in the hope of a decent TripAdvisor review. We do ticketed shows and split the income with the venue. Gaël could let us put on the show but without decent sales, we wouldn't make enough to cover the costs.

'Thanks for calling, Gaël. I appreciate this must have been quite a difficult conversation. Let's hope things pick up again.'

'Yes, of course. I've every faith that we'll be packing the auditorium again next year. I'm so sorry, Kat. If there is anything I can do, or if you decide to put together a family-friendly dance show, perhaps we could do something over winter – we'd have a bigger audience to go at then. The pay would be quite different though, I'm afraid.'

'I'll have a look into it. Thank you, Gaël. I appreciate the offer.'

I say goodbye and end the call.

'More bad news?' Jay asks.

'Did you catch that?'

'Sorry, couldn't help overhearing.'

'He didn't say so, but I'm worried it's damage control after that article. I know the BeachLuxe collapse has had an impact but this just seems like too much of a coincidence. It's frustrating because people love our show. Just last night, the audience were up out of their seats having a great time. Now some crummy journalist has run his mouth and women feel ashamed of having fun.'

'It *will* blow over, Kat and the BeachLuxe issue is temporary. People still need holidays.'

'Part of me agrees but who can say if or when? What do you think about a family dance show?'

Jay rolls onto his side. 'We could modify what we have and wear more clothes, I guess. How much less money are we talking?'

'Without ticket sales, we'd be reliant on what the hotel pays to guest acts. My best guess would be a few hundred euros per performance.'

Jay nods. 'That's not so bad.'

'Per show, not per person.'

'Oh.' I watch his Adam's apple bob up and down as he swallows this information. 'It's still better than nothing. Listen, when we get back to Tenerife, we'll go heavy on our social media promo for the Hunks, and work on a family version of our show just in case.'

'I do admire your optimism. I just hope the others share it.'

Chapter 24

I don't think anyone can ever feel as good as they do the day after spending a whole twenty-four hours in bed. Especially when there's a gorgeous, naked man in said bed. Jay is still sleeping next to me and, for today at least, I've pushed all my business worries to one side. His smooth, bare chest rises and falls with each tranquil breath. His long dark eyelashes fan out across the tops of his cheeks and his full lips pout slightly as gentle puffs of air come out. I smile at the sight of him, and at how special it feels for someone to trust you enough that they can be so vulnerable like that. His arm is above his head so his tattoo is in full view. I trace my finger over it and something pangs inside me. The words show a regret that runs so deep he needed to permanently remind himself to look forwards. He flinches beneath my touch.

'Morning, beautiful.' His voice is thick with sleep.

'Morning, sleepyhead.' I kiss him on the cheek. His skin is warm to the touch.

'Since we're flying back to Tenerife today, we are actually going to have to leave the apartment. Could be hard.' He grins, pulling me in for a kiss.

'Actually,' I say softly, 'I'd like to chat about something.'

'Sounds serious.' He props himself up on his elbow and gives me his attention.

'I was thinking. We never really finished speaking about what happened, in your past.'

He groans and pulls the pillow over his head.

'It's important, Jay; it's obvious you loved your family a lot. I know breaking the law wasn't the best way of going about helping but you saw how desperate they were and tried to fix it.'

'Where are you going with this?'

I take a deep breath for courage. 'I wondered if you'd thought about getting in touch more recently.'

'Kat.' It's a warning. I know this is a painful wound to open but it won't heal until he has some closure.

'Listen, when your mum said she didn't want to see you again, things were raw and painful. She was emotional. You already felt bad for humiliating your family, and then with your dad passing away, you had to deal with the guilt of that too so you accepted what she said.' I stroke his arm. He's rolled onto his back and is staring at the ceiling. 'Then you left town. You don't know if she's ready to forgive you. You've made an honest living for ten years now – that has to count for something.'

'I think staying away was the last good thing I could do for her.'

'I know this has nothing to do with me, but would it hurt to get in touch? If you can that is? I just think that you need to give your mum and brother the chance to forgive you. Time may have healed them now and you could be the final piece of their jigsaw.'

He continues to stare at the ceiling. I've said what I had to say and now it's up to him to decide what he wants to do. I can't force him.

'You have no idea what my family are like. They're stubborn and proud.'

'Fifteen years is a long time to heal, Jay. Even for someone

157

stubborn. Look at me. I've changed my perspective on things and look at how well it's worked out.' I kiss his chest. 'But hey, it's your decision, just promise me you'll think about it.'

He wraps his arms around me and nuzzles his head into my shoulder. 'I suppose I can think it over.'

'Okay, good. Now I suppose we'd better get up.'

'Do we have to?' he asks. I nod and Jay grabs me and rolls me onto my back.

'Well, not straight away.' I say.

He starts to kiss my neck. 'Good. I'd quite like to do more of what we've been doing for the past twenty-four hours.'

I feel him harden against me.

'As much as I want to do this, and I do *really* want to do this, I'm starving. If I don't eat, I'll get hangry.'

Jay raises his eyebrows.

'Hungry and angry, hangry.'

'I know what it means, I just can't imagine you angry.'

'Carry on starving me and you'll see.'

'Relax. Yesterday while you were on your second round of throwing up the entire after-party, I went to get supplies, but then you fell asleep.'

'You're a keeper.' As soon as the words come out I want to claw them back. It's too late. He's heard and he's got a playful look on his face.

'A keeper, hey?'

Heat flushes my face. 'It's just a phrase.'

'Don't backtrack now – you said you wanted to keep me.'

'What supplies did you get?'

'Eggs, croissants, jam.'

'English bacon?'

'No, sorry. I just went to the little shop down the road.'

'Then I can quite plausibly retract my statement. You're not a keeper.'

He grins and goes to the little kitchenette where he busies

himself with butter and jam. I roll over, burying myself in the sheets. I could quite easily go back to sleep.

After breakfast, Jay heads to the gym and I head to the pool for an hour of R&R. We're rehearsing this afternoon and I need to feel as normal as possible, but it's hard when all I can think about is Jay.

I'd sworn off men. I moved here after a horrendous break-up and years of manipulation and emotional abuse. I came here for a fresh start and I've done so well. I became strong, independent and successful. I've been happy since arriving here. A dark feeling swamps me and I can't help but think letting Jay in could change everything. This could be a huge mistake.

***

I stuff the last of the white clothes into the washing machine. They're tightly packed but it seems over the top to split the load. Iain's gym bag is on the floor in the utility room. He came home in his sports gear last night, which must mean the white work shirt he wore yesterday is in there. He hates me going through his stuff – he says he likes it all to be packed a certain way – but I can't stand the thought of one white shirt sitting in the bottom of my currently empty washing basket. I pull the zip. He'll get over it.

I check it over for stains. It's gross, I know, but sometimes the armpits are stained yellow. It's understandable; his job is stressful. I squirt them with my oxy-action spray but I notice more marks: an orange tinge on the shoulder. I rub it with my finger but it's ground in. There are more marks – mauve smears, black speckles. Make-up. Without thinking, I sniff the shirt. There's the stale aroma of sweat after a day in the office, the woody aftershave he always wears, but there's something else, something sweet and floral. Jasmine.

I hear footsteps upstairs and jump, before quickly stuffing the shirt in the washer and slamming the door shut. I fumble with the dial and it takes me three attempts to get the setting right.

'You're up early.'

I jump again.

'Up to no good?' He raises his eyebrow and looks amused. I hit the start button on the load.

'No.' I sound defensive. 'I was just putting the washing in.'

He glances at his gym bag. It's open, its smelly gym paraphernalia spewing out like a disembowelled carcass. 'Please tell me a cat got in or something, and you haven't turned into one of those women who rifles through their husband's gear.' The word 'those' is loaded.

'I ...' I falter. 'I knew there was a shirt in there and just took it out to wash. I wasn't rifling.'

He steps closer to me, his chest slightly grazing mine, and stands tall. I look at my shoes.

'I'm sorry, I know you like everything just right. I'll repack it for you.' I bend down and grab a shampoo bottle that's fallen out when something tightens around my wrist. 'Iain?'

He crouches down so that he's eye level with me. 'I said, don't mess with my stuff.' His voice is cool, calm and barely audible, but the malice in his eyes is unmistakable.

'I'm sorry.' I drop the bottle, get to my feet and scurry away.

When I'm in the bathroom with the door locked, I slump against the wall. Almost as soon as I do, there's a hammering on the door.

'Katelyn, let me in.' Iain's voice is laced with amusement.

I swallow. 'In a minute.'

'Just open the door. I can hear your breathing so I know you're right next to it – you're not on the loo.'

Slowly, I slide the lock. Iain doesn't wait a second before crossing the threshold. He cups my face in his hands. 'Why did you run off?' A V forms between his eyebrows.

'I knew I'd upset you.'

'Don't be silly.' He traces my jaw with his thumb. 'I just don't like you going through my stuff. You know I like things packed a certain way.'

160

I study his face. His features are no longer tight and strained. His muscles are relaxed and expression affable. Now that he's calmed down, the question I want to ask him is burning on my lips. I swallow so hard it hurts my throat.

'Iain, can I ask you something?'

'Of course, sweetheart, anything.' He smiles. Tight and fake. This is a bad idea.

'Your work shirt. It had make-up on it.'

He cocks his head to the side. He wants to know where I'm going with this – surely he doesn't need me to spell it out. It takes everything I have to force the next sentence out.

'Have you been having an affair?'

I'm braced for a torrent of abuse. A rant, or a stream of names. Anything, but not what follows.

He laughs. Cold, hard laughter.

Then he shakes his head. 'You really are a fucking nut job.'

***

The next day, I arrive at Andrea's purposely early. I hear but can't see her unpacking bottles behind the bar.

'You look good. Who is he and why the change of heart?' she asks, popping up from behind the bar. I put my hand to my cheek to try and sense what she means but all I feel is the heat that's no doubt colouring my face a nice shade of pink.

It's not until she laughs that I realise she's teasing me. I compose myself enough to give her a look of mock warning.

'Drink?' She waves an empty sangria jug at me. I can't believe I'm even contemplating this, but there's something about Andrea that makes me fancy a drink and a girlie natter.

I check my watch. 'It's five o'clock somewhere. Make it a small one with lots of orange juice though please.'

As Andrea throws chopped fruit into the jug and adds whatever else is in her famous sangria, I slide onto a barstool.

'The show was great the other night.' She passes me a glass of fruity punch. 'I honestly think you guys are serious contenders.'

'I hope so,' I say, taking a sip.

'But that isn't what's worrying you, is it?'

I draw a breath. It's hard to arrange the jumble of words into a shape that will fit through my lips.

'Come on, Kat, this is a safe space.'

'I've been *sort of* dating Jay.'

She doesn't react, which I'm thankful for, but there's an unmistakable glint in her eye. It's exactly the kind of salacious titbit she loves.

'You mean that god-like hunk of a man who follows you around like a lost puppy?'

I furrow my brow; to some extent that could describe any of the dancers. 'Not sure.'

'The one with the sexy smile and the muscles. The older one, the newest one.'

'The newest one,' I confirm.

'Jeez.' She fans her face dramatically. 'Congratulations.'

'No,' I hiss. 'This is bad.'

'How so? From where I sit on rehearsal days, it's very good.' She winks.

'You know how I had a bad marriage before?'

Andrea's expression darkens. I've never told her exactly what happened in my marriage; she's never asked, and I respect her for that. She understands it wasn't good, and that was all she needed to know and all I wanted to tell her when we met. Years have passed since and we've never needed to expand. 'Look forwards not backwards,' she's always said. Andrea too had a bad marriage before she met Javier so I know she understands where I'm coming from. I also know she won't press me to talk if I'm not willing, but I want her to understand how I'm feeling.

'I can't help thinking that what happened back then will happen again.'

162

Her jaw clenches briefly before relaxing. 'Has Jay given you a reason to think this?'

'No,' I say quickly before she orders a Mafia hit or something.

'Then what are you worrying about?'

'Jay is a good-looking bloke.'

Andrea makes a noise of agreement.

'He literally has women throwing themselves at him each night. He could have any woman and he's chosen me? I can't comprehend that.'

'You're so much more than an attractive woman, Kat. You're a woman with gumption and ambition. What is so hard to understand?'

'I suppose I just think the temptation will be too hard to ignore once the excitement of us wears off.'

'I hardly know him, but from what you've told me, Jay doesn't seem to care about all that attention. You said he doesn't even go out partying with the rest of the dancers.' Andrea looks confused, and I can't blame her. It's hard to explain. It's hard to explain to anyone what Iain was like and how subtle changes in someone's personality over time can go unnoticed, or be dismissed as something like tiredness and stress, until the day you wake up and realise you're too far in. I've got to use my head and not my heart if I'm going to avoid getting hurt again.

'It's complicated. He doesn't, but he had reasons for that. Now he *has* dared to be with a woman, maybe he's taken a step past that. He could have opened the floodgates, so to speak.'

Andrea looks at me like she thinks I belong in a straitjacket.

In essence, I'm scared. I'm scared of being taken for a ride and made a fool of. I'm scared of undoing all the work I've put into myself over the past eight years. I'm scared of falling for someone who doesn't yet realise how amazing they are.

'I just don't want to get in too deep and wake up one day with a partner who hates me and cheats on me every opportunity he gets.'

'Either way, you end up alone. So why not have some fun with Jay and deal with any issues as they arise? That's if you want a man, of course.'

I open my mouth but nothing comes out. In some ways, I'm glad Andrea knows very little about my past because it doesn't influence her thoughts. Her advice is based on the now, which is exactly what I should be basing my decision on.

'Day-drinking?' Pauw slaps me on the back, causing a dribble of sangria to run down my chin. 'You lush!'

'You know what this one is like,' I say, cocking my head in Andrea's direction.

He gestures in agreement. 'Anyway, I've been thinking about a slightly different routine for the semi-final and wanted to run it by you. The judges and crowd have seen our act twice now, and I know Marcus added the thong and that creepy licky-lip thing that everyone seemed to love but I thought we could mix things up a bit more.'

'Okay, what do you have in mind?'

'I know everyone loves the backflips, but I've got a few other tricks up my sleeve.'

'Care to show me?'

'Okay, but I'm rusty, so bear with me.'

He walks over to the dance floor and pulls off his T-shirt, revealing his chiselled physique. Pauw is slightly smaller than the other guys but his boyish good looks are enough to secure him an army of fans. He puts on Avicii's 'Wake Me Up' and starts to stretch his muscles. It's not our usual song choice but it certainly has a lively vibe about it. I like it. When the chorus kicks in, he bounces into the air in a somersault. When his feet hit the ground he immediately propels himself into a double aerial flip. I sometimes forget Pauw is an acrobat by trade. Bringing this into the act could give us an edge.

He turns off the music and walks towards me, raking his hands through his hair. 'It's been a while.' He grins.

'Hey, you've still got it.' I smile, impressed.

'Can you see it fitting in?'

The final is still only a fifteen-minute slot, but I'm thinking it could start the breakdancing segment. With the spotlight of sin currently upon us, I don't think a more talent-driven act would do us any harm and I think after what Paul told me about his disastrous talent competition, he really needs this input to be a success. I think it will be.

'Definitely. Let's run it by the others and see what they think.'

As if on cue, the other guys trickle in, looking well rested after a day off. They start warming up, and when the shirts come off, the masculine smells of shower gel, deodorant and aftershave fill the bar. Andrea grabs a seat next to me.

'It always smells like a boys' locker room when they come in here.'

I quite like it.

Pauw wants to show the guys his tweaked version of the break-dancing set, so they start with that. He swaps places with Ant to be in the centre, does the stunts and goes back to his original position and Ant struts forward. It's a small change but I like it, and Ant is good at strutting. When they're back in their normal positions, the usual routine kicks in. Jay steps forward and licks his thumb, then runs it from his breastbone to the waistband of his jeans. I drink in the triangle of his body and when I raise my eyes, he's looking directly at me. Muscles tighten somewhere deep in my abdomen. Then he throws himself into a backflip and my insides erupt.

'Andrea, you're right. I'm an idiot.'

'Damn right you are. Look at that man.'

'Does your husband know you ogle strippers all day?'

'Of course.' She grins. 'He picks up the aftermath.'

'Eugh! Too much information.'

When the song finishes, I ask them to try it again with Pauw's music choice. It works well; the tune is uplifting and gets the heart pumping. We all agree that it's perfect and makes a change from all the R&B.

After the rehearsal, I tell the guys what went well and dish out a few tweaks before they all disperse. We have a small charity performance tonight, which is sadly unpaid, but it will help raise our profile once more and raise a few euros for a local dog rescue centre. We only have a twenty-minute slot between an auction and a ladies' fashion show, so we've added a few extra bits to our competition entry.

Jay stays behind packing up the props after everyone else has gone. I walk up behind him and snake my arms around his waist, planting kisses across his back. His skin tastes salty and smells deliciously musky.

'Mmm, to what do I owe this pleasure?' he asks, turning to face me.

'Nothing,' I say. I can hardly go into detail about how watching him up on stage has given me certain urges.

'I've got a couple of hours free if you fancy chilling out?' He entwines his fingers with mine and pulls me in, kissing me on the lips.

'Sounds perfect.'

Chapter 25

He didn't even defend himself. He laughed at me. Surely, if he was guilty of having some sort of affair, he'd deny it. It's the knee-jerk reaction of a cheater, isn't it? The excuses would come pouring out, the declarations of love and so on. Not Iain. He's so convinced that I've lost the plot it's amusing to him – so amusing, in fact, he can't defend himself because he finds the whole idea of me being paranoid and jealous hilarious. Of course, I feel like an utter fool now and wish I hadn't said anything. But my brain niggles with the question of what if? I did see make-up on his shirt, that's the thing; it was there in plain sight. I'm an idiot for throwing it in the washer, because now there's no evidence and I have nothing to confront him with. There could be a perfectly plausible explanation: an upset colleague, a corridor collision or some catastrophe near my dressing table, but if so, why didn't he say that? Is it so bad that I asked?

A few days later, when he's in a better mood, I dare to bring it up. He says he's no idea how any make-up got there. He asks if it could have been something else, as he'd had car trouble and had to get under the front end of his Golf. I mean, it looked like make-up, but rolling around on the floor could have attracted all sorts of stains, I suppose. I'm satisfied with the answer. He was so shocked at the allegation that he didn't know how to respond, I guess. I panic-washed the shirt; we all do strange things under pressure. I'm glad to put the whole thing behind us – it's like a weight has been lifted.

***

My head is resting on Jay's smooth chest and when I breathe in, I inhale the comforting musky scent of his warm body. The room is dark and I've been drifting in and out of consciousness for a few hours as Jay sleeps soundly. Being with Jay makes everything seem better; life seems, dare I say it, perfect. It's when I'm alone that the real worry sets in. We're still down on bookings; in fact, they're disappearing faster than sweets at a kids' party. I still need to tell the guys how bad things are. I'd pinned everything on this stupid competition and my silly notion that we could win – and I've led the guys to believe that we can win – but now we've come this far, the acts are really good, and I just don't know if we can.

Even if we did win, it would be a short-term fix for what now seems like a long-term problem. I bury my face into Jay's skin and it almost makes the thoughts go away. I could talk to him about it, but I know what he'll say. What I need to do is have a serious chat with the boys and talk about the next steps.

When the light seeps through the cracks in the blinds I don't think I've slept a wink, but I get up anyway. Jay mumbles something in a sleep-laced voice but drifts back off whilst I dress and slip outside.

I love the early mornings here when the sun is out but it's cool enough to contemplate a cardigan. It's deceptive; it doesn't matter how long I've lived here, I still feel unable to imagine the midday heat that will come in just a few hours. I walk towards the beach. There's nobody here but an early-morning dog-walker in the distance. I step onto the soft grey sand and make my way to the shore, where I sit.

I check the calendar in my phone. We've only got one gig this week and the semi-final tonight – time to get my bottom in gear like I should have done weeks ago. Scrolling through my phone, I go on the Heavenly Hunks Instagram page and set up some fresh ads, then I upload some new photos to our Facebook and Twitter pages, which showcase the more talent-driven aspects of our show rather than the usual hot-guy picks that normally work. Then I use a hashtag generator to try and get them trending, then I read that you shouldn't overuse hashtags anymore so I delete them and put them into a comment. I can't keep up with all the stupid rules.

My phone rings in my hand.

'Hey, Ant, is everything okay?' I ask, concerned. I don't think Ant has ever called me.

I hear him draw a deep breath.

'Ant?'

'Sorry, Kat, I'm here. I just needed to ask you something.'

'Go ahead.'

'Well, I don't normally pay much attention to our show calendar because I'm used to us performing almost every night, but since we've had a few free nights recently, I had a look and I don't think it's been updated. There are hardly any shows on it for the rest of the year.'

I swallow a lead weight that lands heavily in the pit of my stomach.

'Kat?'

'Sorry, Ant. I was going to speak to you all tonight after the semi-final. Business has really quietened down especially since BeachLuxe went bust. People are scared of booking a holiday right now. The hotels seem to want smaller, cheaper acts at the moment and I think some of our regulars are waiting for the bad publicity to blow over. Even the big hotels and the bars are only wanting a show like ours every couple of months, and ticket sales have taken a hit because of the lack of people coming over. I'm putting the word out there, but I'm thinking it might be an idea for us all to consider part-time jobs. Just while we ride this out. I hope by spring we'll be back on track.'

There's a pause.

'Oh,' he says eventually. 'I didn't realise things were that bad.'

I feel a pang of guilt because it's my fault for letting them feel safe. I guess I just didn't quite believe it myself.

'I was hoping the competition might lead to a few bookings but it hasn't really. Just that charity gig last week so far.'

'Is this the end of the Hunks then?'

'No!' I say, far too quickly. 'No, things will pick back up again, I'm sure. The hotels can't keep putting on crap acts for much longer. It might be a tough winter, is all.'

'Do you want me to talk to the guys?'

'That's sweet, Ant, but I think this is something I should do.'

'Okay, well some of them have been talking, so I'd do it sooner rather than later. Marcus is a bit spooked.'

'I'll do it now. Gather everyone around the pool and I'll be there in fifteen minutes.'

When I hang up, I text Jay who is probably still fast asleep on my bed.

Wake up and be by the pool in fifteen minutes. Don't let anyone see you leave my apartment xx

I can't spring me and Jay on them too, not yet. Nobody has noticed him staying at mine because of all the travelling and apartment-swapping that goes on naturally. Some of them suspect he's seeing a local but none of them care enough to dig deeper.

I walk the whole way back with a huge knot in my stomach. When I get there, everyone is gathered around a few loungers. Pauw and Sammy are lying down, Marcus and Ant are standing next to Pauw, and Jay and Hugo sit on the wall behind. My insides clench. This is all my fault.

'Hi, everyone.'

There's an orchestra of mumbled greetings.

'I know some of you have noticed the show calendar is looking

170

quite empty, and you're right to be concerned. I know I mentioned that bookings were down but it's much worse than I expected. I've tried putting the word out there and I've started to run different ads, but until business picks up, I think it might be wise for us to look for part-time work during the day to tide us over. I'm hoping this will be a temporary measure, but the money will dry up pretty soon. I'm sorry.'

I let the information sink in. None of them can look me in the eye, apart from Jay, of course, who gives me a small smile of encouragement.

'We still have the sunshine, and the beaches, and the competition,' I add. 'Even if we don't win the money, it spreads our name.'

'I think Phil's place is hiring,' Pauw says after a few moments, and the relief that his words bring helps to ease the tension in my body.

'That's great, Pauw. Can you let us know the details ASAP?' I say, my words laced with a good smattering of enthusiasm for everyone's benefit.

Pauw looks up from his phone. 'Texting him now.'

'Great!' I force a cheerful expression. Seeing my boys so dejected is heart-breaking, but I have to put on a brave face. 'Let's make tonight's show great. Let's show these hoteliers what they're missing.'

There are a few lukewarm smiles. I think we're going to be all right.

***

Our performance tonight was top-notch. The timings were spot on, nobody missed a beat, and there was chemistry by the bucket-load. I'd be confident for the final too if the competition wasn't so bloody good. Half the guys have disappeared. I think nerves have got the better of them. Me, Pauw and Hugo are left watching the final act of the evening, the dancing duet. Tonight they're doing the *Dirty Dancing* finale sequence and it's brilliant, even I want them to win for a moment. I wait for the lift and then sneak out to round up the others for the results. Ant and Sammy are in the bar at the back of the entertainment lounge.

'Hey, guys, it's almost results time. Have you seen Marcus and Jay?'

'Marcus went to the bathroom, and Jay was outside but you might want to leave him.' Ant snickers. It takes me a few moments to realise what he's implying.

My stomach lurches. 'Oh?'

'Some obsessed fan literally dragged him outside by the band of his jeans. I think he'll be a little bit too preoccupied to care much about who gets through.'

Thunder echoes through me.

'She was pretty decent though, and he wasn't complaining,' Sammy adds. 'I think he'll be fine if we just tell him the results later.'

'Yeah, all blonde hair and long tanned legs. It's what makes the job special, even if we're not getting paid.' Ant winks.

My mind blanks. Tiny visions start to punctuate the void. Jay with a blonde. Jay who I thought was different. The image of Alonso walking outside hand-in-hand with the girl in white hits me. I can remember how carefree he was – he didn't even look like he'd done anything wrong. They're all the same. At least creepy Mike wore a warning badge. Surely not Jay though. Jay who I trusted. Realising Ant and Sammy are still in front of me, I force a smile. 'Let's get in there and see if we've made the final because I *do* care.'

As Ant and Sammy head back into the auditorium, I linger for a moment, taking a step backwards and looking to my left, through the open patio doors, which lead from the bar to the terrace. Sure enough, I see Jay with a leggy blonde woman. Just the sheer sight of her makes me feel doughy and plain by comparison. My chest clenches. As I watch them, I realise I'm holding my breath in anticipation as I try to see a sign or something that tells me this is just a mistake and he's simply brushing off the advances of a fan. The blonde woman places her hands on his chest, gently grazing its defined outline, and then she presses her slender thigh between the bulk of his. She moves her head close to his, tilting it upwards so their lips are just inches apart. He's smiling and looking into her eyes.

There's no mistaking what's happening there and I can't watch anymore. It was only a matter of time before Jay got his confidence with women back, and I was stupid to let myself believe I would be anything more than just a stepping-stone for him. What hurts the most is that he let me believe I was special. After everything I told him about Iain, and my being single for eight years, I thought he'd treat me better than that. Pain sears through the centre of my torso. I practically run back to my seat, sitting down just as the female judge, whose name I should remember by now, appears on stage.

'Ladies and gentlemen,' she starts, but I can't listen. Why would Jay treat me this way? I think back to the woman I saw. Although I didn't see her face, I could tell by her perfectly coiffured hair and the skimpy clothes that clung to her tiny frame that she was probably very attractive. Of course he'd choose someone like her over someone like me. Someone whose shape is blurring at the edges and whose skin is starting to crease. My mind is spinning out of control, replaying every conversation I've ever had with Jay. We never said we were exclusive.

'Ha,' I say aloud. That's it. We're not and never were exclusive. God, I'm an idiot.

'That's not nice,' Marcus whispers.

'What?'

'Laughing at Espectacular not getting through.'

Oh, bugger. 'I was thinking about something else.' Something worse. 'That's awful. They were so good. It, doesn't leave much hope for us.'

I focus on the judge. She's reading out the order differently to last time, one act who are through and one act who aren't. La Leona is through.'

'How the hell did they make that choice?' Marcus asks.

'I don't know. Audience experience? The variety in their performance?' If so, that could be good news for us.

Next up is Ted Sheeran versus Flexibility, the acrobatics act.

'Ted Sheeran is through to the grand finale. I'm sorry, Flexibility, you have not made the next round,' the judge announces. My stomach is twisted up so tightly, like an old washerwoman has wrung it out. Jay still isn't back, but screw him. Everyone else is here for the Heavenly Hunks. He hasn't been with us long enough to know how close we all are and we don't ditch one another at a time like this, especially not for some full-on groupie. Perhaps when this is over we could cut Jay out. Having five guys in the Hunks would be cheaper anyway and I don't think the act would suffer that much, especially if we have to start playing smaller venues; it could actually be a good thing. God! I can't sack him for playing around. I wouldn't sack him if I hadn't slept with him, would I? This is why I shouldn't have broken my golden rule. It's myself I'm cross with.

'Finally, last but not least, we have the Heavenly Hunks versus Daydreamz.'

I hold my breath.

'The last act to go through to the grand final is ...'

Get on with it! I jiggle about in my seat.

'The Heavenly Hunks!'

As soon as we hear our name I leap in the air to cheer. Everyone gets up. They're hugging and quite literally jumping for joy. It's what we needed to hear after the news I delivered earlier today. My chest flutters with happiness. When the excitement dies down and the auditorium starts to clear I realise Jay never came back. It's a strange feeling, sadness mixed with elation; my chest is filled with fizzy warmth whilst my stomach churns with nausea.

'You comin' to celebrate?' Marcus asks.

I put my hand on his arm. 'Not tonight, love. I don't feel great. You guys go ahead – you deserve it.'

'You sure?'

I smile tightly. 'Yes, go and have fun.' Marcus's eyes linger on me for a moment like he's navigating a moral maze: should I leave, should I stay?

'Go! It's an order.' I force a small laugh.

'Okay, okay.' He laughs. 'See you tomorrow, Boss.'

He kisses me on the cheek before bouncing towards the bar with the others.

When they've all gone, I slip out. There's no sign of Jay anywhere and I'm relieved.

Chapter 26

'You're working late a lot,' I say as Iain returns. The second showing of Coronation Street *is just finishing.*

'I'm putting money in the bank, Katelyn.' I can't tell if his tone is condescending or chipper or somewhere in between.

'I know that. I just, well, I feel like I haven't seen much of you recently. I'm always here on my own.'

'I was hoping we could have a holiday this year, Kat.'

'But you said holidays were a waste of money.'

He purses his lips. 'I said they cost a lot of money. If I keep putting in the hours, we can go away for a week, maybe even two. Is there anywhere you fancy going?'

I ponder this; little flutters of excitement fill my belly. 'I've always wanted to go to Italy, see Venice perhaps, or Rome.'

'Venice stinks and Rome is too hot. What about somewhere like Magaluf or San Antonio?'

'They're not our sort of places, are they?'

He shrugs. 'We're young; we like beer and dancing. I don't see why not.'

'We can think about it,' I say.

'Not too hard, your brain might implode!' He laughs to himself and goes upstairs to change.

Later, when he's in the shower, I sneak into the bedroom and take his shirt out of the dirty washing hamper before examining it for stains. There's nothing. I sniff it and there is a sweet smell that's definitely not his cologne, but it could be anything – he could have popped into Boots at lunchtime or have an overscented co-worker. Maybe he's right, maybe I am paranoid.

***

I awake to the sound of hammering on the door.

'I'm coming,' I yell. I touch the screen of my phone and the time flashes: 09.02. There are seven missed calls from Jay. All the visions of him with that woman from the night before flash through my head like a 'Previously on …' section of a TV show and I get that nervous tummy ache that makes you want to vomit.

'Who is it?' I ask before opening.

'It's me, Jay, you silly sod. Let me in – I need to tell you something.'

The fact he tries to make this light-hearted makes my blood boil. I know exactly what he wants to tell me and I don't want to hear it. 'I'm not well, leave me alone.'

'Kat?' he asks, concern fraying the edges of his tone.

'Please, just go away.'

'No, not if you're poorly. Let me come in and look after you.' The familiarity of his gentle voice gives me a lump in my throat, then I remember myself. I won't be made to look a fool. He may want to carry on as normal but I certainly don't.

'Jay, this whole thing between me and you was a mistake. I don't blame you for being you, but I need to be me and that means going back to the way things were. I want to call this off.'

'What?' He has the nerve to sound shocked. 'I have no idea what you're on about. Please let me in.' His voice tremors like he's scared. He's good, I'll give him that much.

'I don't want to see you anymore. It was wrong to mix work

177

and pleasure and, as your boss, I shouldn't have let it happen. This is all my fault for being unprofessional.' I could tell him the truth about what I saw, but that would just give him the chance to worm his way out of it and make excuses I don't want to hear. I'd rather draw a line under the whole thing and move on as friends.

'Have I done something wrong?'

I let out a small humourless laugh. Has he? He's a stripper, for goodness' sake; he's only done exactly what I expected him to. He's a late bloomer, that's all, and I'm a fool for fantasising about us being anything more than a silly fling. I'm an idiot for being shocked at seeing him with another woman. I have nothing left to say, so I rummage through a mental bag of clichés.

'It's not you, Jay, it's me.'

'Kat?' His voice is weak. I want to open the door and I know I need to confront him, but right now I can't keep it together.

***

A few hours of sitting on my balcony reading a book later and there's another bout of hammering on my door. I contemplate ignoring it but I can hear Marcus yelling my name.

'What is it?' I ask, flinging the door open.

'We have some news, Kat.'

'We?'

'The Hunks, all of us. Jay tried to tell you earlier but he said you wouldn't let him in. Are you feeling better, by the way?' Marcus plonks himself on the bed but can't seem to sit still.

'Er, yes. I am. Thank you. What is it?'

'When we were in the bar last night, we got talking to that American judge, Brad. He was telling us how great he thought our performances have been and asked who our manager was. Some of us think he might want to offer us a gig. He lives in Las Vegas, Kat; we think he wants us to go over there.' The corners of his mouth twitch as he tries not to smile, obviously gauging my reaction first.

As the information sinks in, I don't know how to react.

'And ... he wants to speak to me?' My mouth is dry, and my question is obvious, but I'm confused. I don't know what else to say.

'Yes!' His smile finally cracks; he's full of excitement I don't share. I want to vomit.

I think I already know the answer to this question but I ask it anyway: 'And, I'm sure you have your hopes up for nothing, but if he did, you would all want that? To go to Las Vegas, I mean?' He looks up at me with hopeful eyes and then he takes my hand in his.

'We don't want to get our hopes up because we don't really know if that's what he wants to talk about, but ...' he smiles a wide grin, '... pretty much. Pauw might take some convincing and Hugo wouldn't want to leave his family here but think about it, Kat – things are not going well at the moment but we do put on a bloody good show. The clubs in Vegas have all the latest tech, the lighting and special effects and so on. We could be world-class. There would be so many promotional opportunities: TV, sponsors, US tours. We've drained the well here. This is the next step for us. This could be our chance to hit the big-time.'

I sit down next to him and sigh. 'He might just want to talk about how I got things going. Don't get your hopes up, Marc, and seriously, would you all be happy to up and move to another continent?'

'It's a twelve-hour flight back to the UK, it's a four-hour flight from here – what's eight more hours in the air in the grand scheme of things?'

I give an exasperated shrug. I honestly don't think some hotshot Vegas businessman would want an exotic dance act from the hotels and bars of Tenerife.

'The cost of living will be more there you know.'

'We'd manage!' he says. 'Can you call him? I have a card.'

'Fine, I'll call him. I guess it won't hurt to hear what he has to say.'

Marcus hands me a shiny black business card with hot pink writing on it. 'You're a star, Kat.'

Chapter 27

Brad Sharp suggested we meet in a little bar on the promenade. As I head down the palm-lined walkway towards it, the view of the crashing azure ocean below draws me in. It's a view I've come to take for granted. The uncertainty of the Heavenly Hunks' future has made me question whether I would be better off going back to England if things don't work out.

Brad sticks out like a sore thumb amidst the sea of pasty new arrivals that probably came in last night. Dressed in a navy pinstripe suit with a crisp white shirt and a navy tie, he's got that clean-cut American business look. Not quite the T-shirt-and-shorts attire I'm used to seeing here. I don't even ask the server if the man is waiting on anyone; I just head straight over.

'You must be Brad,' I say, holding out my hand. Instead of taking it, he stands up and hugs me.

'Kat, how great to meet you. I've heard so many awesome things.' He gestures for me to sit down. 'What can I get you to drink?' he asks. He's smooth, I'll give him that.

I notice he has a beer but I need to keep a clear head. 'Just a green tea for me, please.'

He gestures to the waiter and places my order then focuses his attention on me. 'So, I've been watching your show throughout

181

the competition and I have to say, I really love your act. Obviously, there's a trip to Las Vegas for the winner, but I want to run something else by you.'

I shuffle forwards in my seat. 'I'm not sure I follow.'

'The winners get to perform a one-off show in Las Vegas but I want to offer the Heavenly Hunks a residency in my new Las Vegas venue, The Forbidden Theatre.'

'A residency?' My head starts to spin.

'Yes, an initial six-month contract, with a view to extending it to a year if the Hunks are a success. We'd cover travel and accommodation and we'd be looking at five shows a week, pretty much guaranteed to sell out.'

It takes a minute to absorb everything he's saying. 'You want the Heavenly to move to Las Vegas and perform in your club?'

He grins a perfect set of white veneers and lifts both arms in the air. 'Why not? Who doesn't love Vegas?'

I'm not sure I would, but it's not just about me, is it? 'It's a lot to think about. I mean, Tenerife is the home of the Hunks.'

'If you want to be a real success in the entertainment industry, Las Vegas is the place to be.'

I think about the gigs we've lost. I've really failed the boys. They deserve this break. Ant wants to make more money, Marcus is still moping about because that girl flew back to England and never called him and Sammy would lap Las Vegas up like an excitable puppy. I'm still furious with Jay and hurt, but I still care about his story and this could be his chance to make it big – show his mum how he's changed and makes a good, honest living now. I'm just not sure about Pauw and Hugo.

'I suppose. How would this even work? I could do with reading the fine print.'

'Of course. You're the business owner, so obviously you and I need to cut a deal and come to some sort of agreement on an asking price.'

Cut a deal? I hadn't considered that he'd want to buy us out.

Selling the Hunks is a big deal. I'd thought he was offering us a permanent gig, but if I put my business head on, I suppose it makes sense: if he wants to pull all the strings, he'd need to own the Heavenly Hunks business. Our choice is a family dance act and day jobs, or doing what we love in Las Vegas.

'Okay, but before I can even think about that, I need more details. What's the exact proposal?'

'As I said, it would be five shows per week at ten p.m. The two days off would be free days, with a show rehearsal on one of those days. It's quite a large auditorium that we've acquired, and we'll have a big-name singer on two nights a week but we haven't signed contracts yet so I can't say who. Anyway, here are the fine details.' He takes a document out of a file and turns it so that I can see.

The pay is monthly, guaranteed and not ticket dependent. The apartments will be shared and free for the initial six-month stint. There is a mutual get-out clause after six months with a view to extend to a twelve-month residency after, just like he said. It all looks promising but could I relinquish all the control and just be a compère?

'What about this bit, here?' I point to a clause.

At least four of the original dancers must sign contracts to be part of the Las Vegas act in the initial six-month period.

'It means I'd need four of the original Hunks to sign a contract for this deal to go ahead. We feel for it to be the Heavenly Hunks, we need to guarantee the original dancers. I can bring two new dancers in but any more than that, I feel like we'd lose the essence of the show. In the early days at least.'

'And you really think the Hunks have got the magic to bring the crowds in?'

'Oh definitely. The guys are electric on stage and the crowd are completely drawn in.'

I smile and carry on scanning through the document. Everything looks pretty straightforward – obviously, I'll get a solicitor to check it over. I know Andrea has a good friend who does a lot of British property purchases; he should be able to understand it.

The last section is entitled 'The transfer of intellectual property', and it talks about the handover of the brand name and my rights to trade as the Heavenly Hunks. I flick back but can't see anything about me as a compère. Has he called us all dancers in the contract? I'm confused.

'Brad, am I one of the four dancers you need?'

The server places my tea on the table and I thank her. When she walks away, I notice Brad's expression has changed and his head has fallen slightly to the side. 'I'm sorry, Kat. I think we've got our wires crossed here. I want to buy the Heavenly Hunks brand from you. To be able to really ramp them up, I'd need full managerial control and that means making sure I have the right person fronting them too. In Las Vegas, we have a great emcee called Jenny Grant. You may have heard of her?'

I nod. Of course I have; Andrea loves her! She's a great comedian who's been on UK TV too, on something like *8 Out of 10 Cats*. My stomach sinks. Where is he going with this?

'Well, we'd like her to emcee with the Hunks. She has a great rapport with the crowd and she has a huge following. She really is what we need to take the Hunks to the next level.'

'Okay,' I say quickly, wondering what my role could be. Then it sinks in. 'So, if you're managing all the bookings, and the guys' contracts are with you, and Jenny is the emcee, what would I be?'

'Kat.' He leans in and speaks in a gentle tone. 'We'd be buying the business *from* you. That's what the section on intellectual property is about. We're buying the brand because we love what you've done, but it's ready for bigger and better things. I'm the guy who can make that happen. You'd be free to do whatever you like, here, in this beautiful place.'

Oh. My heart plummets into the pit of my stomach. Oh God, I'm not included. I almost feel my chest tear in two. On one hand, I should be proud of the fact I've helped create something so amazing that someone like Brad wants to buy it off me and take it to the next level, but on the other hand, I'm part of the Hunks. We're a team. I'm not ready to say goodbye to them.

'I don't think the guys will go if they know I'm not part of the deal,' I say quietly.

He furrows his brow. 'Look, I get that this is a tough decision and I'm sorry. You are great up there but we really want to take the Hunks to a global level and we can't do that without a sell-out name to kick us off. Jen is already a well-known personality. She's loud and brassy but has this charm that works and as I said earlier, she has a massive following. People would book tickets for the Heavenly Hunks just to see Jen. It's a leapfrog move for the Heavenly Hunks with an unfortunate sacrifice. Jen is here and really loved the show too. She has tons of ideas for it.'

I get a flutter of inappropriately timed excitement. 'Jenny is here too?'

'She's an investor in our project. We decided a while ago we wanted to get in on this modern-day male stripper thing that everyone's talking about. We've travelled around looking at different acts for a while now, but they're all very similar or too high profile already and we want something unique to us. The Hunks had a bit more talent between them – it's not just naked guys dry-humping – that's why I wanted to approach you before the competition results because this offer stands whether you win or lose and at least you can make the decision with a clear head.'

'Say this all …' I swallow, '… went ahead, what sort of time frame are we looking at?'

'My club is ready to open and I could get the Hunks on stage in three weeks' time. Needless to say, the legal stuff would have to move quickly.

The thoughts in my head are fighting to be heard. I feel everything: crushing embarrassment at assuming I was part of this, stomach-wrenching sadness at the prospect of losing the boys and giddy excitement at what they could become. 'I need time to think about this.'

'Of course. I need to make a call. You drink your tea, have a think, and we'll chat some more shortly.'

As he leaves, I screw my eyes shut. It's more discreet than banging my fist on the table or letting out the scream contained inside me. I take a sip of my lukewarm tea, which is bitter after leaving the teabag in for too long. I have a lot to process. Firstly, I'm not going to Vegas, but I can live with that – it isn't somewhere I ever saw myself living. Secondly, how do I tell the guys I'm not part of the deal? I should be honest with them and let them make their own decision. I know they will vote to stay with me out of loyalty but the ugly truth is that I have nothing left to offer them. They really want this break. They *need* it. Paul needs the confidence, Marcus needs cheering up, Ant needs to earn some more money, Sammy needs to see the world and Jay, Jay needs to be apart from me. Even if Hugo doesn't want to go it's a flattering offer and he'll have no trouble picking up work here. The guys have given me so much of themselves. It's time I do something for them. The kindest thing I can do is tell them I don't want to go and it's time for me to do something different. I think that if I say that, I can convince them to go.

Brad reappears and sits opposite me. 'Do you need more time?'

I take a breath. 'I can't believe I'm saying this, but how much are we talking?'

'We think this figure would be fair.' He slides a printed banker's draft over. Presumptuous much?

My eyes adjust to the small typeface and almost fall out of my head. 'Bloody hell.'

Brad smiles. 'We realise this is a lot to give up: your livelihood, your team.'

'If the guys want this,' I say past the lump in my throat. 'I can't hold them back.'

'Then talk to them and if they're happy to go ahead, let them go, and do good things with this money. I assume you love living here? This money would help keep you on your feet for a while after the Hunks leave.'

As much as I don't want to admit it, the money will help. 'Of course. Mr Sharp, if the contract looks okay to my solicitor and the guys want this and are happy with their contracts, you'll have yourself a deal.' The words feel wrong and clunky in my mouth.

'Great. You check things from your end, talk to the boys and if the plan is a goer, we'll have to meet up again to sign off all the official paperwork. You're welcome to bring along a lawyer, but it's a straightforward agreement and the money will be yours as soon as we sign.'

I hand him back the cheque. 'Okay, I'll wait for your call.'

Considering what I'm potentially giving up, that all seemed *too* straightforward.

As I leave the bar, I'm filled with heaviness. It's the end of an era but it's so much more than that. It's the end of the life I carved out, the happiness I created. It's the end of living the dream I worked so hard for. Still, it's the right thing for the boys and I can't hold them back. I'm a victim of my own success, I suppose, but that sounds so conceited. I've started from scratch before; I can do it again.

The next task is to tell everyone I won't be going and sell the idea that it's what *I* want. I'm not quite ready for that, so I sit on a stone wall that encases a flower garden on the promenade and look out to sea. It's become a cloudy September day in the time I've spent with Brad and the Atlantic has turned steely and fierce. There are a few die-hard families on the beach but large swathes of it are empty. I can't believe I'm going to lose my boys. A sharp pain pierces my chest as I imagine life without them. I'll miss doling out the advice, setting curfews and just having them around. I know it's selfish to think this way but they're all I've had for such a long time. I'll miss Jay too. I know things aren't great between us now, but in time, we would have been friends again. Now we won't have the chance.

It's all too much. The pressure inside erupts in a flurry of tears and sobs. I face the ocean so nobody can see and I let the wind carry the tears towards my ears rather than down my cheeks. The salt stings, and, in a way, it's a relief to focus on that rather than the aching in my heart.

To distract myself, I check my phone and see an email from Mum and Dad. They've finally booked their flights to come and visit. I almost laugh at their impeccable timing. At least I'll have something to look forward to.

When I arrive back at the apartment complex, Marcus is sitting by the pool in shorts and a hoodie. When he spots me, he leaps up and jogs over.

'What did he want?' I can tell the suspense is driving him crazy.

'It was an offer like you suspected. I need to get you all together to discuss it properly. Can you gather everyone around at the pool in ten minutes?'

'No problem. Are you okay, Kat?'

I force a smile. 'Yes, it's just been a whirlwind few days.'

He accepts that and heads towards Sammy's apartment. As I reach the top of the steps to my apartment, I almost jump out of my skin.

'Jay?' The sight of him sitting on my step sends a jolt through me.

'We need to talk.'

I shake my head. 'I've got a lot on my mind. Please can we do this another time?'

He stands up and forces eye contact. 'You're not being fair. I've racked my brains trying to think what I've done to hurt you and I honestly don't know. Whatever it is, let me put it right.' His eyes are intent, waiting for me to answer. I look away.

'I miss you, Kat.' His voice cracks on my name, torquing my stomach.

I didn't expect seeing him to be quite so painful. A ball forms in my throat, so I swallow hard and step around him to put my key in the lock.

'I've just called a meeting so we'll have to do this another time. Be by the pool in ten.' I fumble for my key and twist it in the lock. Though he's behind me now and I can't see him, his energy engulfs me as he lingers. I pause. I can't let the past haunt me. Jay should know exactly what he did wrong. We should clear the air.

'I wrote to my mum.'

His words pierce my abdomen, sending a wave of emotion through me. I want to turn around and hug him but I can't forgive him for being with that woman.

'Maybe we can catch up after the final tomorrow?' I say. Not waiting for a reply, I go inside.

When the door closes, I throw myself on the bed. What a day. I've barely processed my break-up with Jay, if you can call it that, and now I feel bad for ignoring him when he told me he'd written to his mum. Then on top of that, there's this Las Vegas offer.

As I stare up at the ceiling. I notice it has a yellow-brown stain on it. How have I not seen it before? I suppose Jay has stayed over so often recently that he's distracted me. When I close my eyes, I can almost sense him next to me. His scent is still on the duvet. I can almost feel the heat from his body and the sensation of the soft hair on his arms tickling me as he wraps them around me. A warm tear trickles down my cheek. I shouldn't have gotten so carried away with him. I know exactly what the guys are like, and I love them to bits but none of them are settling-down types. I got so wrapped up in my own fantasy that I forgot all about my vow to never be such a fool again after Iain treated me the way he did. Maybe I'm a sap, and the only way to protect myself is to stay single. It's worked for the past eight years.

I don't know what to think of this whole Vegas thing either. I hug my pillow tighter. God, everything is such a mess. I've had a handle on everything for years and now it seems I've dropped my basket of 'shit togetherness' and spilt its messy contents everywhere. I need to accept that it's the end of the road for us in the Canaries. I'll be okay. I need the sea air and the freedom of walking down the beach in the cool early-morning light. I need Andrea and all the familiar faces at the hotels we work at. I need this life. I need my life but the guys don't. They need the chance to show the world their talents and make something of themselves.

Even if we won the competition, I'd never be able to re-create an opportunity for the guys like the one Brad is offering. We'd get a trip to Las Vegas and some cash in the bank but nothing long-term.

Chapter 28

As I walk down the steps, I faff around tidying my hair and straightening my shorts. It's not like me – I don't normally give two hoots about how I look – but all of a sudden I feel like the spotlight will be shining on me as their leader. The guys will be overexcited and unable to think logically, so I'll have to be the voice of reason.

'Hi,' I say to Marcus as I arrive. So far, everyone is here but Pauw and Jay. There's a tense silence. They know I won't say anything until the whole group have arrived, but I know they're trying to read my expression. I don't like this new dynamic between us, this me and them. We're like a family. I've always said I felt like a mum but today I'm definitely their manager and it doesn't feel normal.

'Hi, everyone.' Pauw comes jogging over. He looks shattered but I resist the urge to say anything. It's a trial-size version of letting go.

'So, we're just waiting on Jay,' Marcus says.

Still, nobody speaks. Perhaps the tension in the air seems worse to me because I'm nervous about seeing Jay.

Someone buzzes and Sam pulls his phone out of his pocket.

'It's Jay. He can't make it but said go ahead and I'll send him the info.'

Can't make it? I saw him about ten minutes ago. 'Okay, as you suspected, Brad had a deal.'

There are a few 'yeses' and 'nice ones'. I explain the deal, the contracts, what they'd be expected to do and so on, but I don't yet tell them I'm not part of the deal. I want them to make this decision for themselves without worrying about me.

'So the accommodation is paid for?' Ant asks.

'For the first six months, then it will be reviewed.'

'And the two nights off are guaranteed?' Marcus asks whilst simultaneously tapping away on his phone.

'Yes, there will be a different performer on at the club on those nights.'

'Jay has just sent a text. He says, "Vegas baby! I have to double-check a few things so can't come to the meeting but I'm one hundred per cent in".'

My heart sinks for two reasons, none of which I understand since I'm still so disappointed with him. One, Jay won't be here with the moral support I've come to value in these tricky situations, and two, Jay is on board with the idea.

'Okay, let's discuss the pros and cons,' I say with as much heart as I can muster. 'It's a good opportunity to progress.'

'Definitely. This could be huge,' Marcus confirms, ignoring my tone.

'I need to call Phil.' Pauw points to his phone. 'This isn't something I can decide on my own.'

'Of course, go ahead. Sammy?' I ask.

'Riches and bitches, dude.' He laughs.

I shake my head disapprovingly. 'Sammy, if that's the level of respect you have for women, we'll be seeking a new dancer.'

'Sorry, Kat, I got carried away.'

'Hugo?'

'It's not for me, Kat. Being in the Hunks is fun but this is my home and I would never leave.' He says. Ant pats him on the back reassuringly.

'Ant? How about you?' Ant has been harder to read through all of this so I'm interested to see what he thinks.

'I think that we have to try. With gigs drying up here, it might be our only choice, if we want to stay in the business, that is, and at the moment, I just don't want a normal job. I love what we do.'

'Pauw, what are your thoughts?'

Paul draws a breath and shoves his phone in his back pocket. 'It's an amazing opportunity and I'm so excited about it, but Phil says it's too much too soon. I'm sorry, guys. I don't know if we can up and leave like that. We own a property here and have great friends here. We're settled.'

'We understand, Pauw. It's a lot to give up.' I turn to the rest of the group. 'Brad said we'd need four of the original Hunks for the deal to go ahead.'

'Man, if you can't make it we understand. We don't need your decision yet,' Marcus says.

'So, downsides?' I say, clapping my hands together. 'There's moving away, leaving what we know and all the people here we're connected to. It will be the end of an era, of what we've built. Plus, *we* won't have full control of our schedule anymore; we'll be reliant upon when they need us so our days off, show dates and whether we can go on tour will depend on them.'

'It's the price we'll pay for more money and exposure, I guess,' Sammy says.

'That's one way of looking at it. Ant?' I prompt.

'I was going to say Kat won't really be in charge anymore if all that is true.' Ant looks at me. 'You're a great boss, Kat, and I for one appreciate everything you've done for us, but you're great on stage too so ...'

My stomach pangs but I manage a wan smile. The truth is, I've been suffering from imposter syndrome since bookings started to dry up, and the praise doesn't sit comfortably.

'Pauw, if you're not a definite no, we need your input too,' I say.

'Moving to another country so far away and making a new life when the one here is so good is a risk.'

'What about you, Marcus?' I ask. He's the only one who hasn't given any feedback.

He shrugs. 'I'm all for it. I share everyone's concerns and it's a scary prospect, but we're a great team. I think we can really become something amazing. If we don't go, I think we'll regret what we could have been. I want us to go for it.'

He makes a good point, and despite my own selfish need to keep them here, I have to do what's best for the Hunks – it's business and we can't afford to turn down a gig like this. 'Listen, I love you all and if the majority of you want in, I'm in.'

'Okay, great.' Marcus grins. 'Now we need to hear from Jay but he seems keen. Anyone know what he's doing?'

'Probably with the blonde chick I spotted him with before we met Brad.' Sammy laughs in a way that suggests he'd be patting Jay on the back if he was here. I'm sick to my stomach.

'I don't want to vote until Jay is here – it's not right,' Marcus says.

'Jay said he had to look into something before he could commit.' Ant shrugs.

Of course! He won't know whether he can even get into America with a criminal conviction, never mind work and live there. Even though I didn't want anyone to go myself less than an hour ago, the thought that Jay could be the one to scupper the dreams of everyone here makes me burn with rage. I know this is perhaps a tad over the top, but I'm angry with him in general so the starting point was already high; akin to roasting a parboiled potato.

'What about the competition?' I ask, steering the conversation away from Jay.

'I think we should still do it. It's still exposure and practice. What do you guys think?' Marcus says.

Everyone nods in agreement.

'Okay.' I can't believe I'm even saying this. 'Well, once my lawyer has looked over the contracts, I'll set up a meeting with this manager guy, Brad, and take it from there.' As the guys go to disperse, I call them back. I was going to tell them at some point that I'd changed my mind and didn't want to go, but I need to be honest with them.

Ant furrows his brow. 'What is it, Kat?'

'Brad and I chatted about the show moving forward. As you've gathered, he would be in charge of the management side of things: ticket sales, promotion and so on. But, there's a but.' There's some uncomfortable shuffling and the guys fold their arms or shift their weight slightly from one foot to the other. 'You'd have a new emcee too – Jenny Grant.'

Their faces are a sea of blank expressions – or a pond rather; there are only four of them.

'So what would your role be?' Pauw asks.

I glance at my feet. My bright orange toes could do with a repaint. 'I'd stay here.'

There are gasps.

'Wait, you never said you weren't coming with us, Kat. This is a game-changer,' Sammy says.

'No, it isn't,' I say calmly. 'Jenny Grant is famous and everyone loves her. She is the perfect person to make you a global brand.'

'But you're brilliant, Kat; the crowd love you here. Why wouldn't they love you in America?' Marcus says.

I smile. 'They might but it's a risk. There's my Yorkshire accent for a start – it could be a barrier.'

'Nonsense,' Ant mutters.

'None of us are going without you, Kat,' Pauw says, looking to the others to rally support. They all nod in agreement.

'Well, I'm your manager and since we have no gigs booked, I'm giving you your one week's notice. You're all fired.'

Chapter 29

Butterflies are going batshit crazy in my stomach. Technically, we no longer need to win this competition. The lads are off to bigger, brighter things. After a full twenty-four hours of freezing me out, they realised I was just doing what was best for them and thawed. On the whole, they seem to have come around to the idea of going to Las Vegas without me and their excitement levels have peaked around the same dizzy heights as the tip of the antenna on the Burj Khalifa. I'll have the money from the sale of the business to tide me over and do something different, and we don't need exposure anymore. But I suppose I want us to go out on a high. I've always believed we had the best act around and winning would consolidate that notion. It would also give the guys a confidence boost before they head off to America.

It's our last show. After working hard to secure new bookings, I've had to cancel the few future shows I had booked because it will be pretty hard to put on an all-male exotic dance show without any exotic male dancers. We head backstage to a small dressing room that we have to share with the other acts. It's certainly cosy. Because it's the final, the event is ticketed, so the acts don't get to sit in the audience this time. Sitting here for our final show makes everything so real, and the lump of lead in my stomach confirms how sad it makes me.

The other reason for the butterflies could be the venue. We're at the fancy hotel that Jay brought me to for our first (and technically only) date. After our encounter yesterday, I thought about him all night. I found myself forgetting why I called it off in the first place. My head is in a mess – what I need to do is confront him and get some answers; I have to know why he betrayed my trust.

Everyone else seems relaxed. In the minibus on the way here Paul announced that he and Phil *would* be going to Vegas because 'YOLO', and they're going to rent out their Tenerife property in the meantime so it's here for when they come back. This, of course, generated a lot of excitement from the guys. I sat in the front next to the driver so I didn't have to talk about Las Vegas or pretend to be happy that the one Hunk in addition to Hugo that I thought I'd get to keep would also be leaving.

As the first act is called up to the stage, I pull myself together – now isn't the time to have a wobble.

'Guys, it's our last huddle,' I say, fighting back a tremor in my voice.

'Ahh, Kat. I'm going to miss you so much.' Sammy pulls me into a headlock, I assume he thinks he's cuddling me.

'Anyway ...' I ignore that. 'I just want to say that it doesn't matter what happens tonight. The Heavenly Hunks have a bright future regardless. That much is set in stone, so let the people judge us tonight, but whatever they say will not shape your success. What we built together here in the Canaries has been fantastic and I'm proud of you all.' I think I've swallowed a golf ball. I have so much more I want to say but I'm scared I'll burst into tears if I try to get any more out.

'Thanks, Kat,' Marcus says. 'It's always been an honour to work with you, and we can't thank you enough for the incredible ride we've had, can we, lads?' There are enthusiastic noises of agreement.

'Okay, let's give it all we've got!'

We linger at the side of the stage awaiting our introduction. My breathing becomes quick and shallow. I can't believe I'm going to do this for the very last time. I give the sound and lighting guy the nod and he starts the music and the dry ice machine. The familiar beat kicks in and I take my final step on stage.

'Good evening, Tenerife! I am here to bring you the men of your dreams – to fulfil your fantasies and give *you* a night to remember. Ladies, I know what you want.' I throw my hands in the air to pump to the beat one last time. I'm in character now; I can get through this.

As the dancers fill the stage and I slink back into the wings, it dawns on me that this could be the last time I watch them perform too. It really is the end of an era.

'You look like you could use a friend.' I turn to see Andrea in a flowing white maxi dress, her blonde curls tumbling down her yoga-toned arms.

I hug her tightly. 'You're a sight for sore eyes.'

'What's the matter?'

'God, it's such a long story.'

She smiles. 'I've got nowhere to be.'

Since this is the short version of the show, I don't have to go back on stage. There's still ten minutes of the act left, so I gesture to an open fire escape. 'Come on.'

We find ourselves in a staff-only section of the hotel. Big metal trolleys filled with fresh linen surround us, and a chambermaid leans against the wall smoking a cigarette. She doesn't seem to care that we're here so I tell Andrea all about me and Jay, what I saw, and how the Heavenly Hunks will be going to Las Vegas without me.

'Wow, that's a lot to take in,' she says.

'I know.'

'A big change for you, hey?'

I nod.

'Let's start with the Hunks moving away. Are you sure you're happy to just let that happen?'

'What choice do I have? I can barely even offer them an income, never mind their name in lights. Some of them are so young – Sammy is only twenty-two. This could be life-changing for them. As their manager, it's my job to seek bigger and better things for them.'

'What does Jay make of you not going?'

'I've been avoiding him,' I say, hanging my head in shame.

'What?'

'Don't judge me, Andri; I'm processing a lot at the moment.'

'Okay, but you should at least set him straight. You can't let him get away with what he did to you.'

'I will, just not tonight. Tonight is about the competition.'

'How do you feel about not being a part of the Las Vegas Hunks? Are you angry?'

I shake my head. 'No, Andri, it's business. Brad just wants to sell tickets and that's the way he knows how. I had nothing left to offer them.'

'What will you do?'

'I have a gorgeous, kind friend who owns a bar. Maybe she'll have some work for me?' I say hopefully.

'Hmm, of course she will. But that isn't who you are.'

'It could be. I'll figure something out. Anyway, the money from the sale of the business will tide me over.'

'I can't believe you're selling your eye candy!' She means it as a joke but it horrifies me.

'No, I'm selling the business. The brand and goodwill.' As I say it, I realise how weak it sounds. What brand? What goodwill? Brad is buying the act. 'Bloody hell, I'm selling the boys, aren't I?'

Andrea shrugs. 'Hey, I was joking. I didn't get a chance because you cut in but I was going to say I'll buy them, again as a joke.'

'You don't need to backtrack.' How bad will I look? It looks like I'm selling them off and running away with the money.

'Hey, it's what they want, remember? It's just the way of the world – business.'

'I can't take that money. It's as much theirs as it is mine.'

'Of course you can. Business sales happen all the time.'

I shake my head. 'No, I'm not selling a shop full of stock, I'm selling humans. It's, it's … like trafficking.'

'You're being ridiculous. It's like selling a football club. It happens all the time.' She flicks her hair off her shoulder.

'I can't take that money. It doesn't feel right.'

'You're well within your rights to keep that money. After all, it's your business and they'll be earning a good whack in Vegas.'

'It doesn't feel right. The lads only agreed to this deal because they thought we could all go. I had to fire them to make them go. It will look like I was after the money all along.'

'Okay. Share it out if you're happy with that.' She sighs, her role as devil's advocate coming to an end. I'm braced for her final challenge.

'Right, now Jay.'

I check my watch. We only have a few minutes left so I look her dead in the eye, ready for whatever she's got, safe in the knowledge that it can't last long.

'Are you sure you saw what you *think* you saw?'

'One hundred per cent. There was no mistaking it. I sell sexual chemistry for a living – I know it when I see it.'

'Fair point. What would happen between the two of you if you hadn't seen what you did? Would you have gone to Las Vegas then?'

'Of course not. I'm still not a part of the Heavenly Hunks Mark II, am I?'

'And how about Jay? Would he still go, if you were still dating?'

'Of course. We weren't really dating. It wasn't anything more than a fling, and this is his career.'

'If it's just a little fling, why were you bothered about some woman all over him? You were hurt when it was Alonso who had another woman dangling from him but you didn't seem this upset.'

'I …' Everything else comes out as air. 'I'll get over it.'

Finally, Andrea's shoulders relax as she backs off. She knows she's got me.

'I really like Jay, that's all. But being with him isn't right.'

'I think you should talk to him. Maybe it was nothing and you can clear the air.'

'It won't change anything,' I say.

'He doesn't know what he's done wrong. You can't part on such bad terms.'

'What does it matter? It's not like I'll ever see him again, is it?'

She cocks her head to the side and sighs. 'We'd better go inside. It's probably announcement time.'

We head back in. The final act is on stage so we go backstage to find the Hunks. Marcus is rubbing the oil off his body with a towel.

'Ooh la la.' Andrea winks at him.

'Guys, can you gather around for a sec?' I say, loud enough to get everyone's attention.

The guys are in various states of undress and trickle over as and when they become decent. 'I just wanted to say I thought you were fantastic tonight. It doesn't matter what the result is. You're all so in sync with one another that I know you're going to smash Vegas.'

I accidentally catch Jay's eye, but he quickly looks down at the floor.

'Anyway, they're going to announce the winner of the competition any minute now, so get out there!' I gesture towards the crowd. I wait for them to leave but Jay hangs back.

'Can we talk yet?'

'After the results,' I say softly, forcing a smile. My chest is tight.

Being so close to him again is too much. In this moment, it would be all too easy to forget what I saw and fall under his spell. I want to fall into his arms, for him to stroke my hair and tell me everything will be okay. I want the citrusy smell of his aftershave to envelop me, but, most of all, I want to feel his warm comfort again. He nods and heads towards the stage wings. Once he's gone, I exhale, but my throat is constricted. I thought I could be professional and treat Jay like the rest of the dancers but I can't.

'Andrea, I need to get out of here. Tell the guys I wasn't feeling well.'

Her mouth opens, but before she has a chance to reply, I dart back out through the fire door, ordering a taxi as soon as I'm in the inky darkness of the night.

Chapter 30

'Kat, wait!'

I'm not running exactly, but I am walking as fast as is possible before it would be classed as running. I can't even tell who shouted at me over the noise of the air whooshing past my ears and the cars on the nearby road. I don't care. I've said all that I can manage for tonight.

'Can you *please* stop walking?' I almost crash into the body belonging to the voice. When my eyes meet those familiar brown ones, thunder roars through my chest and I freeze.

'Jay?' He must have come out through the main entrance and beat me to the hotel drop-off.

'Thank God for that! What's gotten into you?' His eyes are wide and riddled with despair.

'Did we win? I ... I don't feel well.'

'Bollocks. You've been avoiding me ever since the last performance and I don't know why. Now you've fired us all and you're not coming to the States? But forget that for now – first, I think you owe me an explanation. And I don't know if we won. I came straight out after you.'

I look around. There's nobody about but I still don't want the conversation here. 'All right, there's a little bar a mile or so away. Let's go for a drink. I've already booked a taxi.'

His facial muscles visibly relax. I think he expected more resistance from me. We wait in silence for the taxi to arrive. When it does, he holds the door open and I slip inside. 'Did you hear anything back from your mum yet?' I ask, remembering how cold I was yesterday.

'No. I only posted the letter yesterday morning though, so it's too soon. I gave her my email address. I just thought with the move and everything ...' He tapers off.

'I'm sure she'll want to speak to you,' I say. He doesn't reply and we sit in silence for the rest of the short journey. When we get to the bar I choose a table outside whilst Jay grabs a waiter and orders two beers. It's too dark to see the sea, but I hear the gorgeous sound of waves tumbling onto the shore in the jet-black abyss as I wait. I'm too nauseous to enjoy it.

'Okay, what's going on?' Jay's words are out before his bum even touches his seat.

My stomach hardens with dread. Having this conversation seems ridiculous. Things with Jay were so new that I don't know if I even have a right to be upset about him and that woman. We'd not had 'the talk' about relationships or said I love you; that's why I didn't want to say anything in the first place. I suppose if I do fill him in, it should make him think twice about hurting someone else in the future. In Las Vegas. I still can't get used to the fact they're all going to America.

'Right, I have been pushing you away and I do owe you an explanation,' I say cautiously.

Jay settles back into his seat. He looks like a weight has been lifted but I haven't even started yet.

'I've told you I didn't have a great marriage.'

He nods but presses his eyebrows together. 'I thought you were over that?'

'Well, Iain was jealous and possessive, but he was quite controlling and manipulative too.' I stare across the road at the closed shutter of a sunglasses shop. 'He twisted things and lied. He made me question and doubt myself to the point I thought I might be ill.' I let out an exasperated sigh. 'It's hard to talk about because it doesn't seem possible.'

'You can talk to me, Kat. I'm not judging you – I know this stuff happens.'

'Over time, he wore away little chinks in my armour. He'd deny conversations we'd had, to the point where I doubted my own memory. It started off as little things, like him saying he'd pick up a takeaway on his way home from work then swearing blind no such conversation took place. I wondered if he was losing the plot initially, but then he'd have this whole backstory, and parts of that would be true but he'd throw in extra bits that I didn't remember. It's hard to explain. I felt like I had these black spots in my mind. I was embarrassed.'

'Oh, Kat. How about your friends and family? Did they try to help?'

'I lost touch with my friends and family because he made me believe they were just using me. I trusted him so much that I thought I was losing my mind, and he made me believe that he was the only person in the world who was willing to help me … to love me …'

'I'm sorry he did that to you,' Jay says, though I'm not telling him because I want sympathy. I'm telling him because I need him to understand me. To understand just how much his betrayal hurt.

'It's fine, I really am over it, but the experience has shaped who I am now.'

'Did you talk to anyone about what you went through?'

'No. I suppose I was too ashamed. I mean, how can you question your own sanity over what one person says and does? I never *forgot* or *misinterpreted* conversations with anyone else, yet I fully accepted that's what happened with Iain. It could be little things, like he'd say he'd meet me at Pizza Express at seven and turn up at eight and argue with me about how I always make mistakes like that. How could that ever make sense to someone who hasn't been through it?'

Jay presses his lips together but doesn't answer. I don't expect him to.

'When I came out here, I knew I needed to stay in control of myself. I'd fallen into Iain's trap so easily I was terrified it might happen again with someone new, so I decided the safest thing to do was to not let anybody in. When I set up the Heavenly Hunks, I micromanaged the entire thing – the guys, their every move in rehearsals, our every show, every aspect of the tours – because I couldn't risk anyone taking over *my* life again.'

'And you built a successful act. Plus, to be fair, the lads need that level of management.'

I smile. 'Anyway, pity party over.' I slap my hands on my thighs. 'It's all done with now but I want you to understand me. I want you to know how hard it's been to let someone in after being so independent for so long.'

Jay puts his hand out to take mine but I pick up the drinks menu.

'Never feel ashamed of what he did to you.' He locks his eyes on mine and, despite the warm air, a shiver runs down my spine. 'And don't be afraid of it happening again. I was going to say the Heavenly Hunks have your back, and we do, but you don't need us. You're strong, Kat, and it's time to go after what *you* want.'

'What I want doesn't exist,' I say.

He looks hurt. 'What do you mean?'

'After the last gig, I *saw* you.' I give him a look, hoping he'll make the connection himself and I won't have to spell it out.

'You *saw* me?' His brow furrows.

'I *saw* you *outside*.'

Nothing.

'With that blonde woman? At the semi-final.' God, I can't believe he's making me say it.

'What wo—'

I practically see the penny drop.

'Ohh.' He nods. I nod too, with pursed lips to show we're on the same wavelength. Hopefully, now that's registered, we can draw a line under this.

Then he laughs. I wasn't expecting that. Not from Jay. Not after everything I've just told him. The uneasy feeling of history repeating itself engulfs me.

'Really? It's funny to you, is it? After I've just poured my heart out?' I fold my arms defensively but I can feel tears pricking my eyes, defying me, showing him I care too much.

'Let me explain.' His soft words make me wince.

You're losing the plot, Kat.

'I don't need an explanation. I know we were nothing official and we hadn't specifically outlined what the rules were—'

'Rules? Kat, just be quiet and listen for a minute, please.'

Taken aback, I do as he says.

'All right. That woman was Brad's business partner, Jenny.'

I let the words sink in. Jenny? As in Jenny Grant? 'But—'

He holds his hand up. He's not done. 'She was just fooling around and telling me how much she loved our show – she was joking about how we should have a "stroking policy", like a petting zoo. It was a moment of silliness that meant nothing to either of us. That's when Brad was asking about meeting up with you.'

'I'm sorry, but it looked a lot more than a business chat from where I was standing. Was Brad even there?' How did I not recognise her? I suppose I didn't see her face.

'Yes! He'd just walked a few feet away to have a smoke, and if you'd have come outside you'd have seen that. Okay, I get that she was a little full-on, but she was messing about and I stepped away a few seconds later. I had no idea it was because they wanted to sign the Hunks but I knew Brad was a judge and maybe let the joke go a little further because I didn't want to make things awkward right before the final. It was harmless. Brad was laughing his head off.'

'But Sammy saw you too,' I say, unconvinced. I've been here before, and this time around I'm not falling for any lies.

'Sammy wasn't there! If he saw me with her, he hasn't mentioned it to me. They grabbed me straight after the show. I chatted with them for an hour or so whilst the guys were chatting up audience members, then Jenny left to call her husband and I introduced Brad to the guys. None of them were even there. Ask them.'

'But Sammy said she dragged you outside by the waistband.' I'm confused, but if Jay is lying, he's good at it.

'She did drag me out of the bar but I can't remember what by. She was excited to introduce me to Brad. She's like that – hands on and excitable.'

'Surely Sammy said *something* to you about the "hot blonde woman". He told everyone else.' I don't know what to think. I've been here before and fallen for stories just like this one. My whole body is in a vice. 'I can't do this.' I go to stand.

'Please, Kat, don't go. I swear Sammy didn't mention it to me. It won't be a big deal to him and the excitement of Las Vegas took over just after, so that's all we've talked about.'

'Oh,' is all I can manage. Am I overreacting? If so, I feel like a prize twat and this is exactly how I never wanted to feel again. If I'm right, I'm a fool for letting Jay in, and if I'm wrong, I'm a fool for getting worked up. I know Jay isn't Iain but I'm still me. I also know what I saw. Is Jay's excuse plausible? If it was Jenny Grant, I highly doubt she'd be carrying on with someone in public.

'I know you care.' He sips his beer and then his expression changes. I'm expecting him to call me crazy or something, but he doesn't.

'We can talk to Jenny if you like? She was staying for drinks after the show.'

I shake my head. 'No, I need to learn to trust.'

He gives me a small, reassuring smile. 'Were you really not part of the Vegas deal or did you tell Brad you didn't want to go because of all this?'

'I really wasn't a part of it,' I say, sipping my drink. 'But I'm okay with that,' I add.

'You wouldn't leave the Hunks.'

'It's the right thing to do. Besides, whilst living under Iain's manipulation for all those years was wrong, it's also wrong to use my own control over the Hunks as a coping mechanism. The right thing to do is let you all fly and for me to learn how to live with myself. I've focused on the Hunks for eight years and in that whole time, I've not worked on myself. I've been so obsessed with not letting anyone control me again that I've become the controlling figure in my own life.'

'Kat, hang on. You're focused and driven but you're being really hard on yourself.'

I bite down on my lip. 'Jay, in order to truly lay my past to rest, I have to let go.'

'Kat, I get why you're letting the guys go to live their dream but I don't get why you're letting me go.'

I run my fingers through the condensation on my glass. 'Because of the way I behaved, the fact I couldn't trust you or my own instincts tells me that I have to heal, Jay, and you need a fresh start. You deserve someone who can love and trust you and I just don't think I can be that person.'

'What if I think you can? What if I wanted to stay for you?' He takes my hand and pulls me towards him, kissing my fingers. I start to enjoy the feeling of him but it's dangerous territory. I yank it back.

'I'm not prepared to feel that way again.'

'You mean jealous.'

He's being polite but I can't be afraid of the word anymore. 'Crazy.'

'Why would you ever need to? It was a stupid one-time thing.'

'Jay,' I snap. 'I don't like who I become when I'm in a relationship. I don't want to be wondering where you are or who you're with all the time.'

'I thought you were the one person who could see past the bad in me.' He clenches his jaw. I watch the tendons tighten beneath his skin.

'Jay.' I soften my tone. How did my insecurities become offensive to him? This just proves we're a bad idea. 'You know this isn't about you. It's about me and my baggage. You've done nothing wrong. I just can't be with anyone.'

'You know, that ex of yours really did a number on you. If you carry on refusing to trust people, he's going to continue to ruin your life. I'll go to Las Vegas if that's what you want, but just know this.' He leans forward to look me dead in the eye. 'I would stay in Tenerife to be with you. I *want* to stay with you, but I want to hear that you want that too. All you need to do is say the words.' He stands up, looking me in the eye for a moment longer than I'm comfortable with. I remain silent and his eyes glisten with moisture. With that, he walks off, leaving his words hanging in the air.

Chapter 31

When I leave my apartment the next morning, I'm surprised to see Ant, Marcus and Sammy laughing by the pool. I assumed they'd be having a lie-in after the inevitable after-party last night.

'How are you feeling, Kat?' Marcus shouts when he spots me. I head over.

'Better, thanks. How did it go? I can't believe I missed the results.'

'Second place.' He says with a shrug. 'That La Leona bird won.'

'That's great. I'm pleased with second.' I didn't expect to win. The further we got into the competition, the better the acts were, so I'm proud we came so far. La Leona, the opera singer, was pretty amazing.

'Yeah, we went a bit hard on the celebrations. It was light when we got back so we just stayed out here.'

I smile but then pain rips through me. I'm going to miss these lads so much. Just stepping outside my apartment and not seeing them here is going to be too much. I turn towards the pool and pretend to ponder a dip so they don't see my eyes start to well.

'Kat, can we talk?' Marcus drapes his arm across my shoulders, so I quickly dab the corners of my eyes and nod.

He leads me into the garden area. 'Kat, has something gone on between you and Jay?'

His words jolt me. I instinctively go to deny it, but what good is lying now? 'Nothing serious,' I say.

'I knew it! I could sense the tension but everyone else thought I was nuts. Only Pauw agreed with me. Anyway, is he the reason you're not coming to Vegas? If he is, we'll all vote to get rid of him. He's still the new kid in the Hunks and our loyalty is to you.'

My stomach is an uneasy churn of love for Marcus's sweet dedication and sadness for Jay, who loves the guys like brothers. 'Please, that's not necessary. Jay belongs in the show as much as anyone – he's not the reason. What I told you was the honest truth; Brad's offer didn't include me and I want you guys to be a huge success.'

Marcus looks down at me, his big dark eyes checking for any signs of dishonesty. When he's satisfied, he nods. 'Okay. It's not going to be the same without you, you know.'

'It might be better,' I say, forcing myself to sound upbeat. 'And listen, we'll stay in touch. I'll be here if you need advice or anything and I'll be following your shows online. It will work out, I promise.'

'And you could visit?' He grins.

'We'll see. I'm about to beg Andrea for work and I'm not sure she'll pay well enough to cover long-haul flights.'

'Probably not,' he says. 'I can't believe we go in a week or so. It's the end of an era.'

'It sure is.'

'Listen, I need to go and have a nap because I'm going shopping later for some Vegas bits. But we'll catch up tonight if you're free? Maybe we could get the guys together and go for dinner?'

'Sounds good.'

I hug Marcus goodbye and head to Andrea's bar. She's wiping down tables and looks up when she hears me walk in.

'Good morning,' she says. 'Such a shame about the competition last night.'

I shrug. 'It's all a bit meaningless now. I mean, I'm sure the ten grand would have come in handy, but what the heck.'

'Did Jay catch up with you?'

My body tenses. 'Yes.'

'Okay, I can tell you don't want to talk about that. Just tell me one thing – has anything changed since last night?'

'No.'

'Okay. Then I'm guessing you're here about work?'

'Yes, please. I'll do anything you can offer me.'

'I could use an extra bartender in the evening, say eight till twelve, and someone to help with the breakfast shift from nine until noon if either of those suit? The tips are good in the morning.'

'I'll take both,' I reply without thinking. It will be good to stay busy and there will be time for the beach or a nap during the day. Perfect.

'Do you want to start after the Hunks leave?'

I ponder this. On the one hand, it would be great to have some time together before they go, but on the other, the distraction will be good. 'I can start now.'

She raises an eyebrow and throws me a tea towel. 'Okay, I'll show you the ropes.'

After my first shift, I go to the beach and walk along the deserted September shoreline, letting the icy water tickle my feet as they sink into the cold, wet sand. Marcus's words ring in my mind: 'It's the end of an era'. It really is, and the profound sadness that thought brings twists my insides so tightly it almost cripples me. I sit on the drier sand and wrap my arms around my goose-pimpled legs. I want to cry but I can't seem to get it out; I think there's too much despair wrapped in the sadness. I'm at a loss and all I can do is carry on through the next steps of my life.

When I get back to the apartment complex, the pool is quiet. I assume everyone is napping or the shopping spree is in full swing. I walk quickly towards the staircase, keeping my head low to avoid seeing anyone. As I round the corner, I smash into a solid frame.

'Sorry, I …' I pause. Jay's brown eyes send a frisson of electricity through me. No matter how successful I am at pushing him out of my mind, I can't control the visceral reaction I get when I see him.

'Don't mind me,' he says but there's a casual urgency in his tone, which is odd.

'I was just heading for a lie-down.' It's not entirely true but I might need one now.

'I was just trying to gather the guys. I've got some news for them but you need to hear this too.' He rakes his hands through his hair. 'Brad has booked us flights to London to sort out our visas. I ran into him at the hotel when I went to pick up our gear. He tried to call you.'

'I had my phone off at work and forgot to turn it back on.'

'We're leaving in three days and there won't be time to come back here before we fly to Las Vegas.'

'Three days!' No, that's too soon. My throat constricts.

'We have to have interviews at the US embassy to get our P-visas. I still don't know if I'll get one yet because of my past. I never expected I'd be attempting to move to the States. It all feels quite surreal.'

I don't reply.

He looks at me imploringly, his warm eyes searching my face for something … a reason to stay?

'Good luck,' I mumble and practically run up the steps to my apartment.

***

There's a knock at my door as I'm making coffee. 'Who is it?' I shout.

214

'Paul.'

I breathe a sigh of relief and open the door.

He looks me over. 'God, you look like crap.'

I can feel that my face is puffy from crying. 'Late night,' I say unconvincingly.

'I thought you were ill.'

'That too.'

'Kat, it's not too late to come with us if you've changed your mind.'

'No, I haven't. It's time we went our separate ways. It's just our time, Paul.' The words almost choke me. 'I am going to miss you all though.'

'We'll miss you too.' He wipes his glossy eyes with the back of his hand. 'Anyway, Marcus mentioned going out for dinner and I just came to let you know he's booked that Chinese restaurant down on the promenade for seven.'

I check the clock on my phone; I have an hour. 'Great, shall we meet downstairs at quarter to?'

'Perfect – see you then.'

I close the door behind him and slump against it. I just need to get through the next two days. Once they've gone I'm sure I'll find it easier to cope.

As I get ready, a consuming feeling of loneliness creeps over me. It's a darkness that descends from nowhere, constricting me. It slides down my throat, filling my stomach and chest with unease. I haven't felt like this since I was with Iain and I've a feeling it's going to stay with me for a while. I have to take a minute to convince myself I'll be okay.

When I'm ready, I drag myself downstairs. I'm five minutes late so everyone is there waiting.

'About time,' Ant teases as I join them.

'You look stunning, Kat.' Paul kisses me on the cheek. I catch Jay's eye and he quickly looks away. 'Shall we make a move?'

We set off walking en masse towards the restaurant. Jay and

Marcus walk ahead, and I walk with Paul at the back while the rest prat about in the middle, their excitement for Las Vegas bouncing off them.

We take our seats around the table, order food and drinks quickly, and then start chatting. The buzz of excitement coming from them helps me push aside the sadness I feel at them all leaving soon.

'What's the first thing you're going to do in Vegas?' Marcus asks the table.

'Bellagio fountains,' Paul says.

'Shopping at the Venetian,' Phil adds. 'Since I'll be a gentleman of leisure.'

'I really want to go to a Hooters,' Sammy says.

'I want to gamble on Fremont Street,' Ant says.

'Sleep,' Jay says, to a table of gasps. 'What? It's a long way, we'll be jet-lagged.'

I laugh with everyone else but Jay purposely avoids making eye contact.

'What about you, Marcus?' Paul asks.

'I want to see the lions at the MGM Grand.'

'Hang on a minute, Sam, you're in Las Vegas and you want to go to a Hooters?' Ant asks.

Sammy shrugs. 'I always see them in movies and they look fun.'

'It's like sneaking a McDonald's burger into the Ivy,' says Marcus. 'There's a bloody Spearmint Rhino there.'

'I don't want a strip club, I just thought ... you know what, never mind. The first thing I want to do in Vegas is ditch you lot.'

'Ahh, Sammy, who'll buy your beer for you if you ditch us? The drinking age is twenty-one you know,' Marcus says.

'I'm almost twenty-three, you dick, and you know it. You're just jealous because you're past it, old-timer.'

'If he's an old-timer, what am I?' I ask, though I'm enjoying the banter.

'You're our queen, Kat,' Sammy says with a wink that sends a warm glow through my body.

'Bloody old-timer.' Marcus shakes his head. 'I can still rock a red G-string better than you.'

'The red G-string is all yours, mate. Anyway, it's Jay who's going to be pole-dancing around a Zimmer come opening night,' Sammy continues. We all look at Jay, who glances up from his beer glass, startled like he's just woken up.

'Sorry, guys. I was miles away.'

'Hearing's going already.' Marcus laughs and the banter continues. Jay's eyes sink back down to his beer glass and my chest sinks with them. I hate to see him look so broken.

The food arrives and changes the focus, with everyone diving in to secure their dumplings and pieces of shredded duck.

'We've all been talking about Vegas and getting excited, but we've got some other things to say,' Marcus says as he drizzles plum sauce onto a pancake. 'Kat, we have so much to thank you for. You've been the rock that we all needed at some point. You've been our surrogate mother, our leader and our best friend.' He chokes a little and my chest aches.

'It's true.' Paul picks up where Marcus left off. 'We all needed you more than you'll ever know. The Heavenly Hunks *is* you, and the fact we're all going to continue the journey without you is unimaginable.'

'But we understand why you're staying,' Ant says.

'And we respect your choice,' says Sammy.

'Thank you for everything, Kat,' Hugo says in his accented English.

Emotion swells in my chest and erupts in a sob before I can stop it. 'Guys, obviously the Heavenly Hunks is a business and Brad offered me a lump sum to buy the business. Taking it didn't feel right—'

'You've earned that fair and square,' Marcus chips in. I hold my hand up to quieten him.

'After thinking about it, I agree. I have earnt that money fair and square, but so have you, so I've split it equally between us.' Paul opens his mouth to protest. 'It's not a huge amount each but it's enough to treat yourselves and have a bit to get you going in Las Vegas. It's already in your bank accounts.'

'Kat, you shouldn't have done that, love,' Marcus says.

'I wanted to, and besides, I have a job working for Andrea so I won't be short. I've loved every minute of working with you all. I love you all so much,' I manage as tears roll down my face. Paul and Ant stand up and give me a joint hug, which gives me a chance to compose myself.

'Thanks you two,' I say, patting them both. Jay still hasn't spoken. To be fair, his feelings about leaving differ to the others and he's said his piece already.

'Right.' I clap my hands together. 'Enough of that. Let's eat!' Everyone tucks in, but I still have a huge ball of emotion stuck in my throat. I nibble a prawn cracker but the pieces just cling to my oesophagus.

The conversation soon turns back to Las Vegas and some horrific-sounding ride at the top of the Stratosphere Tower that they're all mouthing off about going on. All except Sammy, who point-blank refuses and says they're all nuts. As I take in the scene of my Tenerife family, I know I'll cherish this moment forever.

Chapter 32

The day after the meal, everyone was busy clearing out their apartments and packing so I left them to it and went to work. Since today is their last day, we've decided to have a few drinks around the pool at the complex. The guys are in the mood to party and I just want to spend time with them all.

'I can't believe it's our last night,' Ant says, popping the lid off a bottle of Estrella. 'Doesn't feel real, does it?'

Everyone agrees with varying sprinkles of melancholic inflection.

'Brad won't be as good a manager as our Kat,' Paul says, and I can't help the smile that spreads across my face.

'I think we should share our favourite Kat memories,' Paul says.

I protest loudly, covering my face with my hands.

'Okay, I've got one,' Sammy says, ignoring me. 'It was when I'd only been with the Hunks for a few weeks. I wasn't used to all the, er, female attention and this one girl wouldn't leave me alone. She was pretty fit, and anyway, one thing led to another and she ended up back at the apartment. The next morning, she was still there, so I made her coffee and she followed me to the pool for a bit. I dropped hints about being busy but she still wouldn't leave. It got quite late so, eventually, I politely told her I had to get to rehearsals and she said she'd come. I panicked, thinking I'd never get rid of her, but then Kat came in and gave her a dose of no-nonsense honesty.'

'Ha,' I laugh. 'I remember her. I told her that until you guys stopped acting like players you would never settle down and she deserved better.'

'Then you gave me a right rollocking about treating women with respect,' Sammy says.

'Yes, and not for the first or last time.' I give him a pointed look.

Marcus sips his beer. 'I've had "the talk" too.'

'I think we all have,' Ant says, laughing.

'Anyway,' Marcus says, 'I think my favourite Kat memory is when I got that awful sickness bug and you twats buggered off and left me—'

'Not true! I got you a can of Red Bull,' Ant interrupts.

'Er, yeah, and an adult nappy! Plus it was half a can of Red Bull, and completely flat. Very helpful, mate. Angel Kat went to the pharmacy for some Imodium and then sat with me for a whole forty-eight hours until I was feeling better. I'll never forget that, Kat.' He stretches over and pats my leg.

'Mine was after I'd had that back, crack and sack wax when it was all the rage,' Paul says.

'When was it ever all the rage?' Marcus interrupts.

Paul gives him a wry look and carries on. 'I thought it would be good for the show but I came out in the most horrendous spotty rash. Kat had to put aloe vera gel on me for the next couple of days when Phil wouldn't go near it. Above and beyond, that, Kat love.'

Gentle laughter follows.

'Sorry, Kat, but my favourite memory of you was when we did karaoke that time and you did a full rendition of Sir Mix-A-Lot's "Baby Got Back",' Ant says.

'Oh yeah, I was pretty good at that.' I chuckle at the memory. I did it for Andrea when she was at the height of her *Friends* obsession.

Eyes naturally fall to Jay who, as of yet, hasn't spoken. He must sense the attention as he looks up from the label that he's peeling off his beer bottle. 'My favourite Kat memory ...' He drums his fingers lightly on the bottle, like he's working up to something. 'All of them,' he says.

I feel like I've been punched in the gut. The fact he can say that after everything I've put him through just shows he deserves better than me.

'The first time I met Kat, she thought I was going to mug her and almost decked me.' He lets out a dry laugh. 'I didn't know what to think really. On one hand, I liked her feistiness, but I also feared for my life.' A few of the guys laugh knowingly. 'If I had to pick a favourite memory, it would be the first time I saw her smile. I'd just finished my audition and felt nervous as hell. I was sure she was going to turn me down, then she smiled and her eyes lit up and melted all my fear away. It was the first time I realised she was beautiful inside and out. When she kissed me and I thought we could be together, I felt like the luckiest guy in the Canaries.'

My heart feels like someone has prised open my ribcage and grabbed it. I'm crushed and I hate Iain for screwing me up so much. He's winning and I'm letting him. I hate myself for giving in, but Jay deserves something simpler. I know he doesn't see it now, but when he's been away for a while he'll look back and thank me.

Slowly, everyone turns to look at me. Awaiting my reaction.

'Er ... okay. Brilliant memories, guys,' Paul says, trying to mask the awkwardness. 'I think it's safe to say we'll *all* miss Kat incredibly, but our minibus is coming bright and early tomorrow so I think we should all go to bed now and sleep off the beer.'

Everyone except Jay rises.

'Night, Kat.' Marcus kisses my cheek. 'Are you seeing us off in the morning?'

'Of course,' I say, rubbing my hand over his upper arm.

'I will see you around sometime. I've got a job at the new bar at the marina.' Hugo says.

'Definitely. You know where I'll be.' I embrace him warmly.

I say goodnight to the others and they vanish quicker than Magica's iguana.

'What about you, Jay? Don't you want some sleep before your flight tomorrow?' I'm seething with him but 'Manager Kat' can't just leave him out here in his current state.

'I'm fine. Just leave me alone.' He makes a lame shooing gesture with his hand.

Rage surges through me. I can't believe what he just did. 'You had no right to say what you did in front of everyone.'

'I was sharing my favourite Kat memory, just like everyone else was.'

'You've had too much to drink.' I shake my head. I know he's hurt but there's no point going over old ground. 'Let's get you up to bed.'

'I've had two beers.' He glances at the bottles beside him. 'Maybe four.'

'Jay?' I add weight to the word, hoping it's enough to make him stop and remember why I'm doing this.

He looks down at the beer bottle and picks at the label. The muscles in his jaw tense. He looks as though he's about to speak but doesn't.

'Come on,' I say, with more authority this time.

'For once, can you just let *me* make a decision? I want to sit out here for a while.'

I hold up my hand. 'Fine.' Then I turn to walk away.

'You're like Fort Knox,' he calls after me, 'locking your precious feelings in and shutting me out because of things that happened to you in the past, and it breaks my heart that you can't let go and allow yourself to be happy.'

Why doesn't he get it? 'It's not about *allowing* myself to be happy, Jay. It's about *keeping* myself happy, and there's a difference.' I've given men a try. Iain was a manipulating control freak, Alonso was a womaniser; I see what the Hunks get up to with their fans and after just a few weeks with Jay, I suspect him of cheating. Relationships just don't work for me.

He rolls his eyes. 'It's like talking to a brick wall.'

'You'll get over it.' I bite my lip. I didn't mean to sound quite so harsh and patronising but I can't backtrack now.

'Don't you get it? It's not about how *I* feel. It's about you. I want *you* to be happy.'

'Then just let me be,' I whisper.

He looks past me to the glowing blue water of the pool. His facial muscles have relaxed and the light gives him a hollowed-out, gaunt appearance, almost like the soul has gone from inside him and left him deflated.

My instinct is to go to him and stroke his hair, but instead I turn and walk towards my apartment. When I'm inside with the door shut, my mind turns to all the things he said earlier. I don't think I've ever been called beautiful before. As I replay what he said over and over in my head, my stomach twists tighter with each memory. The feelings I experienced each time we were together pelt me like stones: the first time I laid eyes on him, our first date, our first kiss. Each pleasurable memory turning to pain.

This will be easier after tomorrow.

Chapter 33

'I can't believe this is it,' I say. Paul, Marcus, Jay, Ant and Sammy are lined up by the minibus with their cases and backpacks slung over their shoulders. Five pairs of watery eyes; five sets of slumped shoulders and sombre faces before me.

'I can't believe you're not coming,' Paul says. 'I'm not even bothered about leaving Phil because I know he's joining me in a few weeks, but you, Kat, I don't know how I'll get by without you,' he chokes out. My own throat is so full of emotion that I can't speak; instead, I wrap him in the tightest hug possible.

'Bye, *Pauw*,' I whisper once I'm able.

'Gonna miss you, Kat,' Sammy says.

'You too, love. Stay out of trouble!' I squeeze him tightly and move along to Ant.

'Keep them all in line for me, won't you?'

He smiles and nods with watery eyes.

'I'm going to miss you,' Marcus says as I move towards him.

'I know.' I nod. 'Me too.' God, this hurts. Marcus, seeing the pain on my face, wraps me tightly in his arms.

'Jay,' I say, pulling away from Marcus.

He doesn't speak. Instead, he steps forwards and wraps his strong, thick arms around my waist, holding me so close our lips brush against one another's. His eyes are intent on mine, and everyone else evaporates around us. He lifts his hand to gently brush away the hair that's blown across my face, and a tingle spreads from my neck to the base of my spine. I'm in a trance as he moves the extra inch and presses his warm, full lips to mine. Heat fills my body as each cell magnetises, desperate to pull Jay even closer. Before I know what's happening, my body melts into his as our lips move in sync, wanting more.

The sound of whoops and cheers brings me back to reality. What the hell am I doing? I pull away but Jay doesn't release me straight away. I look him in his pleading eyes. They're willing me to change my mind and ask him to stay, but I won't do it. Eventually he releases me.

'Things could have been different,' he whispers.

'Goodbye, Jay.'

The minibus driver starts rushing them, gesturing frantically for them to get inside. I can't blame the poor guy; he probably has plenty more jobs to get to today and we could be here forever. When they're all seated safely inside, he slams the door with a huff. I can see Marcus and Jay through the window. They're both looking at me. Marcus gives a watery smile whilst Jay's eyes burn through me. It hurts so much to see them leaving, and to see the anguish on Jay's face, that I have to look away. I wave as the minibus moves off. When it's out of sight, unable to bear the weight any longer, I allow the crushing sensation to take hold. It's so intense I can't breathe. I step backwards and stumble over the kerb. I feel myself give way to the overbalance and start to fall.

My arms flail, seeking something solid to grasp, when all of a sudden, something grabs me from behind and stops the inevitable.

'I got you.'

Strawberry-scented hair wafts in front of my face.

'Thought you might need a friend today.'

When I'm steady, I turn around and bury my face in Andrea's

hair as she wraps me in a tight embrace. I can't speak, the lump in my throat is so painful, so I just let her hold me.

'So, do you feel like a momma bear who's just waved her beloved cubs off into the wild?'

'I feel like part of me has been ripped away.'

'I know, honey.' She strokes my hair. 'It was always going to be hard, but it will get easier – especially when you hear from them and you know they're doing okay.'

'I know,' I whisper. 'It's just that my whole life has gone in a flash – my work, my friends, my family. What do I have left?'

'You have me,' she says. 'And a new job at a bar where the boss hates tardiness, so you'd better move your butt. You start in fifteen minutes.'

I laugh and dry my salty tears. I know Andrea is only trying to keep my mind off things but I just want to curl up in bed and cry.

'I'll be there. Let me go and do something with my puffy face first.'

She smiles. 'I'll see you there when you're ready.'

***

The next few weeks pass by in a blur of work and sleep. It's surreal, like one life ended and another began. I've only vaguely existed in both realities. Andrea has kept me busy between shifts with either cocktails, cups of tea or extra hours, so I've not had much of a chance to process how I feel. She's been very sweet, but now the plasters she slapped over all the wounds in my life are starting to peel away. Last night, I couldn't sleep and went down to the pool for some air, and I half expected to see Jay sitting there. I don't know whether the surprise at him not being there was irrational disappointment or a symptom of losing my mind.

I think a part of me doesn't quite believe I've lost my boys for good. It's like they've gone off to the waterpark for the day, every day. I check my phone and almost leap in the air when I see a message from Marcus.

Hey Kat,

Sorry none of us have been in touch. There's been loads to do. We've all got our visas sorted now after a few issues. We fly out to Las Vegas tomorrow. Can't wait! We'll be in touch when we're there.

We all miss you loads and hope you're enjoying your freedom. Love ya!

M xxx

My chest pangs as I key out a reply, letting him know I'm okay and wishing them well. Jay must have managed to get a visa then. I get a sinking feeling. Perhaps I didn't expect him to. Perhaps I thought that if his visa was refused, he'd come back here and there would be less pressure on us because I wouldn't be the reason for him staying. I hate myself for feeling this way.

Letting him go was the right decision and I'll be happier for it in the long run. I just have to stay strong.

Chapter 34

'Kat!' Phil shouts excitedly from across the bar.

I walk over to him and gesture to a table. 'Sit down and I'll get you a drink.'

'A Coke Zero would be great.'

I return a few moments later with two Coke Zeros. 'So, what brings you here?'

'I leave tomorrow,' he says, jiggling with excitement.

'Oh gosh, has that much time passed already?' I run the mental calculation. The guys have been in Las Vegas for just under a fortnight. I've been following their new Instagram page, but so far it's just been rehearsals.

'Paul has been on the phone to me every day telling me how amazing the apartment is, and the Strip and the malls and everything. I can't wait to see it all for myself.'

A pang of sadness strikes. It's so much more than I ever gave them or could even imagine offering them. I'm so happy they've got this opportunity but disappointed that I couldn't give it to them.

Phil is so excited, I raise a smile. 'It sounds amazing.'

'Do you regret not going out there?'

'No.' My throat is dry so I sip my Coke. 'I love being here, and besides that, I had no job to go to so would never have gotten a visa.'

'You could have done the ninety days like me.' He grins.

'I don't have the benefit of a high-earning life partner to live with. What's your plan after the ninety days?'

'I'm hoping the guys have an idea by then on whether or not they're going to be staying six or twelve months.' He starts wittering about visas and ESTAs but I'm barely listening.

I shrug. 'I've no idea. I think the US visa system is a mystery to most.'

'Did you know they're doing their first show tomorrow night?'

'No,' I say, unsure of why it hurts so much that I didn't. I'm not their manager anymore. I suppose it's the kind of thing I thought at least one of them would let me know about.

'There's a live stream on IGTV and I think highlights will be going on their YouTube channel.'

'Great.' I force a smile. To be honest, I've been cyber-stalking them since the minute they left. Their followers are blowing up and they've only done a few promo appearances.

Phil reaches across the table and covers my hand in his. 'It's okay to feel weird about all this. The Hunks were yours for so long, and you made them great. You don't have to hide the fact you're finding this difficult. I know that in many ways, they are too.' I don't say it, but I'm glad he doesn't mention Jay specifically. As much as I miss the Heavenly Hunks, it's Jay who I find myself thinking of the most.

'Thanks, Phil.'

'I didn't do anything,' he says.

'For understanding.'

He accepts that with a knowing look, then sips his drink. 'Listen, I have to go and get the rest of my packing done but I wanted to say goodbye.' He stands up and rests his hand on my shoulder. 'I hope you find your happiness.'

'Thanks, Phil. Give my love to the boys.'

***

My mum and dad arrive a few days later. After a tearful reunion, we head to one of the bars on the promenade.

'So, love, it must be a bittersweet feeling for you at the moment?' Mum asks. She's put on about three stone since I last saw her and her red frizzy hair has grown outwards in all directions. Both have given her a jolly, amiable appearance.

'If you mean about the Heavenly Hunks going on to bigger, brighter things then you're right,' I say. 'It's the end of an era but I'm incredibly proud of what we achieved together.'

'You should be,' Dad says, patting my hand. 'A right little business brain you've got there – just like your old man.' Dad hasn't changed much. He's always had a big beer belly and a jovial-looking face. Just his hair has thinned and the grey is starting to turn a snowy white around his temples.

It's nice they're here. Things feel normal again – I think they feel it too because we're chatting like old times. They've never brought Iain up and I moved here so soon after I left him that I never got a chance to explain.

'You know Iain?' I ask, prompting my dad to sit up straighter.

'Mmm,' he says, setting his lips in a hard line.

'I was going to ask what you thought of him but I think I can tell.'

'You were too good for him,' Mum says. 'We never said anything, but we didn't get a good vibe from him at all.'

'You seemed to have to give up a lot for him, Kat, and he never gave anything up for you.'

I look down at the table. 'Things were worse than you even knew.'

'Oh?' My mum presses her eyebrows together and I fill them in. There're lots of 'oh loves' and 'why didn't you talk to us?' type comments.

'I'm only telling you because I'm sorry about the way I treated you. I didn't see what he was doing and I pushed you away.'

'Kat, we knew it was him but we also knew you wouldn't listen to us – we were scared you'd cut us off completely if we meddled. When you said you were moving to Tenerife to start afresh, we were so pleased because we knew you'd be away from him. Of course, we knew we'd miss you but the fact you were safe was more important. We didn't want to push you to tell us anything; we knew you would in your own time.'

I stare at the table.

'And here we are, eight years later.' My dad means it as an affectionate joke but it tips me over the edge and I burst into tears.

'Kat? I was joking, love.' He stands up and puts his arms around me.

'I know.' I wipe my eyes. 'Now I think I've messed up the next phase of my life too.'

'How so?' Mum asks softly and I find myself telling them all about Jay.

'He sounds like he thinks the world of you,' Mum says.

'Hang on, Janet,' he says to her. 'If he's trying to pressure Kat into a relationship when she's not ready, he's as bad as Iain.'

I shake my head. 'No, Dad, it's not like that. Jay respected me. He knows about my marriage and he didn't pressure me. He wanted me to see that we would be great together but I let old demons take over and I couldn't shake them.'

'Can I be frank?' Mum asks.

'It's the twenty-first century, Janet, you can be whoever you bloody want to be,' my dad says, prompting Mum to roll her eyes.

'Relationships take work, even the good ones. The key to making them last is communication. Every topic should be on the table for discussion.'

'Can I interrupt?' Dad asks. 'I'm happy to talk to your mum about periods or emotions or whatever but if she comes home with stories of her bloody knitting club shenanigans, I shouldn't have to listen to that. I'm not a saint.'

231

I laugh softly. 'That's not what Mum's saying and you know it.'

He winks. I've missed my dad's knee-jerk humour in a crisis.

'*Anyway*,' Mum continues, 'if you can't talk to your partner about anything, it probably won't work out. What you need to do is stop questioning yourself and asking if you are strong enough to be in a relationship and start asking if Jay or whoever comes along next is a good listener.'

I ponder this and it makes sense. 'I wish I'd have talked to you before I sent him off to another continent.'

'There's not much you can do about him now, but there are plenty more fish in the sea, love.'

Chapter 35

Andrea was great about giving me flexible hours so I could spend time with my parents. They left yesterday and I think our relationship is stronger than it's been in over a decade. Now they've gone, the desperate feeling of losing everyone around me has hit me again with a vengeance and Andrea has made it her duty to cheer me up.

'Okay, I have Sex on the Beach, I have potato chips, the iPad is charged – let's do this.' Andrea insisted on having a Heavenly Hunk debut screening in her boxy little office at the bar. She said she was desperate to see how Brad has ruined my legacy, but I know she's just ripping off the plaster, making me get the first viewing over and done with in a calm, controlled environment. I think that she thinks it will make things easier in the end. Part of me can't bear to watch, but another small part of me is dying to see the guys in all their glory and my stomach flutters with excitement.

'I'll take one of those,' I say, reaching over for one of the cocktails whilst Andrea fiddles with her iPad. The show was hours ago, but I wasn't getting up at ridiculous o'clock to watch it live.

'Here we go,' she says, propping the iPad up in a stand on her desk.

The lighting is intense, like on *Britain's Got Talent* or *The X Factor*. That Jenny Grant woman comes on stage. She makes a few innuendos, which the crowd seem to love, and then she introduces the Heavenly Hunks. Then the music kicks in and the boys storm the ginormous stage. The music and dry ice that we used here are still the same, just on a much bigger scale. Hugo's replacement is some incredibly hot, dark-haired stack of a guy. I wonder if they all get along.

The routine so far is pretty much unchanged, which comes as a relief to me. It just looks bigger and better on the huge stage, and the expensive lighting gives it a top-class appearance. I'm watching, and I'm actually doing okay. I like that Brad and Jenny have stayed true to our act and 'new Hugo' can even play the piano. I'm doing so well I could cry.

Then, the camera zooms in on Jay. It's close enough I can see the depth of his chestnut eyes. I can see the skin of his torso that my hand has felt every ripple of and his tattoo is just visible on his inner bicep. I can almost smell his soft brown hair, and as he uses his large hands to press his body into the floor, I can practically feel them on me. Then a stronger feeling takes over. A monkey wrench yanking and turning my stomach over.

'I'm sorry, Andrea, I can't do this.'

I leave, walking as fast as I can back towards my apartment. When I arrive, I throw myself on the bed and let the tears that I'd barricaded in for the entire walk home stream out.

My pillow is damp. I'm empty. I stopped crying an hour ago, but still, I can't get my brain to function in any sort of rational way. I don't know what's the matter with me. Seeing Jay physically hurt and yet I feel compelled to watch the video again. I take my phone off the side and search for the video. When it pops up, I don't hesitate in hitting play. I don't know how many times I watch it, but somehow I end up searching #HeavenlyHunks on Instagram. It brings up hundreds of images that audience members have taken. I scroll through them, enjoying the comfort seeing them brings. Every time I spot Jay, I get the familiar pain in my stomach, but I still stare at him for too long.

Chapter 36

A few days ago, Paul sent me a message to say the Heavenly Hunks had been invited onto *The Celia O'Donnell Show*. I snuggle into my duvet and prop up my iPad.

The show's theme tune kicks in and Celia walks onto the set waving to the audience. I sit up straighter in bed and hold my iPad closer.

'Ladies ... and some gentlemen, have we got a treat for you this evening. Think hot, naked men. Think silky-smooth torsos and moves to make your dear granny blush. They've completely sold out of tickets for the next six months and women are offering to sell their own mothers just to get a seat. They are the hottest act sweeping Las Vegas right now. Brace yourselves, because tonight we welcome none other than the Heavenly Hunks!'

The audience erupts in applause. There's cheering, and from certain camera angles, I can see that some people have even stood up. I'm still in awe of how the Hunks have made such an impression on America in such a short space of time. As the boys walk onto the set, my heart stops.

They look so well. Dressed in different variations of jeans and T-shirts, they all look effortlessly gorgeous. Jay's hair is a little longer; it's ruffled messily and a piece falls into his eyes. I have to look at someone else. It's easy to see why the crowd are so excited. They've not even spoken yet and I'm already gnawing my nails like a rabbit with a carrot.

'Hello, and welcome,' Celia says as the guys squeeze onto the adjacent sofa. 'So, you guys must have the women falling at your feet?' She fans herself dramatically. My Hunks laugh awkwardly while new Hugo looks towards his feet comically. Ant scratches the back of his neck, which has subtle red blotches emerging, and Paul hasn't been able to make eye contact with the host yet. It makes me smile because they used to be like that around me in the early days. It's a moment before I can bring myself to look back at Jay. The familiarity of his features makes my stomach twist.

'I guess there have been a few admirers,' Marcus says sheepishly.

'Just a few, huh? What do you say, audience members: do they have a few admirers in the room tonight?' Glass-shattering 'woos' that only dogs should be able to hear ensue.

'Okay, okay, let's get serious. You guys seem to have come from nowhere and taken Vegas by storm. What's your story? How did the Heavenly Hunks come about?'

'It was actually a lady from the UK called Kat who brought us all together,' Marcus says. I sit up straighter when I hear my name. The boys go on to tell brief stories of how they came to be in Tenerife and how the Hunks began. My thermostat seems to kick in and eye-pricking warmth floods me.

When Celia announces that they're going to show a clip of their Vegas show, I realise my eyes are dry and sore from not blinking. Just as the clip starts, my phone rings.

I exhale impatiently when I see the name on the screen. 'Andrea, what's up?'

'What's up with me? What's up with you, more like? You're late!'

'What?' I check the time. I should have been there an hour ago. 'Bugger. I'm so sorry, Andri. I'll be there right away.'

'Kat, is everything okay?'

'Yes, I was just watching the Hunks on *The Celia O'Donnell Show* and lost track of time. I'm so sorry, I'll make my hours up.'

'I'll see you when you get in.' She hangs up the phone and I reluctantly lock the screen on my iPad.

'I'll see you boys later,' I whisper.

When I arrive at the bar, Andrea is sitting at a table with a pair of glasses perched on the end of her nose, mulling over some paperwork.

'Hi,' I say guiltily.

'Kat, sit down. Please.' She gestures to the chair opposite and my chest sinks. I don't think I've ever seen her so serious before and I'm ashamed of myself for letting her down. If one of the Hunks had been late for a rehearsal or show, I'd have been livid.

'Andrea, I'm not taking liberties, I promise. It was an accident and I'll be more careful.'

'Kat, look around. The bar is empty, so your lateness has actually saved me money.'

Oh, she doesn't need me. I close my eyes, bracing myself. She's going to let me go.

'I'm worried about you.'

My eyes open with a start. That wasn't what I expected.

'This obsession with the Hunks isn't healthy. You need to move on.'

'What are you talking about?'

'I'm talking about spending all of your free time online, on their Instagram page, their Twitter feed, their website, their YouTube channel—'

'All right, all right. I get what you're trying to say but you have it wrong. Of course, I'm interested in their careers. I helped build them.'

'You're not interested, you're obsessed. This isn't the first time you've been late because you've been glued to some show they're on, and you spend every spare minute you have looking at your phone.'

I make a noise of exasperated frustration.

'Kat, you're living and breathing your past. It's not healthy and it's sure as hell not moving on. You don't even look like you've showered.'

Words jumble and jam in my mouth so I shake my head.

'When was the last time you went out and did something fun?'

'I—' I deflate. 'I can't remember.'

'Take the day off and go to the beach. It's warm enough to lie there and read a book. There are some in my office that tourists have left behind. Go and choose one and relax ... away from your screens.'

'Are you sure you don't need me?'

'The place is dead. Go!'

I nod and head into her office. There's a shelf full of bestsellers from over the years: a faded copy of *The Da Vinci Code*, a well-thumbed *Fifty Shades of Grey*, a dog-eared *Big Little Lies*. I settle on a yellowing copy of *Me Before You*. I haven't read it or seen the film but, as is always the case with popular books, I know how it ends and it'll suit my mood.

'Got one.' I wave the book at Andrea.

'Okay. Enjoy your day and I'll see you for your shift tonight.'

I almost go straight to the beach, but I don't have a towel or anything to lie on, so instead, I do something I never do. I head into a little bar overlooking the beach and order myself a small jug of sangria – I'll have a drink, go home, get a towel, and *then* go to the beach. Andrea has every right to be frustrated with me. She was kind enough to give me a job and I haven't even had the decency to try. We both know my heart isn't in it. The beach-front is quiet today. The only people I see walking by are older couples. They all have something in common; they all seem content. They're not chasing their pasts or futures, they're happy in their now. I suppose for years I've sort of been suspended in a bubble. I thought I was happy but perhaps I was just too busy to feel sad, and it felt like happiness. The closest I've come to true happiness recently, that wasn't work-related, was my time with Jay.

I have an idea. If I'm going to be content in my now, I need to do something I enjoy. I take out my phone and dial Gaël, the manager at the Grand Canarian. He answers almost straight away.

'Kat?'

'Hi, Gaël. Listen, this is a bit out of the blue, but I wondered whether your offer of being an entertainment manager still stood?'

He pauses and my stomach twists. Oh God, I bet he was just being polite. 'I think you're great at organising acts, Kat. The only problem is, we are still quiet. I could offer you a few hours though. I'm currently running around like a headless chicken trying to sort out guest services, bar staff and our pool refurbishment.'

Excitement jolts me. 'That would be fantastic.' I still have some of my sale money left but it won't last long and I'm not earning much at Andrea's bar anyway. Maybe I could do both jobs.

When I've finished my sangria, I head home. My iPad is on the bed where I left it. The sight of it catches me by surprise, which is silly since I left it there and I was hardly expecting burglars. I could just watch the end of *The Celia O'Donnell Show* and then go to the beach, couldn't I?

Before I know what I'm doing, I'm back in bed, snuggled under the blankets, watching the clip of the Heavenly Hunks show in Vegas. I smile at the moves I recognise and get a warm feeling of nostalgia when it includes a snippet of Marcus singing in his smooth caramel voice. When it ends, the studio cameras cut back in and the audience are going crazy.

'Woo.' Celia fans herself once more. 'I'm beginning to see why this show has sold out now.'

They talk in more detail about the schedule and the 'amazing things' Brad and Jenny have done. My stomach clenches and I have to tell myself that bigging up their managers on TV is probably in their contracts.

'Well, you've really been an overnight sensation.' Celia draws that particular part of the chatter to a close and I love her for it. 'But what I'm sure our audience members really want to know is who are the Heavenly Hunks?

'We thought we'd have a little fun with you and play a game of truth or dare.' She raises her eyebrows comically at the camera. 'Now, I can't remember all of your names so I'm going to go along from left to right. Starting with you.'

The camera pans in on Ant.

'Truth or dare, young man? Give me your name and your choice.'

'I'm Ant, and I'll take a dare.' He flashes a wicked grin and the audience cheers.

Celia glances at the crowd. 'Okay, I think I know what they want. Ant, it says here that you're a classically trained ballet dancer. I mean, that in itself is amazing, but you've combined that with *erotic* dancing. I think we have to see this. I dare you to show us some erotic ballet.'

Ant walks to a carpeted area behind Celia's sofa and, to everyone's amusement, Taylor Swift's 'Shake It Off' begins to play.

'We thought we'd mix it up a little,' Celia says with a wink.

I watch as Ant makes tiny, rhythmic movements with his body as he gets in sync with the tempo. He takes his T-shirt off (much to the audience's delight) and throws it to a charmed Celia. Then he's ready, throwing himself into fast spins, press-ups and groin pumps. The whole sequence is fast, fluid, and perfectly in time to the music. The camera takes in Celia and the other dancers who're clapping along in the background. The audience goes wild and he plays on this by lunging into a mid-air front split.

To finish, Ant blows kisses to a wolf-whistling audience and takes a bow as Celia joins him on the carpet. 'Take it all,' she says, stuffing green bills in the waistband of his jeans.

When Ant takes his seat back on the sofa, his smile spreads from ear to ear.

'I've lost the ability to speak,' Celia says, causing an eruption of laughter. 'Okay, we have time for one more and believe me, if *CSI Miami* could wait, I'd extend the show. Next hot guy along, what's your name and do you want truth or dare?'

I swallow hard. Jay is the next hot guy along.

'I will take truth,' he says. It surprises me and I don't know why.

'Okay, strippers get a bad reputation. I want to know if it's true. Do you live up to that womanising stereotype?'

'Wow.' He laughs nervously. 'Okay. Well, I get it and there is a lot of female attention that comes our way, but no, I'm a professional and I don't mix work with my private life.'

'Tell us more about your private life. Are you in a relationship?' Celia pries.

'I'd never really thought about settling down, but back in Tenerife I did meet someone special who I saw a future with.'

There's a chorus of 'awws' from the audience.

'Wait a minute. Who is this girl and where do I find her to beat her up?' Celia jokes.

Jay laughs nervously. 'She wouldn't want me to say.'

'Did you love her?' Celia is like a dog with a bone.

Jay's presses his lips together tightly. I can feel how awkward this is for him but I don't care, I want to know.

'Yes,' he says, eventually.

'Oh my goodness. So what are you doing in Las Vegas talking to me when the girl you love is on an island in the Atlantic?

'It wasn't the right time for us. She wasn't ready to settle down so we parted ways.'

'Ladies, we have a devastated Hunk on our sofa. Who wants to comfort him?' Celia teeters over to him on her heels and hugs him comically in a 'there, there' sort of way as the crowd screams. Jay squirms uncomfortably.

'Who would do that to such a fine specimen?' Celia shakes her head playfully. 'Well, there you go, ladies, there's a heartbroken Hunk on the market and all you need to do is get yourselves to Las Vegas to go cheer him up.' The camera closes in on Jay's face. There's a look of shy discomfort at the attention, but above the watery smile, his eyes hold something that I can't put my finger on but that resonates with something inside me. I want to reach into my iPad and hug him.

'Okay, we're almost out of time.' Celia finishes by thanking the guys and wishing them luck.

I don't know how long I've been staring at the iPad for, but when I come to, the screen is black and it's locked itself. Jay has been away for weeks now and he's still thinking about what we had. He said he loved me. I must have meant something more to him than I ever imagined. Without reason, I considered him the same as every other man I've ever been close to. He didn't deserve that. My mum said a partner needs to be able to listen and Jay listened to me so much. I have a crushing feeling that I've made a terrible mistake writing us off like that. I'm an idiot.

'What have I done?' I whisper.

Chapter 37

'Your hair is still unwashed, yet sand-free, and you're wearing the same clothes as you were this morning. You didn't go to the beach!' Andrea's eyes narrow on me the second I walk into the bar.

'At least I'm on time,' I say with false cheer.

'Oh, Kat, were you on the internet again?' Her soft tone does nothing to comfort me; instead, it ignites bubbling frustration. I pause before answering, as I don't want to snap or sound defensive.

'No, actually, I wasn't.' Not the whole time at least. 'I got my life in order instead.'

A look of relief washes over her. 'Tell me more.'

'You're right. I've been miserable and that's partly because I'm pining for the boys but I'm also stuck in a rut and not doing anything to help myself. After having a good think, I called Gaël and I'm now his entertainment manager at the Tenerife Grand!'

I take in her shocked expression. 'Don't worry, I can still work here too as Gaël only needs me for a few afternoons or evenings a week.'

'That's great. Doing what you love is exactly what you need.' She smiles. 'Now can you take the order from table two please.'

Later, when the bar is quiet, I find myself checking my Instagram feed. There are a few new posts on the Heavenly Hunks' page, including a few Boomerangs and videos. I lean on the bar and watch them.

'Kat!'

I jump out of my skin and turn around to face Andrea.

'You just said you're making changes! This is not doing you any good.'

'You think it's wrong of me to keep up to date with their success?' I ask defensively.

'No. I think it's unhealthy to be so obsessed. You do nothing but follow the Hunks around the internet like a virtual lost puppy. It's more than keeping up with their success and you know it.'

I do know it.

'I'm sorry, but someone needs to tell you to pull yourself together.'

I glance down at the thick rubber mat on the floor of the bar area. You can drop a bottle of vodka on this mat and it wouldn't smash, yet here I am, standing on top of it, broken in a thousand messy pieces.

'I know.' I choke on the words.

'Oh, Kat.' Andrea pulls me into a tight embrace. 'It's normal to feel sad, but you have to deal with it in order to move on. I'm sorry I upset you, but watching the videos online every second of the day is just you putting your emotions on hold – you need to let go.'

'You're right, but it's not only that I miss the guys. It's …' I can't bring myself to say it so I pull out my phone, prompting an unimpressed look from Andrea. 'It's not what you think. Just watch this.'

I fast-forward the video of *The Celia O'Donnell Show* to the truth or dare part and hand it to Andrea. She looks impatient but takes it anyway and presses play. As the segment progresses, I watch her expression change from frustration to something more sympathetic. Through the tinny speaker on my phone, I can just about make out Jay's voice. It's enough to give me a sharp pain in my chest.

When the clip ends, Andrea looks at me with heavy eyes. 'You love him too, don't you?'

'Love?' That's a strong word. I'm about to deny it but the memories come back to me. Swimming at the Ritz Carlton, lying in bed all day, the butterflies, the tightness in my abdomen, the swelling in my chest and the happiness that flooded my body when we were together. The tearing pain of saying goodbye. Andrea is right but it scares me to admit it.

'Yes, *love*. Why does it scare you so much?'

'Because the last time I thought I was in love it ruined my life.'

***

I sit waiting. It's gone dark and I'm shivering. I hug my legs tighter to my chest and the moisture from my face transfers, making my prickly knees soggy. I should get up off the floor, turn the heating on and sort myself out but I can't. The clunk of the key turning in the lock makes me jump. My heart is racing. He's home.

'Katelyn?' he shouts up the stairs. There's uncertainty in his tone like he thinks I'm out. He's mad. I shouldn't be out at this time.

'Katelyn?' he calls again, impatient now. I hear him stomping from room to room. The lounge, then the kitchen and the small utility room at the back. Blood pumps thickly around my eardrums. His heavy feet climb the stairs.

The door swings open followed by a blinding light. 'There you are. What the hell are you doing on the floor?'

I look up slowly. His eyes are filled with hatred.

'I know everything,' I say. My words are barely audible.

'What are you talking about? Get up off the floor, you daft cow.'

'I started recording us. You. I wanted to keep a record of things

for my own sanity. I was embarrassed, Iain. I wanted to make sure I didn't make any more mistakes.'

'*You've lost it.*'

The fact that he's carrying this on when I know the truth helps me turn my fear into rage.

'*No,*' *I yell.* '*You've lost it, you twisted freak! I recorded everything; when you said you'd pick me up and didn't. You left me in the snow for three hours, Iain, and when I rang you in tears, you tried to make me believe you told me you couldn't pick me up. But I have it all here.*' *I thrust my phone out in front of me and hit play.*

'*Course I'll pick you up at the bus stop. It's going to snow later so I don't want you walking.*'

He laughs. The audacity makes me shake with anger.

'*Then after that, I told you I had to work late.*'

'*You didn't. Your mind games are not going to work on me anymore. At first, I thought maybe your mind was going. I felt sorry for you.*' *I spit the last few words out.* '*But your mind is fine. When I eventually decided to walk the last five miles home, Margaret Penistone from the village store drove past and gave me a lift. She is lovely, but I've only just learnt that because you always manage to persuade me to stay in, don't you?*'

He stands there, stony-faced, giving nothing away. It causes me to falter.

'*Anyway, she's seen your car, parked up in the lay-by on the road out towards the river—*'

'*So?*' *he spits.*

'*Most nights, Iain.*' *I rise to my feet. I can't have him looking down at me whilst I do this.* '*You're not alone in the car, are you?*'

He sits on the edge of the bed, plotting his next move no doubt. His hesitation gives me strength.

'*You're having an affair and you've been screwing with my head, making me feel stupid whilst you get away with screwing God knows who every night.*'

'Katelyn, it's not what you think.'

'It's exactly what I think. I want you to get the hell out of my house,' I shout.

'But—' His lip falls slack and wobbles.

'Get out!'

***

'I know you had a bad experience but whatever happened is in the past. You have to move on. Your feelings *now* are the ones that matter.'

I tense. 'I know and I've already decided that I won't shy away from relationships from now on.'

'But you've let the man you love go.'

'I gave him the opportunity of a lifetime,' I correct.

'You pushed him towards something he didn't care about.'

I can't speak because I know she's right.

'Listen, I know you believed in your heart it was the right thing to do but it's okay to admit you were wrong.'

'What good is that now? He's gone for the next five months at least – if the success of the Hunks continues it will be another year after that. I've lost him, Andri.'

'For someone who sought safety by micromanaging every aspect of your business, you're missing a glaringly obvious solution here.'

I frown. If she thinks I can up sticks and move to Las Vegas to be with Jay, she's watched one American romcom too many. I have no chance of getting a work visa because I have no work to go to and I can't afford to live there without a job. He probably wouldn't want me now anyway. 'No, I'm not. I can't just go halfway around the world to chase a guy I monumentally screwed over. He's better off without me and my emotional baggage. He might think he loves me, but when he finds love with someone else, he'll see that too.'

She folds her arms. 'Katelyn.'

'What?'

'You've sabotaged your own happiness for far too long. I'm making you redundant. I'm going to ask Gaël to do the same because being stuck in a rut with your career isn't what's wrong. It's being stuck in a rut with your love life.'

'What? You can't sack me because I won't chase after someone who lives over five thousand miles away.'

'I can. Here.' She hands me a brown envelope.

'What's this?'

'Take it,' she says. 'It's your redundancy package.'

Redundancy package? 'What are you talking about?'

I'm at a loss. What kind of friend would do this? I'm at my lowest ebb and she's sacking me when she knows I hardly have enough euros to last the next few months. 'I know I was late this morning but it was a one-off. Please, Andri, I need this job.'

'Take the envelope.' She thrusts it at me and, tentatively, I do as she says. What choice do I have? At this point, I'd go and beg Alonso for a job in any of his bars.

I go to open the envelope but Andrea places a firm hand over mine. 'I just want to hear you say it.'

'Say what?'

'That you love Jay.'

Why is she doing this to me? 'What, because if I admit that I love Jay you'll give me my job back? Brilliant.'

'No, I'm not going to give you your job back.'

'You're a piece of work.' I shake my head.

'Just admit it!'

'Fine!' I'm almost screaming. 'I love Jay. For all the use it is.'

I throw my head in my hands and start to cry. It's not just a few tears; it's shoulder-hitching tears with involuntary sobs that pop out like hiccups. It's what millennials call 'ugly crying'.

'Okay,' she says softly, sliding her hand away. 'Now open the envelope.'

I look up at her through stinging eyes, my vision almost opaque.

'Go on,' she prompts.

Carefully, I slide my nail down the seal and slide out a piece of paper. I scan the document and it's a few seconds before it registers.

'You bought me a plane ticket?' I clutch my hand to my mouth.

She nods, a sheepish smile playing on her lips.

'But …' I'm lost for words.

'It's a return ticket. Just go to Las Vegas and figure things out,' she says.

'What about work and my life here? I can't just put everything on hold.'

'I hear you've been fired, and I think what you mean is "thank you".'

'Thank you,' I say, still shell-shocked. 'I can't accept this though, it's too much.'

'You're my friend and I want you to be happy. You've been miserable ever since they left, and I thought it would help to pay them a visit. Maybe you could talk to Jay …'

I glance at the date. 'Gosh, this is for tomorrow!' Thoughts of speed-packing and leg-shaving race through my mind.

'If I left it any longer you'd talk yourself out of going.'

She knows me too well.

'I can't believe you bought me a ticket to Las Vegas,' I say, still absorbing her generosity.

'It was either that or smash your phone and iPad, so either way, I was parting with a large sum of money,' she says drily.

'How did you even manage to do this? Don't you need personal details?'

'Remember when you started here and I photocopied your passport and made you fill in all those employment contracts?' She winks.

I lunge forward and wrap her tightly in my arms. 'Thank you so much, Andrea. I will pay you back every penny, I promise.'

'I don't want the money. I want you to be happy,' she says with earnestness etched into her features.

'I don't know what to say. It's so generous of you.'

'Say that you'll go with an open mind and come back with a clear head. Jay loves you and you love him.'

I nod, overwhelmed with a feeling of fullness. This is the kindest thing anyone has ever done for me. 'You are a wonderful person, Andrea.'

'Tell me something I don't know.'

Chapter 38

The tug starts the pushback and the plane gently moves away from the terminal. It's my second flight of the day, as I had to fly via Gatwick but I'm no more relaxed. I hate flying. The flight-safety film comes on. Even though I know the ropes after thirty-odd years of flying, I still normally give these things my undivided attention, but today I can't concentrate.

We puncture the grey clouds, and ten minutes later we're sailing through gorgeous blue air atop a fluffy white pillow that masks all of Earth's ugly problems. The seatbelt sign turns off and the sound of unclicking buckles is instantaneous. I leave mine on, but it's not just the fear of plummeting into the Atlantic that's causing the uncomfortable knot in my stomach and no amount of seatbelt-wearing will make that go away. I'm consumed by the gut-twisting fear of seeing Jay and explaining why the hell I've travelled halfway around the world to see him when I'm pretty sure he hates me. How do I explain that I was wrong and I want to be with him?

I accept a mini bottle of wine from the drinks trolley and browse the movie selection. When nothing catches my eye, I play *Who Wants to Be A Millionaire?* for a good hour and, frustratingly, never get past two hundred and fifty thousand pounds. It was a good distraction while it lasted. Dinner breaks up the next hour, but once that's been cleared away, the lights are dimmed and people begin to snuggle up beneath blankets. There's not a chance I'll be able to sleep with the concoction of unease bubbling away in my stomach, so I wander to the loo, for something to do more than anything, then purposely walk down the opposite aisle and through the back galley to get back to my seat. The man next to me gives me a weary glance as I sit down and I'm worried that my fidgeting has started to annoy him.

When everything fails to offer distraction, I let my mind go to where it's been trying to go ever since Andrea gave me this flight ticket. Jay. Once I do, I'm pelted with little pebbles of doubt. What if he was wrong about his feelings and is happy now? What if he's moved on and seeing me will be his undoing? What if he's mad at me for messing him around? What if he's met someone else? I think (and this 'think' lacks any form of confident backing) that I can cope with all scenarios but the last. At least I will have tried, and I'll have closure. But if he's met someone else, then I'll be too late; he'll be gone completely and I'll have nobody to blame but myself.

Perhaps it would be better to change my flight home to tomorrow or something and put this little adventure down to Andrea filling my head with nonsense. The plane hits an air pocket and bounces violently. The seatbelt sign pings on and my heart races as the plane continues to shake and rattle. I glance around nervously. Nobody else seems in the slightest bit fazed, but I can't settle now.

I hit the service button, probably with a little too much vigour as the man next to me gives me another *look*. I ignore him since I have enough to worry about without adding him to the list. The flight attendant appears within a few moments.

'Is there something I can get for you?' she asks before plastering a red-lipped smile on her face. I feel a bit sorry for her having to do that and almost tell her she doesn't have to smile on my account.

'Can I get another one of those little bottles of white wine please?' Then I remember Andrea's kindness and how I've irked the man next to me and add, 'And whatever he's having. It's on me.'

I'm quite proud of myself; I've never completed a random act of kindness before.

'Funny, aren't you?' he says, and my head spins around so quickly I almost break my neck.

'Excuse me? I was just trying to do one of those random-acts-of-kindness things.'

He narrows his eyes and studies me for a second or two. 'Sorry, I thought you were joking, because, you know, they're complimentary.'

I feel myself blush. Of course they are; I had one earlier. 'Sorry, too many Ryanair flights,' I say sheepishly. 'I was genuinely trying to apologise for disturbing you.'

To my relief, he smiles. 'I'll have a beer,' he says to the flight attendant. 'And she's paying.' He winks at me, and the air flight attendant, who has probably heard that joke a thousand times, gives a wry smile and heads to the galley for our drinks.

'I'm Simon,' he says, holding out a hand for me to shake.

'Kat.'

'Been to Vegas before?' he asks.

'No, it's not somewhere I've ever wanted to go before but I'm visiting someone.'

'I've been twice. It's mental! I'm meeting some of my pals for a stag do. The missus wouldn't let me do the full week so I'm having five days over there.'

I smile. I get the impression his loyalty to his 'missus' runs quite deep and he's not actually bothered about his shortened jolly.

'So, who you visiting? Celine Dion?' He laughs at his own joke. It isn't funny but it helps me warm to him.

'Something like that. I used to manage an all-male exotic dance act called the Heavenly Hunks and I'm going to see them now they're performing in Las Vegas.'

'You're kidding?'

I widen my eyes. 'No.'

'My missus has been watching those guys on all the chat shows. They're becoming quite a name now. Bet you're gutted you're just the ex-manager, aren't you?'

If only he knew. 'No, it's a long story, but I wish them well.'

'Wow.' He sits back in his chair. 'I can't believe that. Wait until my missus finds out about this. She'll hate this Vegas trip even more.'

'You'll have to bring her next time,' I say, and he laughs like that's the most ridiculous suggestion he's ever heard. The flight attendant brings our drinks and a mini bag of pretzels each and the turbulence seems to dissolve.

'Cheers to Las Vegas,' he says, pressing his plastic glass to mine.

'Cheers.' I take a sip.

'So,' he says through a mouthful of crumbs, 'you're heading out to Vegas to see a bunch of strippers who you used to manage? Aren't you even a bit gutted that you're not their manager anymore?'

'Like I said, it's a long story, but the short version is that to hit the big time, they had to go with a new manager. I'm happy for them.'

'That's very diplomatic of you. I bet they can't wait to see you.'

'They don't know I'm coming.'

'Why not?'

Because if I warned them, the one person I'm most desperate to see would probably go into hiding. 'It's a long story.'

'You say that a lot.'

'I—' The rest comes out as air, and I chuckle. 'I suppose I do.'

'Well, this is a twelve-hour flight and so far we've not quite done three of 'em, so I might just be up for one of your long stories.'

I eye him suspiciously and when I determine he's being serious, I begin. 'All right, but I'm starting from the beginning. And don't say I didn't warn you!'

***

Simon fakes falling asleep as I'm telling him about the date at the beach Jay took me on. I elbow him playfully in the ribs. It's surprising how well you can get to know someone when you're cramped up in a metal tube, hurtling through the air. I've gone from apologetic stranger to touchy-feely (borderline violent) BFF in record time.

'Okay, so then there was the competition,' I say.

'Competition? Please tell me this was the lady-stripper competition and your memory is vivid enough to provide wonderful imagery?'

'No.'

'In that case, we're going to need more drinks.' He hits the service button. 'And this time, they're on me.'

The flight attendant looks weary. She doesn't even plaster on the fake smile or ask what she can get us this time, and I sense there is some kind of drinks quantity etiquette that we've breached.

'Do you think we're supposed to be asleep now?' Simon whispers as she walks away.

'Maybe. We're probably spoiling what should be a quiet overnight shift.'

'I bet they don't have this problem in the front seats.' Simon gestures to the curtain at the front of our cabin.

'Probably not. I think they have golden taps by their lie-flat seats that pump out champers.'

'Oh, how the other half live.'

256

The flight attendant returns with our drinks. This time, there are no pretzels.

'Good job I'm not starving,' Simon says wryly. 'Anyway, tell me about this competition.'

So I do. I fill him in on the acts, both dodgy and awesome, the guys' dedication and, of course, Brad and Jenny.

'I know that Jenny bird. She's a bit of all right.'

I give him a look.

'So after you dumped muscle-man because you didn't want to be taken for a ride, he went off stripping in Vegas and you stayed in Tencrife.'

'Yes.'

'But now you've realised you made a terrible mistake and are flying to see him, without his knowledge, after he's been in the biggest adult playground in the world for the past four weeks, as a single man.'

'Yes.'

Simon makes a 'phew-ee' type noise, indicating that he thinks I'm mad.

'Excuse me, do you mind keeping your voices down? I have a conference to get to as soon as we land and need to get some sleep,' a man across the aisle says.

'Sorry,' I say quietly and shuffle round in my chair to face Simon. 'Do you think I'm making a huge mistake?'

'What do I know? I'm just some guy on a plane whose wife has very strict rules about Vegas. I dread to think what I'd get up to if I was single.'

'Oh God.' I throw my head in my hands. 'I should have stayed in Tenerife. My friend put me up to this. She bought the ticket and everything.'

'Look.' He places a well-meaning hand on my shoulder, but removes it quickly, obviously unsure of the boundaries of in-flight friendships. 'Ignore what I just said. Seriously, what do I know? If your mate thought you were so mopey she wanted to chuck a fortune in your direction, there was obviously more to you and this Hunk than I'm privy to. If he has similar feelings for you, you're on to a winner.'

'Do you really think so?' I ask, clinging to that shred of hope.

'Course I do. Anyway, what's the plan? Land and head straight to his hotel room?'

I shake my head. 'No, I'm going to check in to my hotel, sleep, freshen up and then go to their show tonight. I called ahead and Brad, my replacement, has managed to squeeze me in and get me a backstage pass, and he's promised not to tell the guys I'll be there.'

'Wow, that will be a massive surprise. Aren't you worried that they'll have moved on?'

'Bloody hell, you give with one hand and take with the other, don't you?'

He chuckles. 'I'm just making sure you're mentally prepared. What if you turn up and Mr Loverman has a lover*woman*?'

'I haven't got the capacity to mentally prepare for that. I'm going to say sneak out, fly home and pretend I was never there.'

'Wrong answer.'

'I didn't know I was on the *Wheel of* bloody *Fortune*.'

'Shhh,' Aisle-man says again, this time with considerably less patience.

'So sorry,' I say, embarrassed to have caused a scene again.

'Look, you've flown all this way. If you see him with another woman, that's not his fault. Remember, at this point, he owes you nothing. He's single in a new country and might feel lonely. If he's as good-looking as you say, he won't be short on offers, will he?'

'No,' I whisper, sullenly.

'There's no saying this scenario is going to happen, but be prepared that it might not be roses and daffodils like in those movies I never watch.'

'Those movies you never watch, hey?'

'Maybe I've watched one with the missus,' he grumbles. 'The point is, you still have to tell him how you feel. Even if he has Pamela Anderson on his arm, he deserves to have all the information available to him before he makes his decision.'

He's right. If Jay is with someone else, I can't blame anyone but myself. 'Maybe I should have told him I was coming. At least that way, if he has met someone else, he could have told me not to come.'

'Or told her he's not that into her.'

'Isn't that the name of one of those films you never watch?' I tease.

'Wouldn't know.'

'Anyway, it is what it is. I just have to be brave.' I don't feel brave. I feel like I need to shut off any form of emotion just to have the courage to face him and that's before I say any of the awkward 'feelings' stuff.

'Exactly,' he says. 'If you've messed him about in the past, you need to prove to him that you're ready to be with him.'

'How do I do that?' I ask, lapping up the advice from this stranger.

'If I knew that, I'd have my own book out.'

I sigh. I suppose I have to figure that out on my own.

Somehow, we natter for the entire duration of the flight, and when the captain announces our descent, I'm a little bit sad at having to say goodbye to Simon.

Chapter 39

After four hours' sleep and a shower, I feel much more human. The flight in and meeting Simon is a fuzzy memory now and all I can think about is the show tonight. It's dusk when I peel back the curtains; I'm taken aback – it is quite a view I've got.

'Jesus!' I say aloud, as giant floodlit fountains go off. That must be the Bellagio; I've seen it in movies. Thinking of *Ocean's Eleven* reminds me of Iain, and I shudder.

I check the e-ticket Brad sent me when I got in touch to tell him I was flying out. The show starts at ten in the Forbidden Theatre in the Jackson Hotel. Google Maps shows me I've got a bit of a walk on my hands, even though it's only a few hotels along. I'll grab some food and do some sightseeing on the way.

The theatre is intimate but deceptively spacious. Each small table seats four patrons, all forward facing, and the floor slopes gently upwards from the stage to give everyone a good view of the action. There is also an upper tier. I spot podiums and all sorts dotted about – it's going to be a much bigger production than what we had in the Canaries.

As the room fills up, so does a cavity of apprehension inside me. I order a giant frozen margarita from the waiter and take in more of the elaborate surroundings. The stage juts out so the audience can sit around three of its four sides, and when I look up I can see all sorts of fancy lighting and suspended platforms.

As the lights dim and the music starts, my stomach tenses. I'm more nervous than I was during the competition. I check my phone as a distraction and see a WhatsApp message from Simon.

Go get 'em, tiger!

I smile. At this moment in time, that small jumble of words from a virtual stranger is just what I need to read.

My margarita arrives just as Jenny floats down onto the stage in a suspended harness. She's wearing a red chiffon dress that dances elegantly around her as she descends. I'm not going to lie – seeing her in my old spot is hard to watch, especially with the upgraded set, but I can't process that right now because I'm desperate to see someone else.

I sip my drink, and as I place my glass down, the boys come on stage. I gasp.

'Divine, aren't they?' the woman next to me says as she bounces in her seat excitedly. I nod before turning back to the stage.

The first set is pretty similar to what we did back in Spain. The routine, the music and the dry ice. There's a background stage set that looks like a grand staircase, which we never had, and the lighting is much better – there's an actual person controlling the sound and lighting, which apart from the competition final, is a huge step up from having a spotlight and a few coloured lights set on a random sequence at best. It's funny; this is what I'd dreamed about for the Heavenly Hunks – not Las Vegas, but a big production drawing the masses.

The next song comes on – 'Freak Me'. Not one of my choices, but I recognise it from the first few bars. Jenny comes on stage and says something about treating the much-deserving women in the audience, but I miss most of what she says because I'm draining the last of my margarita.

The woman next to me screams, causing me to jump. I look around and see she's smiling and clapping – eyes fixed on the stage. As I move my gaze, I see what the fuss is about. Marcus has jumped off the stage onto one of the tables and is gyrating his groin just inches from an audience member. This is new. I scan the room. Paul is massaging some lady's shoulders, Sammy is giving out a foot rub, and Jay is giving someone a lap dance. The audience is going wild; they love it. Then the boys move around, circling the room, seeking more participants.

I tense. I don't want any of them to see me, not yet. It will throw them off their game and ruin the performance. They're going everywhere. I shrink in my seat. Please gods of exotic dancing, let me go unseen. Marcus has even climbed a rope and is on the top-tier balcony. Nowhere is sacred. I slink into my seat. Surely, my body language will be enough for them to see I'm not up for a shoulder rub. Keeny McKeenson next to me, however, is like a stripper beacon, bouncing around and clapping excitedly.

Two warm hands land on my shoulders. They arrive from nowhere. I go rigid. Apparently, body language is not commonly recognised amongst the male population. I fix my eyes to my lap as whoever it is gets to work, albeit far too gently, on my shoulders. Part of me wants to glance to see who it is but I resist the urge. It can't have lasted more than twenty seconds, but it feels like an eternity before he leaves me alone.

'I'm so jealous,' the girl next to me says, punctuating it with a dramatically sour pout. 'He's my absolute favourite one.'

'Which one was it?' I ask, far too eagerly.

'The one with a tattoo on his inner bicep.'

My stomach tightens. Jay. I look at the stage where they're now all assembled and study him for signs of upset or shock. But he's smiling and working the room with his eyes and groin. He didn't know it was me. I don't know whether to feel relieved or a little bit miffed.

By the time the show has ended, I've been through so many emotions that the thought of going backstage and surprising everyone seems like too much to tag on to the day. *Go get 'em, tiger*. I repeat Simon's words. What exactly do I have to lose? Even if Jay isn't happy to see me, the others will be, and even if Jay has moved on and met someone else, I still get to see my boys. This is not a wasted trip. I have no idea how to get backstage or what the process is, so I ask a surly-looking member of the security team, who takes me through after checking my ticket.

'First door on your right,' he says before going back out to the foyer to help disperse the crowds.

I'm in a stark white corridor, lit with awful fluorescent strip lights that hurt my eyes after being in near darkness for a few hours. The door is closed. There's an actual star on it that reads 'Heavenly Hunks'. How do I do this? Do I knock? Do I barge in? Do I run?

'Do you have a VIP pass?' a female voice chirps. I turn around to see a petite lady with shoulder-length blonde hair. She has headphones on with one of those attached mics that reminds me of Britney Spears circa 1998.

'Yes,' I say meekly.

'Wonderful. I think you're our last one, so I'll take you straight through.'

She knocks three times. For the record, I would have gone with the knocking too.

She peeps around the door. 'Hey, everyone, I have one more fan for y'all.'

'Awesome,' a male voice says. I think it's Marcus.

Morris-dancing centipedes fill my stomach as she guides me through the door. They're having photographs taken with a giggling bunch of young women in front of a screen with 'Heavenly Hunks' splashed all over it. It's very Hollywood-esq. Once the pictures have been taken, a different member of the events team beckons me over, and the guys turn their attention to me. The plastic smiles on each of their faces dissolve at slightly different rates as they recognise me in turn.

'Kat!' Sammy is the first to jump up and dart towards me. He

263

picks me up and spins me round. When he puts me down the others are gathered around too.

'Hi,' I say. It comes out all pathetic and unsure.

'I can't believe you're here,' Paul says.

'I didn't expect to see you, Kat, but it's great you made it,' Marcus says, hugging me. 'Welcome to Vegas! You should have told us you were coming – we could have made arrangements.'

I bat his words away with my hand. 'I wanted to surprise you.'

'Job done,' Ant says.

As they all ask questions about flights and hotels and how it's going at Andrea's bar, I can't help but scan the room for Jay. He was there a second ago; I saw him smiling away and hugging one of the fans.

I notice an open door behind the screen, which leads into another room. Has he disappeared at the sight of me? Perhaps he's gone off with that woman. My skin starts to prickle. This is bad.

'He's in there,' Marcus says, following my line of sight.

'Who?' I say, pitifully.

Marcus cocks his head to the side. 'Just go and see him.'

I look at the doorway. There's no sign of Jay.

'You have to actually walk through the door,' Marcus whispers in my ear.

I look at the opening. Beyond it is a sofa and one of those lightbulb-framed make-up mirrors. It must be the dressing area. Slowly, I make my way towards it. There might as well be a wild bear in there for all the terror I'm filled with.

When I get to the doorframe, I peer in.

'Hi,' I say.

Chapter 40

'A little heads-up might have been nice.' Without looking at me, Jay pulls on a navy Ralph Lauren hoodie; the action ruffles his hair. He's got the matching joggers on too. I haven't seen him this covered up before. He looks so good it hurts.

'It was last-minute,' I say. 'A long story.'

He nods whilst throwing items into a rucksack.

'I got in this morning.' I'm trying to lead him into some kind of conversation but I'm struggling.

'Well, it's a great city. Enjoy your stay.' He slings the bag over his shoulder and walks towards the door. I don't plan to, but as he passes me, I reach out and grip his arm. He looks at my hand and flinches as if it's on fire and I've just scorched his skin.

'Jay,' I say softly, 'I came to see you. Can we talk?'

He looks me in the eyes for the first time this evening, and the familiar, enjoyable, zingy feelings fill my body yet they conflict with the tearing pain in my heart. I try to ignore them.

'I think we talked enough in Tenerife, don't you?'

Okay, I didn't expect a warm greeting, but I did think he'd be more willing to hear me out, especially after travelling so far just to speak to him.

'Listen, it's good to see you looking well.' His tone softens.

'And the guys will be so happy to see you, but I'm tired and this is a lot to take in. I'm sure I'll see you around.'

Everything inside me is urging me to strike, to convince him to hear me out, but the words turn to sand in my mouth. I've messed him around enough and if he needs some time, I have to let him have it.

'Goodnight, Jay. And great performance.'

'Cheers.' With that, he leaves.

A few seconds later, I'm engulfed in the comforting warmth of two strong arms wrapping themselves around me. My chest leaps as I spin around hoping Jay has realised he's missed me and has come back to rekindle our romance.

'He's hurting. Give him some time.'

'Paul,' I say, trying to mask my disappointment.

'Thought you might need a friend,' he says with a sympathetic expression.

'Yes.' I smile. 'More than ever.'

As we walk through the backstage corridor to the theatre exit, Paul natters away without taking a breath. I am listening but I'm also thinking about Jay's reaction, so I do miss bits.

'So the others have gone off clubbing with some of the crew but they're all dying to catch up, so we're going to do a breakfast buffet tomorrow if you're up for it?' I hear him say.

'Some things never change,' I mutter. 'But breakfast sounds good. Where's Phil?'

'His mother is over from the UK so he's taken her to the Venetian for supper.'

'Nice.' I've met Phil's mum. The image of her fuzzy white hair and floral frocks is a stark contrast to the flashing lights of Las Vegas.

'It really is great to see you, Kat,' he says. 'We've all missed you so much. Don't get me wrong, this has been quite a wild ride and we've loved every minute, but you should have been a part of it.'

266

I reach out and rub his arm. I hate that he feels guilty. 'Don't worry about me. I could never have taken you this far and I'm proud of you all. I really am happy for you.'

We've come through an alley beside the hotel, and facing us is the Flamingo. The strip is lined with cars, bumper to bumper and going nowhere. The shining lights of the hotels and casinos are like nothing I've ever seen before, and I've been to the Blackpool Illuminations – several times.

'It really is a crazy place,' I say. 'Intimidating even.'

'You get used to it, and once you have your bearings it's not so bad; it's actually a lot of fun.' He grins wickedly.

'I'll take your word for it.'

'You'll do no such thing,' he says. 'You'll see for yourself! We'll make sure you have a great time, starting tomorrow.'

'Thank you,' I say, thickened with meaning. He heard how Jay reacted and I'm grateful to him for discreetly letting me know I'm not alone out here.

'Okay, meet us at the Grand Lux Café in the Venetian at eleven tomorrow morning and we'll kick off the sightseeing.' He kisses me on the cheek and waves me off.

When I get back to my hotel room, I can't shake the look on Jay's face. Maybe my mind has morphed it into something much worse than it was, but his tone was so cold that I can't be sure. I slump on the bed, unable to focus on taking off my shoes, never mind getting ready for bed. He hates me. I could have handled him being with someone else – that would have been awful timing and my own fault – but him hating me is too much to bear. Jay has obviously started to move on and I've just come and whacked him back to square one like a giant piñata. My stomach churns the curdling sadness; I'm a terrible, terrible person. With no other lifeline, I dial Andrea.

'I shouldn't have come; I need a flight home ASAP.' My breathing hitches, breaking up the words.

'Kat? What's happened?' Andrea says with concern in her tone.

'I've just ruined everything for Jay. I've messed him about and it's not fair. I told him I wanted to be with him, then broke it off and let him fly all the way to Nevada and then I changed my mind again and came to see him and he's confused and hates me and it's all my fault.'

'Whoa, Kat, slow down and breathe.'

I sniffle and wipe my nose on my sleeve because the tissues are out of reach.

'Sorry, what time is it there?' I don't have my bearings yet and hadn't even thought to check.

'It's early but I'm up, don't worry. Now, back to you.'

'I need to leave here and forget about Jay. He deserves someone normal.'

Andrea laughs.

'Oh, so I'm a joke now, am I?'

'No,' she says firmly. 'You are not a joke but leaving Las Vegas now is exactly what you *shouldn't* do. That's what Jay is struggling with – all this changing your mind. Leaving when things get tough just proves his point. I get that you had a bad marriage and you don't want to end up there again, but this isn't just about you anymore. You need to show Jay that you know what you want and you're all in. Tell him you're there for a week and you're going to prove to him you know what you want.'

I press my palms to my face. 'How do I do that?'

'Just show him.'

'How? Am I supposed to follow him around like a lost puppy? He doesn't want to see me, Andri.'

'He loves you, Kat and love doesn't just go away. He'll come around. He's wounded and probably in a state of shock. Just stay there through this awkward time to prove that you can stand it when the going gets tough.'

'Okay, so I'll just stay in Las Vegas when he said "I'll see you around", which is obviously code for "don't bother trying to talk to me". Great advice.'

'Kat, calm down. You're lashing out because you're scared of rejection. That proves to me how much you *don't* want to lose Jay. Now all you have to do is show *him* that.'

I don't say anything. I feel terrible for shouting at Andrea but I feel constricted like I've been squished into a corner and there's no easy way of getting out.

'I'm sorry,' I say, eventually. 'I'll stay. Of course, I'll stay.'

'Good! Now go get him.'

I put the phone down feeling no better. Andrea is right of course; I can't run away from this but staying isn't going to be easy.

Chapter 41

When I wake up, I'm groggy. I feel like I spent all of last night partying, which is a little way away from the reality of one (admittedly large) margarita and a midnight bedtime. It must be jet lag. There's a message on my phone from Andrea telling me to stay strong and that I can do this. I hope she's right. I take a deep breath before going to have a shower. Today is a new day.

The Grand Lux Café is exactly that: grand and luxurious. It has a traditional New York vibe, if that's a thing? Not that I've ever been to New York – this comparison is purely based on my imagination and the fact that the yellowish lighting is slightly Tiffany-inspired. I spot Marcus first, sitting at a table with the others.

'Hi,' I say apprehensively, taking the empty seat.

The chorus of 'Morning, Kats' is just like things used to be in Tenerife and relaxes me a little. Most of them are already eating. Jay, who's shovelling scrambled eggs into his mouth, has his eyes fixed on his plate.

'It's a buffet, so fill your boots,' Paul says. Feeling the prickly weight of Jay's presence, I take Paul's statement as a cue to leave the table and get some food, breathing a sigh of relief when I get to the hot food station.

I ponder the eggs and hash browns and decide on a pancake with some streaky bacon. I'm drizzling on thick maple syrup when I sense someone come up beside me.

'Experiencing the culture?'

I look up to see Jay standing there.

'Something like that.' I prod at the sausages with some small metal tongs but stop short of taking any. I don't have the appetite for them.

'Look, I'm sorry for being so off with you last night. It was a bit of a shock to see you here and, if I'm honest, I don't really get why you're here – it's not like the flights are cheap and I know Andrea isn't paying you that well.'

I feel awkward and almost say that I came to see the boys, but my mum's words ring in my ears and all I can think about is communication. I have to be honest.

'I saw you on TV.' I hold his gaze and watch as the cogs slip into place. It takes a while but, granted, they've been on a few shows now.

He gets there eventually. '*Celia O'Donnell*?'

I feel my cheeks flush. 'Yes.'

'I was on live TV. She pressured me.' He makes a sweeping gesture with his hand.

My chest deflates. 'Oh.'

He rubs his face with his hands, 'I'm sorry, Kat. I don't know how to feel. Of course I meant what I said on *Celia*. I didn't know you'd see it and I never in a million years expected to see you here. Did you come all this way to admit that you were wrong?'

'Well, as good as they look, I didn't come for the pancakes.' I'm backed into a corner here really and although this isn't the way I planned to tell Jay how I feel, I'm done playing games.

He stares at me intently and rakes his hands through his hair. His expression is so pained I can almost see his two halves: the one wanting to push me away to protect his heart and the one wanting to believe we have a chance.

I want to reach out and wrap him in my arms but I can't. Instead, I add some extra maple syrup to my pancakes, rendering them inedible. Then, picking up my plate, I turn to him before heading back to the table.

'I know. I get that you've probably moved on, maybe met someone else or whatever, but I had to come over and at least tell you how I felt because I'd never forgive myself if I didn't and it isn't fair to you to not have all the facts but I totally understand if—'

He places his hand lightly on my shoulder. His touch is enough to freeze my entire body. Still clutching my plate, I'm rigid.

'I just need to think, Kat.'

My heart leaps but I don't want to seem too hopeful.

'Do you think we can talk somewhere more private? Preferably not over greasy bacon?' I ask, chewing my lip nervously as I await his reply.

'We have a rehearsal in a few hours and then the rest of the day off. When you've finished here you won't want lunch, so how about a bit of sightseeing?'

A smile builds on my face. 'I'd love that.'

'Meet me at the Bellagio fountains at three.' He pulls a tourist leaflet out of his back pocket and points to an area. 'I'll wait around here, on the sidewalk.'

'Okay.' I stop myself from saying 'It's a date' because I don't want to jump to any potentially embarrassing conclusions.

We head back to the table and Paul raises his eyebrows questioningly. I give a slight shake of my head to indicate 'not now'.

'Pancakes look good,' he says, and I'm glad he got the message.

'So, I want to hear all about Vegas,' I say, taking the first, cold bite.

The guys revel in sharing their exploits. Gambling, women, drunken escapades – you name it, I hear it all.

'Sounds like you're having a ball.' I snap a piece of crispy bacon and put it in my mouth, enjoying the salty taste.

'It's a whole other world. Brad has been fantastic, and the brand name has started to really get out there,' Marcus says before adding, 'Couldn't have done it without you though, Kat.'

'Listen.' I cover his hand with mine. 'You don't need to keep attributing your success to me. You guys are the ones with the talent – I didn't teach you how to sing or backflip and I sure as hell didn't show anyone how to do the splits. You guys are the talent.'

'But still,' he says, patting me on the back.

Once breakfast is over, we part ways and agree to meet at Caesars Palace for a late dinner. I leave with a feeling of fullness that I haven't had for a while.

Chapter 42

I spend the next few hours exploring the Venetian. I watch in awe as a bride and groom sail along one of the hotel's canals in a gondola, and for a moment, as I cross a bridge beneath a fake blue sky dotted with fluffy white clouds, I feel like I could be in Venice. I browse some of the fancy shops and visit the casino before spending a good forty minutes trying to find the exit. When I finally break out onto the Strip, my eyes need time to adjust to the iridescent sunlight. When I check my watch, I realise it's time to head to the Bellagio. I walk as fast as I can through the throngs of tourists, feeling a bit like a salmon swimming upstream. I'm not sure how long I've been walking, but I haven't even reached the Flamingo yet. I'm convinced the sidewalk is actually a treadmill.

When I cross the bridge over the Strip near the Venetian, I have to take a second to compose myself. I'm warm and sweaty from the speed-walking. Since I don't want to meet Jay for the first time in months looking like I've cycled twenty miles through the desert to a Bikram yoga class whilst eating a vindaloo, I powder my shiny face and pop a bit of lip gloss on. It's the best I can do with the tools that I've got in my messenger bag.

When I reach the meeting point, it's more crowded than I expected and I can't get a glimpse of the water, never mind Jay. The music starts and the crowd start to cheer. I stay on the outskirts, craning my neck to try and spot Jay.

'Kat!' His recognisable voice comes from somewhere to my left but I can only see a swarm of heads facing the other way.

'Kat!' he calls again; he sounds nearer now but more to the front of me. I move my head left and right trying to spot him. Eventually, I lock on to his mesmerising brown eyes. He fights his way through the throng of people until he reaches me.

'Sorry, I didn't think. Three p.m. is the first show today and I forgot how busy it gets. Let's go for a walk around the edges and come back in ten minutes or so.'

Above the sea of heads, huge jets of water leap hundreds of feet into the air to the tempo of Lady Gaga's 'Bad Romance'. I let Jay lead the way and I can tell he's been here a while; he dodges tourists like a pro. On one hand, his mission takes away from any awkwardness there may have been, but on the other, it's undoing all of my good powder work – I'm melting.

We end up in an impeccably well-looked-after garden area near the main entrance to the hotel.

'Let's stop here for a minute,' Jay says when he reaches a small but still impressive traditional round fountain with a central spout.

'At least we can see this one,' I joke, even though I can't because the sun is blinding me.

'So …' He takes a breath and puts his hands on my upper arms, guiding me into a shaded spot. It's an instant relief – I can open my eyes properly. When he's satisfied I can see, he starts again, 'I brought you here because I really did want to show you the fountains.'

I nod. 'I know,' I say, trying not to appear too disappointed.

'But now you're here and I'm actually looking at you, I don't care about the fountains. I don't know what it is, but you do something to me, Kat. You suck me in and make me want to be around you … be *with* you.'

A shiver ripples over me. I don't know if it's from Jay's words or the cool spray blowing off the fountain beside us.

'I know coming here has upset the apple cart. It's completely my fault you're confused. I didn't want to hurt you, but I had to let you know that what I said back in Tenerife was wrong. It took you leaving for me to realise that. I know I put you through hell and you've spent the last month adjusting to your new life here … without me, and I don't want to ruin any of it.'

'Then why did you come?'

The words are like a fishhook in my gut. I can't answer. What am I supposed to say?

'I'm selfish,' I say. My mouth is freewheeling.

'No.' His tone softens. 'I get it. This connection we have means something. I'm glad you've realised that it's too strong to ignore.'

My chest lifts in hope.

'I've been imagining this scenario almost every night since I got here. I haven't been able to sleep because I lie in bed going over conversations in my head, planning what I'd say to you if I ever saw you again.'

And then it deflates again. When I try to speak, the words stick, so I nod in agreement.

'Listen, should we go and get a drink? I don't think that we should be having this conversation whilst we're standing right next to the valet-parking attendant. Let's go inside and sit down.'

'Okay,' I croak.

We walk through the revolving doors into the huge, impressive lobby. The echoes of the clatter and chatter of people passing over the ornate marble flooring gives the space a vibrant feel. Everywhere I look, something grabs my attention. Above us is a huge sculpture of colourful glass flowers. There must be thousands of them of all different sizes.

'I wouldn't fancy dusting those,' I say to Jay, who isn't really listening. I think he's trying to focus on finding a place to sit and have a drink. We continue through the lobby, past some marble pillars to a conservatory area at the back. The room is much brighter thanks to the glass ceiling that floods it with natural light. It isn't until I look down that I notice the flowers.

'This must be the botanical gardens,' I say. I read about them in the in-flight magazine.

'We'll head in there.' Jay points to a green entrance with gold lettering above that reads 'Sadelle's'. It looks fancy but I suppose he's earning the big bucks now.

We walk into the grand restaurant and the waiter takes us up some steps to an elevated bar area. She seats us at a small dark wood table with two wooden chairs with wicker inlays.

'I haven't been in here before,' Jay whispers. 'I think it's a bit posh for me.'

'Well, how much can a cup of coffee be?' I say, picking up the menu. My eyes bulge when I discover the answer. 'Crikey – they're double what I'd normally pay!'

'We'd better make sure we get our free refills then.' Jay grins and something in my chest leaps.

'At least it's a nice place,' I say.

'I saw my mum when I went back to England,' he says. Pain rips through me. How did I not know that?

'How did it go?' I ask gently.

'She'd opened my letter but wasn't sure what to do. It was frosty but we talked.'

'That's good, isn't it?'

He nods. 'It's going to be a long road but in time I think we'll patch things up. I'm glad I did it.'

I give him a reassuring smile.

Jay orders two coffees and two glasses of water as I take in the elegant duck-egg blue and white surroundings.

When the waiter leaves us, Jay draws a breath. 'I was awake

most of last night thinking of what to say to you. Like I said I've been through the scenario so many times … sometimes I yell at you to leave me alone and others I wrap you in my arms. Last night was the first time I had to think about this for real.'

I pick the skin around my nail as I wait for more.

'My first reaction was to miss the breakfast today and spend the week avoiding you.'

I cock my head to the side. 'Jay.'

'Well, isn't that what we do?'

'Touché.'

'Then I realised I had too many unanswered questions for that, so here we are.'

'Ask me anything you want,' I say as the waiter places our drinks on the table.

'Why now? Why did you let me leave Tenerife and settle here before coming to tell me how you felt?'

'I told you, I thought I was doing the right thing letting you go—'

'*Letting* me go?'

'You know what I mean.'

'No, the problem here is that I *don't* know what you mean. One minute I'm in your bed and you're telling me you never want the moment to end, the next you're saying you made a mistake and you don't want to be with me. Now you're saying *that* was a mistake? Put yourself in my shoes, Kat. It's like trying to date Dr Jekyll.'

I stare down at my cup as tears press against my eyes. He's right. I've messed him about too much. Coming here was a huge mistake and I can't blame him for being confused. I'm confusing myself. I sip my coffee. It's too hot. It scorches the back of my throat, causing me enough pain that a tear I'd been holding on to escapes and rolls down my cheek.

'Don't cry.' Jay reaches across the table and takes my hand. 'It's all just a lot to process. Just when I thought I understood you, I realised I didn't know a bloody thing. I thought I'd finally found someone who got me, Kat; someone I could trust. You blindsided me back in Tenerife and now you're doing it again.'

I swallow some water to push down the painful ball in my throat and pick up my bag. 'I know, I'm sorry.'

I scramble around for my purse but my tiny bag is packed so tightly that it's wedged in and I can't get it out. 'Stupid bloody thing.'

'These drinks are on me.' Jay gently removes my hand from my bag.

'Thank you,' I say, looking into his eyes. 'I'm going to go.'

'You don't have to go. Finish your drink. Your gut reaction doesn't have to be to push back when things get a little bit awkward.'

'I know, I just thought ...' I don't know what I thought. I don't know what I'm doing here messing Jay about again.

'I did love you, you know.' The past tense hurts. 'It's been hard being here, adjusting to a new life, being back on the path of being a single guy enjoying the life that I thought I would have all along, but I have now ... adjusted, I mean.'

A pain sears my gut. 'I understand and I don't want to ruin everything for you, so for that reason, I am going to go. Thank you for the coffee.'

I hurry out of the restaurant, back past the beautiful displays in the botanical gardens and out of the hotel. That's how far I get before the tears come, thick and fast. People stare at me as I make my way back to the Strip. A kind lady with a Southern accent asks if I'm okay and if there's anything she can help me with, but I can't speak. I shake my head and force a smile of thanks before continuing on my way back to the Flamingo. When I get to the bridge, I turn to climb the steps and knock into a woman carrying a McDonald's cup. The drink goes everywhere. Her nostrils flare. She looks like she's about to lay into me.

'I'm so sorry,' I say. When her eyes meet mine, her face softens. I dread to think what I look like.

'It's all right, honey. Just be careful.'

When did I transition into that person who screws everything up?

Chapter 43

When I'm halfway across the bridge, I stop. I'm doing it again. I'm running away at the first sign of awkwardness. Andrea's words buzz around my head:

Show him you can be trusted.

Prove you're there to stay.

I think back to what my mum said about listening and I *did* listen. I heard him loud and clear. I broke his heart.

Did I listen?

Relationships take work, even the good ones.

'Oh God.' What the hell am I doing?

I run back over the bridge towards the Bellagio. I collide with the doors and burst into the foyer before sprinting towards the café. Jay has just walked out.

'Wait,' I shout. Several people turn around but he doesn't. I carry on running until I'm close enough I can touch his shoulder.

When he turns it's a moment before he realises it's me and when he does, he looks dazed like he's in shock but I press on regardless. 'I'm not leaving you,' I say, panting. I double over and rest my hands on my knees to try and catch my breath. 'Running away is exactly what I've been doing wrong so here I am, running

'... to ... you.' I almost cringe at how cheesy that sounds but his mouth curls up into a grin.

'Jay, I'm not going to let Iain control me anymore. You were right; you listened to me and everything you said was true. If I can't trust you, I can't trust anyone.'

'I've never seen you run before – you must have it bad!' His mouth curls up again and it gives me hope.

'I meant it when I said that all the stupid things I did were to protect us both but all I've done is cause us both a great deal of misery and pain. Listen, I have no idea how this will work. We live thousands of miles apart and you're a big star now, but if you want to give it a go, I'm done pushing people away. If you'll have me, I'm yours.'

He takes my hands in his and looks me in the eyes. I melt into them. 'I've waited a long time to hear you say that, Kat.'

He leans forwards and places his soft, warm lips on mine and my body fizzes with delight. As he kisses me, the buzz of colour, people and lights spin around me – like I'm suspended in a parallel reality from which I've no desire to return. Then he pulls away, planting three little kisses on my nose as he does.

'Let's go out after dinner tonight. It can be our first official date as a couple – no more secrets.'

'I'd love to,' I say.

Chapter 44

'Jay has spent the past month pining for you, Kat. He wouldn't come out and have fun – he performs and goes to bed. He doesn't come to the pool on our days off or anything,' Sammy says.

'He's been an all-round miserable git,' Marcus says. 'We were going to send him back to Tenerife! You came in the nick of time, Kat.'

'He's missed you, love.' Paul covers my hand with his.

'Shut up you lot, you'll find out what it's like to love someone when you grow up,' Jay says and we all laugh.

'Now, let's order some drinks.' Ant does a mini drumroll on the table.

As we're tucking into our food, I look up and catch two brown eyes looking at me. My body fills with warmth and I know this is how I want to feel always.

When the meal is finished, I film a short video of the boys saying hi to Simon's wife and send it to him. It should earn him a few brownie points and it's the least I can do after he helped get me through my flight here. After that, Jay and I head for a walk. There are some childish wolf whistles as we leave and I find myself grinning uncontrollably.

'We might make the last fountain show of the night if we hurry,' he says.

We speed-walk to the Bellagio next door and find a vantage point just as the show is starting. The tin whistle of the *Titanic* theme tune begins, and despite the warm temperature, a shiver runs down my spine. The fountains start to gently sway like a slow Mexican wave, and to be brutally honest, they're disappointingly small.

'It's a bit like the waves at sea,' I whisper, but I don't know if Jay is listening to me. His eyes are glistening.

'Are you okay?' I ask a little louder.

'It's this bloody song. It gets me every time,' he says, dabbing the corner of his eye. I giggle.

'Only a monster can get through this song without getting emotional,' he says when he notices my laughter. He pulls me close and kisses the top of my head.

As the song moves into the second verse, the jets propel the water higher into the air and Jay squeezes me tighter and my whole right-hand side tingles with the warm fizz of electricity.

As the chorus builds again and Celine Dion adds even more power to her voice, the fountains erupt into the air higher than I ever could have imagined. I gasp and tears prick my own eyes.

'There you go.' Jay bumps me playfully with his hip.

As the song ends and the fountains fade into the lake I get a wave of sadness. It's everything: the *Titanic*, the happiness of being with Jay and the realisation that I'll have to go back to Tenerife without him.

As the crowd disperses, we're left as alone as you can be on the Las Vegas Strip, by the blue-black water. The warm lighting of the Bellagio's bars and restaurants glitter on the far side and the sound of traffic comes from behind us.

'I love you, Kat.' Jay's words come from nowhere and fill me with warmth.

'I love you too. I know that now,' I say softly, standing on my tiptoes to plant my lips on his.

'Mmm. I could get used to that,' he says, making me smile. I feel like the Cheshire cat.

'How will this work?' I say, unable to shift the concerns I have about the thousands of miles between us.

'Things are complicated now. I'm locked into my contract for almost another five months.'

My heart sinks. 'I know.'

'I won't re-sign after the next five months are up but I need to know it's real this time. I can't walk away from what I have here only to find in a couple of months you've had a wobble again and decided to call it off – I need you to promise.'

'I know, I understand. You'd be taking a chance on me and my track record is awful.'

'I'll say.' His eyes glint mischievously.

'All right! I'm trying here.' I prod him in his side playfully.

'How about we stop trying, and start doing?' He intertwines his fingers with mine and pulls me into his big frame. I look up into those soft chestnut eyes and melt into the shape of him. How was I ever scared of this?

'I don't know what the right thing for us to do is, but I know what feels right, and it's this.' He leans down and I tilt my head up and our lips meet. Sparks erupt through my body as we find our familiar rhythm.

'Get a room,' some lad with a giant sippy cup says as he walks past.

Jay laughs and rests his forehead on mine. 'Shall we get out of here?'

'I'm just over the road if you want to come back to my room?' I ask as Jay raises his eyebrows in mock hopefulness. I thump his chest playfully.

'I didn't mean for *that* but maybe we *could* do that.'

***

The sky outside is a soft grey-blue. The sun isn't up yet but it must be peeking over the horizon somewhere. I'm lying on the super-king-sized bed wrapped in Jay's sizeable biceps and I could stay here forever. Our bodies are warm and naked beneath the covers and it feels right.

The mattress compresses as he lifts his head and kisses me on the cheek.

'You're awake?'

'Couldn't sleep.' I snuggle into him.

'I hope you're not worrying again.' I don't blame him for thinking that.

'I'm just happy.'

He kisses me on the head.

'So what do we do now?' I ask. 'You've still got five months left on your contract here and I don't have the money or visa to stay here.'

'You could stay here for three months and live at my place,' he says.

'I can't do that. I want to earn my own money and I can't work here.'

He kisses me on the head. 'Five months isn't that long. You can come and visit again. I can see to the tickets.'

'Jay, I don't want you paying to keep flying me around the world like a high-class escort.'

He laughs softly. 'Listen, we have the rest of the week together. I'm going to take you to the Grand Canyon and the best restaurants in town. Let's enjoy this time and then we can figure out the next five months.'

I snuggle into his chest and listen to the slow, rhythmic beat of his heart. 'I like the sound of that.'

Epilogue

'I've missed this magician,' Jay says, pulling me into a seat near the stage.

'I can't believe I waited five months for you to come back and you've brought me to watch Magica on our only night off,' I tease.

'Oh, come on. He's had months of practice since we last saw him. Besides, you've had me for three months now – it's time to spice things up.' He winks at me and I shake my head. We've been working seven days a week since Jay got back, trying to get our entertainment agency off the ground. It's been tough but we're starting to get somewhere. We have some fantastic acts now too, which makes our night with Magica even stranger.

I glance around the small cabaret lounge at the Sunseeker Life hotel in Costa Adeje and am not surprised to see we're the only ones in here. 'At least we won't be fighting for table service.'

I raise my hand to grab the attention of the waiter and order us two mojitos each, since it's happy hour.

The magician appears on stage, dressed in all his highly flammable livery.

'Ooh, the cape is swirling,' I say with mock excitement in my tone. Jay shakes his head. 'Sorry,' I whisper.

There's a loud bang, followed by some smoke, and Magica's hat appears from nowhere.

'Okay, that was pretty good.'

He pulls out a string of handkerchiefs as our cocktails arrive. As I'm taking my first sip, Magica points at me.

'Oh God, audience participation,' I whisper to Jay.

'Just go with it.'

Mr Magica asks me to pick a card and show it to the audience (Jay) before hiding it on my person. He then proceeds to prance about with the rest of the cards and does some elaborate arm wafting before splitting the deck.

'Is this your card?'

I glance at the eight of diamonds with shock. 'Yes, yes it was.'

I pat myself down as I walk back to my seat but I can't find the one I tucked in the back of my waistband. I'm sure he didn't come anywhere near me.

'You're right. He's improved,' I say to Jay. 'But I think I preferred him when he was one iguana short of a reptile house.'

Magica leaps off the stage and holds his hat out to me.

'Me again,' I whisper to Jay. 'I swear, if he makes me pull a live animal out of that thing I'll scream.'

I look to Jay, expecting to see him smiling, but his face is deadpan and his jaw hard-set. I hope I haven't spoilt his night. His eyes are fixed on the magician and now I feel bad for spoiling the show. Magica's hat explodes with a bang, and when the smoke disappears, a mini hat sits in its place in his hands. He gestures for me to pull out whatever is inside.

I put my hands in and fish around before grasping something small and round with a hard lump on it. I pull it out. It's a shiny diamond-looking ring. At least it isn't an iguana.

Confused, I look to Jay to see if he's also bamboozled. I'm in complete shock when I see that Jay is down on one knee, looking at me with expectant eyes. The music changes from the upbeat cheese Magica had on, to something soft and instrumental.

Magica swirls his cape and vanishes (by quickly scurrying behind the curtain, not by some amazing magic trick).

Jay takes my hand in his. 'Kat, I don't know if this is the best way to ask, but I played out all sorts of scenarios in my head, from the most simple to the outrageously wild and, well, this seemed the most fitting.'

He rubs his thumb across the bumps of my knuckles.

'Anyway, when I stepped off the plane and landed back in Tenerife, I knew I needed a new life. The UK wasn't working out for me because I couldn't escape my past there and there was always something missing in Las Vegas. Tenerife is my 'just right' and that's because of you, Kat. You know my past and have accepted me anyway. You've accepted me as the person I am today, and I wake up every morning wondering why this beautiful, kind, caring woman is with me. I love you, Kat, and I want to wake up next to you every morning until that final day where I don't wake up at all.'

I swallow hard. I'm ready.

'Katelyn Shepherd, will you marry me?'

I look down at the man who is all I want in this world, and my whole torso feels like it's filled with helium. Emotion courses through me and erupts in the form of watery eyes.

'Yes.' I kneel down too. 'A thousand times, yes.'

He pulls me in and kisses me as my heart feels like it might burst.

After a few moments, he pulls away. 'I almost forgot.'

He slides the ring on my finger. It's a platinum or white gold band with a pretty cushion-cut diamond that picks up the colours of the stage lighting and refracts it in tiny rainbow beams.

'It's beautiful,' I whisper through my damp salty lips.

'I had a little help choosing, in the form of an outspoken Spaniard with expensive taste.'

I laugh. 'Andrea is a good egg.'

'I don't know that Barclaycard will agree,' he says, kissing me again. 'I'm teasing. I thought it was perfect and Andrea simply agreed.'

'Well, I love it.'

'Sorry, but can I take a picture of you showing off the ring? It's for my mum. She's desperate to know what you said.'

'Yes!' I squeal excitedly. 'Take as many photos as possible. Send it to my mum too,' I say, already trying out different poses. When he's sent several pictures, he takes me by the hand.

'Come on, I have a surprise for you.'

'I think the whole proposal is supposed to be the surprise,' I say as he takes my hand and leads me out to the pool area. We walk through an access gate onto the beach and he leads me to one of the hotel's Bali beds. A bottle of champagne sits in an ice bucket, and rose petals are scattered on the white cushions, upon which is a silver tray holding chocolate-covered strawberries.

'It was going to be my commiseration corner if you said no, but we'll use it to celebrate instead.' He winks.

I take a strawberry and listen to the crashing of the waves as Jay pops the champagne cork. 'This is perfect.'

'You're perfect.' He places his lips on mine.

I get a shiver.

Jay's phone buzzes. Whilst he checks his messages, I lean across and finish pouring the champagne.

'I hope it's someone important. Don't they know you're busy?' I tease.

He ignores me and raises his glass. 'To us.'

'Cheers, to us,' I echo.

We lie back on the bed as the white voile drapes billow in the breeze. Above us, the sooty sky is dotted with stars that are actually twinkling. It could be that my eyes are still a little watery, but the whole moment is perfect.

'Oi oi.' A loud, brash, baritone voice comes from near the hotel.

'Who would spoil this moment?' I say under my breath.

I can make out someone, or maybe two someones, stomping through the sand in our direction. Great, some British nobs are coming to take the piss.

Jay jumps up and springs towards them. For a second, I think he's going to have a go at them but he wraps his arms around the first dark figure.

'Marcus!' he shouts.

Marcus? My mouth goes dry. Marcus? I scream and leap up too, and when I get beyond the voile I can just about make out his moonlit face. 'Marcus!' I wrap him in my arms and he squeezes me back tightly.

'Hi, Kat.' The other figure steps out of the shadows.

'Sammy!' I hug him too.

'The others got your text message and are on their way,' Marcus says.

'What are you all doing here?'

'We couldn't miss the proposal of the century!' he says.

'Well, you sort of already did!' I hold up my hand to show off my ring, which sparkles under the moonlight.

'The boy done good,' Marcus says as three more figures emerge from the hotel's gate.

'Ant, Paul, Phil!'

'And Hugo is on his way!' I recognise Paul's voice.

'Did you do all of this?' I turn to Jay who nods sheepishly.

'That's not all, Kat,' Marcus says.

'What do you mean?'

'We've arranged with Gaël to do a one-night only show, tonight. It's a sell-out so I hope you've still got your chicken fillets.' He winks.

'Oh my God, Jenny isn't here?'

'Jenny isn't a patch on you,' Ant says. 'You're our Tenerife compère and always will be!'

'Was this you too, Jay?' I ask and he nods.

'Oh my God. I love you. I love you so ...' I can't even finish because tears are streaming down my face. Jay takes me in his arms and squeezes me tight. 'I love all of you,' I manage. I can't believe I get to go on stage with the Hunks again. I don't even care that I'm just dressed as me and not 'stage me'.

For this moment, under the moonlight, I have everyone I ever wanted, together in one place. I know now that Jay will always have my best interests at heart. I know that he loves me for who I am and I know I've found my happy ever after.

Acknowledgements

As always, this book would not have been possible without many people. Firstly, I'd like to thank Abigail Fenton, Cara Chimirri and all at HQ Digital, for commissioning this book. A few years ago, publishing a book was beyond my wildest dreams; now I've published six with a seventh on its way and I'm forever grateful for the opportunity. I'd also like to thank my wonderful editor, Belinda Toor, for her honest and supportive feedback and for spotting all the random errors that I missed. On that note, I'd like to express huge thanks to Helena Newton for her eagle-eyed proofreading and lovely comments and for providing me with solid proof that I should never be in a position of trust whereby I'd have to look after several people. Thank you for making sure I didn't forget any of the Hunks! Thank you also to Kia Thomson for your much-needed help and support with my first draft.

The writing community is so supportive and I'd like to say a massive thanks to the Yorkshire Writer's group, Rachel Burton, Rachel Dove, Rachael Stewart, Lisa Swift and Katey Lovell, for always being there to lift spirits, give advice and tell funny stories about loo roll. One day we'll get that champagne afternoon tea and it will be epic.

Huge thanks to Lucy Knott, Maxine Morrey, Belinda Missen,

Lynsey James and Sarah Bennett for social media inspiration, support and laughs. In addition, all the HQ Digital writers are incredibly supportive – there are too many to name but thank you all.

Rachel Gilby at *Rachel's Random Resources*, thank you so much for all your support with marketing and blog tours over the past few years and for your own wonderful reviews. They mean the world to me.

The Chicklit and Prosecco chat group is a great place for readers and writers who love this genre to connect. Anita Faulkner deserves a huge thank you for setting the group up. On a similar vein, ChicklitChatHQ on Facebook is a wonderful place full of supportive authors and bloggers, and has given me so much support over the years.

Last but not least, thank you Vicky Rayner for coming to London with me on our very important 'research trip'.

A Letter From Victoria.

Dear reader,

I just wanted to say a huge thank you for taking the time to read *Sun, Sea and Sangria*. I'm a huge fan of the Canary Islands and after visiting several of the islands and enjoying lots of hotel entertainment, felt they made the perfect setting for this book. Writing the book during the 2020 lockdown helped provide me with some much-needed sunny escapism and I hope it does for you too whatever your circumstances.

If you've read any of my other books, you'll know that travel features quite heavily, from Scotland to Las Vegas. I love swapping travel stories so do get in touch and let me hear your thoughts if you've ever visited any of the places mentioned in any of my books – you can find me on Facebook, Twitter, Instagram and TikTok (although I don't really know what I'm doing there other than making a fool of myself).

Reviews long and short, good and bad are incredibly valuable to authors. They let us know how we're doing, how we can improve and give us warm fuzzy feelings when people like our work. If you can spare a few minutes to leave one on your chosen retailer's website, I do read them and would love to hear your feedback.

Finally, thank you again for your support in purchasing this book and, if you liked it, please check out my others.
Best Wishes,
Victoria Cooke

Dear Reader,

We hope you enjoyed reading this book. If you did, we'd be so appreciative if you left a review. It really helps us and the author to bring more books like this to you.

Here at HQ Digital we are dedicated to publishing fiction that will keep you turning the pages into the early hours. Don't want to miss a thing? To find out more about our books, promotions, discover exclusive content and enter competitions you can keep in touch in the following ways:

JOIN OUR COMMUNITY:
Sign up to our new email newsletter: hyperurl.co/hqnewsletter
Read our new blog www.hqstories.co.uk
🐦 : https://twitter.com/HQStories
🅕 : www.facebook.com/HQStories

BUDDING WRITER?
We're also looking for authors to join the HQ Digital family!
Find out more here:
https://www.hqstories.co.uk/want-to-write-for-us/
Thanks for reading, from the HQ Digital team

ONE PLACE. MANY STORIES

Keep reading for an excerpt from
A Summer to Remember …

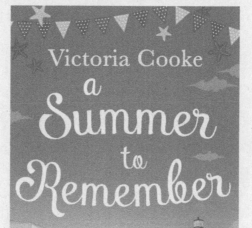

Prologue

2010

The black and white chequered floor whizzes past. Like a psyche-delic trip, it isn't real. I know that I'm running. I can't feel my limbs moving, just the vague sensation of the air resistance caused by the motion. I'm on autopilot, and the only thing tying me to the reality of where I am, is the pungent smell of disinfectant that's been with me at every turn.

I stop abruptly, almost colliding with a person dressed head-to-toe in baggy green scrubs. My heart pounds in my chest. I look down at my hand, the knuckles white, still clutching my phone from when I got the call. It can only have been twenty minutes ago. It's hard to tell because it feels like a lifetime has passed. The surgeon seems to understand that I can't speak; his features are barely displaced, neutral, but there's something lurking in his earthy eyes. Sympathy? 'Mrs Butterfield?' he asks. I nod, my mouth like Velcro, my brain too disengaged to speak.

'Mrs Butterfield, I'm sorry. We did everything we could.'

Did?

You can't have.

The blood pumping in my ears is deafening. Barbed wire is

wrenched from the pit of my stomach, right up through my oesophagus. I've never felt pain like it. My legs give way, unable to bear the weight of the surgeon's words and my knees crash to the floor.

I'm vaguely aware of a low, drawn-out wail. It's me. The surgeon crouches down and looks me directly in the eyes. The warmth of his chestnut-brown gaze anchors me, and I'm able to gather tendrils of composure. I take a breath.

'Mrs Butterfield, is there anyone we can call for you?'

I shake my head. I only have one person, and now he's dead.

Chapter One

2018

'Eurgh.' I slam the pearlescent invite down by the kettle. '*Plus one*,' I say in a mocking tone. Coco cocks her head to the side like she's trying to understand me, and I cup her fluffy face.

'I know, I don't get it either.' My cat's emerald eyes are still intent on me so, glad of an audience, I carry on.

'Why Bridget has to assume I need someone by my side is beyond me. As if I'm not capable of going to a wedding without a *plus one*. It's not nineteen blooming twenty. I don't need a chaperone. Perhaps I'll take you, Coco. That'll teach her.' I tickle her under her chin and she stretches out lazily. I'm only half joking.

As I pour my first coffee of the day, my phone rings. 'Someone's ears are burning,' I say on answering.

'Really?' Bridget also ignores the need for pleasantries.

'I got your wedding invite,' I say dryly.

'Well, don't sound too enthusiastic about the happiest day of your best friend's life,' she retorts.

'Aren't we a bit old for best friends?'

'Don't change the subject.'

303

I rub my temples with my thumb and forefinger. 'I'm sorry, Bridge. I just, well … I'd specifically told you I didn't need a plus one.'

'It's just a formality, Sam. Don't be so sensitive. I just wanted you to know the option is there if you did want to bring someone.'

'Well, I don't,' I say, before feeling a little guilty. 'It just seems so old-fashioned, like, the *lil lady* needs a gentleman to escort her.' I put on my best 'Southern Belle' accent, and Bridget giggles.

'I'm sorry,' she says. 'It wasn't meant to offend you.'

'I did warn you,' I scold. 'Look, I'm not on the lookout for a man, nor am I *resigned* to being alone – I'm *happy* with it. People need to stop assuming I need someone. I got the bloody cat everyone thought I should get, okay!'

'I know, I'm sorry. Everyone else will be coupled up, so I just thought if you wanted to bring a *friend*, then you could, that's all.'

'All of my *friends* will already be there.' I'm aware of my exasperated tone so I soften it a little. 'I was just telling Coco that *she* could be my plus one.'

'You'd better bloody well not.' Bridget's stern tone amuses me. I sense that she wouldn't put it past me.

'Oh, now you've made her sad.' Coco looks far from sad as she rubs her face on my balled-up fist. 'I've seen some gorgeous cat dresses on eBay.'

'Bring her and I'll have you both escorted out,' Bridget replies.

'Then stop assuming I can't be single and happy.'

'Fine!' she sighs. 'But send me a picture of one of those cat dresses, it's been a miserable week.'

I'm happy it's time to drop the subject. It may seem like an overreaction, but Bridget knows as well as my other friends do that my frustrations are the result of a good seven years' worth of do-gooders trying to set me up with brothers, colleagues, friends of friends, and even a sister at one point. I'm happy on my own. It's like the saying goes, 'It's better to have loved and

304

lost than to have never loved at all.' All I need are my memories and my cat.

'How's work?' she asks.

I groan, wondering where to start. 'I'm still working my backside off to make the US team. Seventh time lucky, hey?' Every year five people from our offices are chosen to go to Boston for three months to work on a global marketing project with the American head office team. I've tried for seven years – yes, seven years – to make the cut. It's become my obsession.

'Oh Sam, this year has to be your year,' she says sympathetically.

'It's like no matter how hard I try, someone else shines brighter. This year I've worked my backside off and if I'm not chosen, I might start looking somewhere else.' It sounds like I'm being a drama queen, but I've given everything to Pink Apple Advertising and I've been pretty open about wanting to go to Boston. If they don't choose me this year, I don't think they ever will, and that Boston trip is the only real catalyst to a promotion.

'Well, if they don't pick you this time, they don't deserve you.' Bridget sounds distracted, like most people do when I talk about work.

I stifle a sigh. My friends will never understand how much it means to me. 'The invites are gorgeous, by the way,' I say, stroking the silver ribbon running down the thick, shimmery cream card with embossed dusky pink lettering. She was right when she said it will be the best day of her life.

2003

My breath catches in my throat. There he is, chewing the corner of his thumbnail nervously. He looks so vulnerable standing there in his navy suit and tie. When his eyes set upon mine, I can feel their warmth envelop me. His head tilts ever-so-slightly to the side and his watery eyes crinkle when he smiles. I glance down at my simple ivory dress, self-consciously smoothing out non-existent wrinkles. My mum had steamed the thing to death, fussing about invisible creases and generally adding to my overall nervousness.

The music starts, a piano instrumental of Canon in D, and butterflies beat venomously in my stomach when the expectant faces turn towards me. My mum is there, at the front with her new olive-coloured organza hat on. She's clutching a tissue to her face.

'Are you ready, pumpkin?' my dad whispers in my ear. Normally, I'd tell him not to call me that, but today I'm too nervous to care.

I grip my dad's arm tighter in mine, clutch my bouquet of white lilies with the other and take a deep breath before setting off. It's a blur as we walk down the small aisle, past a handful of close friends and family, to where Kev is waiting. When I join him, he gives my hand a gentle squeeze and leans in close and breathes into my ear.

'You … are … beautiful.'

I feel his words.

Suddenly the room is ours and ours alone.

Chapter Two

I smooth down the skirt of my Ted Baker dress as I walk into the church, smiling as I take in the beautiful flower displays. Bridget has chosen pageboys and flower girls instead of bridesmaids so that she didn't have to choose between her closest friends or fork out for a bazillion extortionately priced dresses. To be honest, I was quite relieved when she told me. Being plucked, waxed and spray-tanned within an inch of my life didn't really appeal, though I have shaved my legs for the occasion. I've worn this dress to three recent weddings because it fits my slender five-foot-five frame perfectly. It has a pencil skirt in shades of metallic pink and rose gold, with a plain white chiffon top. My make-up is minimal, and my dark hair hangs in loose waves which look like they dried that way after my morning surf but in actual fact took the hairdresser thirty minutes of wanding, teasing and praying to the hair gods for. I've never surfed in my life. I don't go in the sea ever – too much uncertainty lurking under that strange foamy stuff which floats on the surface.

Viv, Sarah and their husbands are easy to spot as I make my

way down the aisle. I slide into the spot they've saved for me next to Viv.

'It could be you next,' Viv gushes as I place my bag on the floor. Seriously, I've just sat down. It's as if she doesn't know better, except for the fact that she bloody well does. I'm about to say something about hell freezing over first but second guess myself. Can you say the word 'hell' in church? The last time I paid any attention to religion was the Harvest festival in 1996, and that was only because the vicar looked a little bit like Mark Owen. Am I about to be struck down by lightning? Maybe I should cross myself.

'So, you didn't bring anyone then?' Sarah leans across to ask. She kind of purses her lips in a sympathetic way. I don't reply, but seriously, it's okay to go to a wedding alone. It's like these people don't even know me, despite the fact we've been friends since Bridget introduced us over seven years ago.

When I first met these women, I'd just moved to London. I couldn't bear to stay in our village after losing Kev. I needed a clean slate. My old life had finished, and I needed something completely different. It was almost a year to the day I'd lost Kev when I bumped into Bridget in the foyer at work. And I mean literally bumped into her, knocking her espresso out of her hand so hard that it flew over her shoulder, luckily without spilling so much as a drop on her cream suit. She worked for a different company in the same building, and being new to London, I was hugely intimidated by her. She laughed off the faux pas and said I looked like I needed a stiff drink. We met up after work, I told her my story, and the rest is history.

Viv and Sarah are Bridget's close friends, but soon became mine too. At first, they took pity on me, listened to my endless stories about Kev and offered sympathy whilst I revelled in my new friendship group. But before long, they started to talk about me 'putting myself back out there'. I've been defending my single-hood ever since.

I give her a tight smile and nod. It's the same old story. Sympathetic glances when people learn you're single in your mid (okay, late) thirties, and the comments are always along the lines of 'you'll meet someone soon.' In some ways, I feel sorry for them, thinking you need a man to make your life better. A man can't make your life better. Only a soulmate can even come close to doing that, and I'd already found mine.

The organ starts to play. The dull sound of pressurised air being forced through the pipes reminds me of death. Why they play this instrument at weddings is beyond me. Everyone turns to catch the first glimpse of the bride. Bridget looks stunning in a simple silk gown with capped lace sleeves and a diamanté-encrusted waistband. Her blonde hair is in a neat chignon with some loose curls framing her face. She smiles at us as she walks past, her rosy cheeks and sparkling eyes radiating happiness. I remember that feeling too, and I cherish it.

***

Thank god. I swipe a welcome Pimm's on arrival at the hotel reception, and it goes down rather too easily. Churches are tinged with the memory of Kev's funeral. Whilst the funeral itself is a blur, I've never felt comfortable in one since.

'Slow down, Sam, it's only noon,' Sarah says, taking mouse-like sips from her own.

'You do you, okay?' I say, before realising I sound harsh. 'Sorry. I love weddings and I love seeing my friends happy, but they do bring back memories.'

Sarah strokes my arm. 'We get it, hon, but if you get sloshed and make a prized tit out of yourself, you'll regret it.'

'That happened one time,' I say with an eye-roll.

'Yes, and I forgave you because everything was still raw and because I wasn't letting anything spoil my big day. You need to be here for Bridget today.' Her eyes bore into me, but their intensity is broken by the waiter offering more Pimm's. I decline and look pointedly at Sarah, who wears a smug expression.

Across the foyer of the hotel, Bridget and her new husband Alex are posing for photographs. The photographer is shepherding miniature humans into a line. It's like a comedy sketch: just as he manages to get one end of the line straight, he loses a child from the other end. His face is starting to redden.

'We should find our table,' Viv says, moving us on.

The tables are not numbered or named like usual. Instead, we have to find ours by working out the punchline of a joke. 'Well, Mrs Killjoy, you'll never find your table,' I whisper to Sarah, who gives me a tight smile and shakes her head. The joke for our table reads: 'What happens when Iron Man takes off his suit?' Viv and Sarah exchange confused glances.

'Oh, come on,' I say. 'Seriously?'

They both shake their heads. I look to John and Mark, their husbands, who are wearing equally blank expressions.

'He's Stark naked! Tony Stark?' I say, chuckling in response to a few groans. I remember Bridget running that one past me and I thought it was hilarious.

We find our table, and sure enough, the centre plaque reads 'He's Stark naked'. As we sit down we watch several bewildered guests wandering around in confusion.

'Are you struggling?' I say to an elderly gentleman hovering by our table.

'Just a little.'

'What's your clue?'

'RIP water.' Puzzlement is etched into his brow. 'It doesn't even sound like a joke.'

I stifle a smirk. 'You will be *mist*,' I say, gesturing to the table to my right. I turn to the others. 'I think this is more fun than the actual wedding.'

'I'm just glad Bridget and Alex found one another, because they're the only two people who get these jokes.' Sarah takes the wine from the centre of the table and fills us up.

'So, I'm allowed to drink now?' I say sarcastically.

Sarah rolls her eyes. 'I was just looking out for you.'

I'm about to retort when Viv's husband, John, interrupts me.

'So, Sam, no handsome prince on the horizon yet?'

'Nope.' I take a long sip of wine in place of a groan.

He tilts his head to the side. 'You'll meet someone soon.' And there it is. I notice Viv giving him 'a look', which I'm grateful for. Maybe Bridget has had a word.

A loud gong interrupts the slightly awkward silence which ensues. 'All rise, for the bride and groom.'

There's a loud cheer and a round of applause as Bridget and Alex enter and take their seats at the top table. The happiness radiates from the pair of them and whilst I'm finding this whole day a little difficult, the smiles they wear are infectious. Not all romances are doomed and the love they have for one another is real, it only takes a quick glance in their direction to see that. They look beautiful together and the solid block of ice in my chest starts to thaw with the warmth that breaks through from just looking at them. I genuinely wish them a long lifetime of happiness.

Want to read on? Order now!

If you enjoyed *Sun, Sea and Sangria*, then why not try
another delightfully uplifting romance from HQ Digital?